Jerry Muskrat looked up at Blacky and winked.
See page 78.

BIG BOOK OF ANIMAL STORIES

Thornton W. Burgess

*Original Illustrations
by George Kerr and Harrison Cady
Adapted by Thea Kliros*

DOVER PUBLICATIONS, INC.
Mineola, New York

Bibliographical Note

Big Book of Animal Stories, first published by Dover Publications, Inc., in 2001, is a new compilation containing the unabridged texts of the following four editions: *Old Mother West Wind,* originally published by Little, Brown, and Company, Boston, in 1910; *The Adventures of Peter Cottontail,* originally published by Little, Brown, and Company, Boston, in 1914; *The Adventures of Grandfather Frog,* originally published by Little, Brown, and Company, Boston, in 1915; and *The Adventures of Buster Bear,* originally published by Little, Brown, and Company, Boston, in 1916. All of the original illustrations by George Kerr (*Old Mother West Wind*) and Harrison Cady (*The Adventures of Peter Cottontail, The Adventures of Grandfather Frog,* and *The Adventures of Buster Bear*) have been adapted for the Dover edition by Thea Kliros. An introductory Note has been specially prepared for this edition.

Library of Congress Cataloging-in-Publication Data

Burgess, Thornton W. (Thornton Waldo), 1874–1965.
    Big book of animal stories / Thornton W. Burgess.
        p. cm.
    A new compilation containing unabridged texts of works originally published by Little, Brown and Company between 1910 and 1916.
    Contents: Old Mother West Wind—Adventures of Peter Cottontail—Adventures of Grandfather Frog—Adventures of Buster Bear.
    ISBN 0-486-41980-0 (pbk.)
    1. Children's stories, English. [1. Animals—Fiction. 2. Rabbits—Fiction. 3. Frogs—Fiction. 4. Bears—Fiction. 5. Short stories.] I. Title.

PZ7.B917 Bb 2001
[Fic]—dc21

        2001028698

Manufactured in the United States of America
Dover Publications, Inc., 31 East 2nd Street, Mineola, N.Y. 11501

Introduction

Born in Sandwich, Massachusetts, in 1874, Thornton W. Burgess wandered the shores, meadows, and forests of this Cape Cod town during his boyhood, gaining a love and appreciation of nature that formed the spirit of his later work. As a grown man, he told bedtime stories about animals and nature to his young son. This was the beginning of Burgess' career as a much-loved children's author as well as a highly respected naturalist. In his first book, *Old Mother West Wind* (1910), Burgess did more than just entertain: he was careful to present his stories so that children could gain a better understanding of the ways of wild creatures. As his popularity grew, Burgess recognized the educational value his work had in teaching children about the habits of animals, and at the same time, he developed in his readers a reverence for nature. It was his aim that those who read his stories would grow to share both his love of nature and his concern for the natural environment and its preservation.

Contents

Old Mother West Wind   1

The Adventures of Peter Cottontail   71

The Adventures of Grandfather Frog   135

The Adventures of Buster Bear   203

Old Mother West Wind

by

Thornton W. Burgess

"Where are you going in such a hurry?"
asked Bobby Coon.
See page 52.

I. Mrs. Redwing's Speckled Egg

Old Mother West Wind came down from the Purple Hills in the golden light of the early morning. Over her shoulders was slung a bag—a great big bag—and in the bag were all of Old Mother West Wind's children, the Merry Little Breezes.

Old Mother West Wind came down from the Purple Hills to the Green Meadows and as she walked she crooned a song:

"Ships upon the ocean wait;
I must hurry, hurry on!
Mills are idle if I'm late;
I must hurry, hurry on!"

When she reached the Green Meadows Old Mother West Wind opened her bag, turned it upside down and shook it. Out tumbled all the Merry Little Breezes and began to spin round and round for very joy, for you see they were to play in the Green Meadows all day long until Old Mother West Wind should come back at night and take them all to their home behind the Purple Hills.

First they raced over to see Johnny Chuck. They found Johnny Chuck sitting just outside his door eating his breakfast. One, for very mischief, snatched right out of Johnny Chuck's mouth the green leaf of corn he was eating, and ran away with it. Another playfully pulled his whiskers, while a third rumpled up his hair.

Johnny Chuck pretended to be very cross indeed, but really he didn't mind a bit, for Johnny Chuck loved the Merry Little Breezes and played with them every day.

And if they teased Johnny Chuck they were good to him, too. When they saw Farmer Brown coming across the Green Meadows with a gun one of them would dance over to Johnny Chuck and whisper to him that Farmer Brown was coming, and then Johnny Chuck would hide away, deep down in his snug little house under ground, and Farmer Brown would wonder and wonder why it was that he never, never could get near enough to shoot Johnny Chuck. But he never, never could.

When the Merry Little Breezes left Johnny Chuck they raced across the Green Meadows to the Smiling Pool to say good morning to Grandfather Frog, who sat on a big lily-pad watching for green flies for breakfast.

"Chugarum," said Grandfather Frog, which was his way of saying good morning.

Just then along came a fat green fly and up jumped Grandfather Frog. When he sat down again on the lily-pad the fat green fly was nowhere to be seen, but Grandfather Frog looked very well satisfied indeed as he contentedly rubbed his white waistcoat with one hand.

"What is the news, Grandfather Frog?" cried the Merry Little Breezes.

"Mrs. Redwing has a new speckled egg in her nest in the bulrushes," said Grandfather Frog.

"We must see it," cried the Merry Little Breezes, and away they all ran to the swamp where the bulrushes grow.

Now someone else had heard of Mrs. Redwing's dear little nest in the bulrushes, and he had started out bright and early that morning to try and find it, for he wanted to steal the little speckled eggs just because they were pretty. It was Tommy Brown, the farmer's boy.

When the Merry Little Breezes reached the swamp where the bulrushes grow they found poor Mrs. Redwing in great distress. She was afraid that Tommy Brown would find her dear little nest, for he was very, very near it, and his eyes were very, very sharp.

"Oh," cried the Merry Little Breezes, "we must help Mrs. Redwing save her pretty speckled eggs from bad Tommy Brown!"

So one of the Merry Little Breezes whisked Tommy Brown's old straw hat off his head over into the Green Meadows. Of course Tommy ran after it. Just as he stooped to pick it up another little Breeze ran away with it. Then they took turns, first one little Breeze, then another little Breeze running away with the old straw hat just as Tommy Brown would almost get his hands on it. Down past the Smiling Pool and across the Laughing Brook they raced and chased the old straw hat, Tommy Brown running after it, very cross, very red in the face, and breathing very hard. Way across the Green Meadows they ran to the edge of the wood, where they hung the old straw hat in the middle of a thorn tree. By the time Tommy Brown had it once more on his head he had forgotten all about Mrs. Redwing and her dear little nest.

Besides, he heard the breakfast horn blowing just then, so off he started for home up the Lone Little Path through the wood.

And all the Merry Little Breezes danced away across the Green Meadows to the swamp where the bulrushes grow to see the new speckled egg in the dear little nest where Mrs. Redwing was singing for joy. And while she sang the Merry Little Breezes danced among the bulrushes, for they knew, and Mrs. Redwing knew, that some day out of that pretty new speckled egg would come a wee baby Redwing.

II. Why Grandfather Frog Has No Tail

Old Mother West Wind had gone to her day's work, leaving all the Merry Little Breezes to play in the Green Meadows. They had played tag and run races with the Bees and played hide and seek with the Sun Beams, and now they had gathered around the Smiling Pool where on a green lily-pad sat Grandfather Frog.

Grandfather Frog was old, very old, indeed, and very, very wise. He wore a green coat and his voice was very deep. When Grandfather Frog spoke everybody listened very respectfully. Even Billy Mink treated Grandfather Frog with respect, for Billy Mink's father and his father's father could not remember when Grandfather Frog had not sat on the lily-pad watching for green flies.

Down in the Smiling Pool were some of Grandfather Frog's great-great-great-great-great-grandchildren. You wouldn't have known that they were his grandchildren unless someone told you. They didn't look the least bit like Grandfather Frog. They were round and fat and had long tails and perhaps this is why they were called Pollywogs.

"Oh Grandfather Frog, tell us why you don't have a tail as you did when you were young," begged one of the Merry Little Breezes.

Grandfather Frog snapped up a foolish green fly and settled himself on his big lily-pad, while all the Merry Little Breezes gathered round to listen.

"Once on a time," began Grandfather Frog, "the Frogs ruled the world, which was mostly water. There was very little dry land—oh, very little indeed! There were no boys to throw stones and no hungry Mink to gobble up foolish Frog-babies who were taking a sun bath!"

Billy Mink, who had joined the Merry Little Breezes and was listening, squirmed uneasily and looked away guiltily.

"In those days all the Frogs had tails, long handsome tails of which they were very, very proud indeed," continued Grandfather Frog. "The King of all the Frogs was twice as big as any other Frog, and his tail was three times as long. He was very proud, oh, very proud indeed of his long tail. He used to sit and admire it until he thought that there never had been and never could be another such tail. He used to wave it back and forth in the water, and every time he waved it all the other Frogs would cry 'Ah!' and 'Oh!' Every day the King grew more vain. He did nothing at all but eat and sleep and admire his tail.

"Now all the other Frogs did just as the King did, so pretty soon none of the Frogs were doing anything but sitting about eating, sleeping and admiring their own tails and the King's.

"Now you all know that people who do nothing worth while in this world are of no use and there is little room for them. So when Mother Nature saw how useless had become the Frog tribe she called the King Frog before her and she said:

"'Because you can think of nothing but your beautiful tail it shall be taken away from you. Because you do nothing but eat and sleep your mouth shall become wide like a door, and your eyes shall start forth from your head. You shall become bow-legged and ugly to look at, and all the world shall laugh at you.'

"The King Frog looked at his beautiful tail and already it seemed to have grown shorter. He looked again and it was shorter still. Every time he looked his tail had grown shorter and smaller. By and by when he looked there was nothing left but a little stub which he couldn't even wriggle. Then even that disappeared, his eyes popped out of his head and his mouth grew bigger and bigger."

Old Grandfather Frog stopped and looked sadly at a foolish green fly coming his way. "Chugarum," said Grandfather Frog, opening his mouth very wide and hopping up in the air. When he sat down again on his big lily-pad the green fly was nowhere to be seen. Grandfather Frog smacked his lips and continued:

"And from that day to this every Frog has started life with a big tail, and as he has grown bigger and bigger his tail has grown smaller and smaller, until finally it disappears, and then he remembers how foolish and useless it is to be vain of what nature has given us. And that is how I came to lose my tail," finished Grandfather Frog.

"Thank you," shouted all the Merry Little Breezes. "We won't forget."

Then they ran a race to see who could reach Johnny Chuck's home first and tell him that Farmer Brown was coming down on the Green Meadows with a gun.

III. How Reddy Fox Was Surprised

Johnny Chuck and Reddy Fox lived very near together on the edge of the Green Meadows. Johnny Chuck was fat and roly-poly. Reddy Fox was slim and wore a bright red coat. Reddy Fox used to like to frighten Johnny Chuck by suddenly popping out from behind a tree and making believe that he was going to eat Johnny Chuck all up.

One bright summer day Johnny Chuck was out looking for a good breakfast of nice tender clover. He had wandered quite a long way from his snug little house in the long meadow grass, although his mother had told him never to go out of sight of the door. But Johnny was like some little boys I know, and forgot all he had been told.

He walked and walked and walked. Every few minutes Johnny Chuck saw something farther on that looked like a patch of nice fresh clover. And every time when he reached it Johnny Chuck found that he had made a mistake. So Johnny Chuck walked and walked and walked.

Old Mother West Wind, coming across the Green

Meadows, saw Johnny Chuck and asked him where he was going. Johnny Chuck pretended not to hear and just walked faster.

One of the Merry Little Breezes danced along in front of him.

"Look out, Johnny Chuck; you will get lost," cried the Merry Little Breeze, then pulled Johnny's whiskers and ran away.

Higher and higher up in the sky climbed round, red Mr. Sun. Every time Johnny Chuck looked up at him Mr. Sun winked.

"So long as I can see great round, red Mr. Sun and he winks at me I can't be lost," thought Johnny Chuck, and trotted on looking for clover.

By and by Johnny Chuck really did find some clover—just the sweetest clover that grew in the Green Meadows. Johnny Chuck ate and ate and ate and then what do you think he did? Why, he curled right up in the nice sweet clover and went fast asleep.

Great round, red Mr. Sun kept climbing higher and higher up in the sky, then by and by he began to go down on the other side, and long shadows began to creep out across the Green Meadows. Johnny Chuck didn't know anything about them; he was fast asleep.

By and by one of the Merry Little Breezes found Johnny Chuck all curled up in a funny round ball.

"Wake up, Johnny Chuck! Wake up!" shouted the Merry Little Breeze.

Johnny Chuck opened his eyes. Then he sat up and rubbed them. For just a few, few minutes he couldn't remember where he was at all.

By and by he sat up very straight to look over the grass and see where he was. But he was so far from home that he didn't see a single thing which looked at all like the things he was used to. The trees were all different. The bushes were all different. Everything was different. Johnny Chuck was lost.

Now, when Johnny sat up, Reddy Fox happened to be looking over the Green Meadows and he saw Johnny's head when it popped above the grass.

"Aha!" said Reddy Fox, "I'll scare Johnny Chuck so he'll wish he'd never put his nose out of his house."

Then Reddy dropped down behind the long grass and crept softly, oh, ever so softly, through little paths of his own, until he was right behind Johnny Chuck. Johnny Chuck had been so intent looking for home that he didn't see anything else.

Reddy Fox stole right up behind Johnny and pulled Johnny's little short tail hard. How it did frighten Johnny Chuck! He jumped right straight up in the air and when he came down he was the maddest little woodchuck that ever lived in the Green Meadows.

Reddy Fox had thought that Johnny would run, and then Reddy meant to run after him and pull his tail and tease him all the way home. Now, Reddy Fox got as big a surprise as Johnny had had when Reddy pulled his tail. Johnny didn't stop to think that Reddy Fox was twice as big as he, but, with his eyes snapping, and chattering as only a little Chuck can chatter, with every little hair on his little body standing right up on end, so that he seemed twice as big as he really was, he started for Reddy Fox.

It surprised Reddy Fox so that he didn't know what to do, and he simply ran. Johnny Chuck ran after him, nipping Reddy's heels every minute or two. Peter Rabbit just happened to be down that way. He

Johnny didn't stop to think that Reddy Fox
was twice as big as he.
See page 11.

was sitting up very straight looking to see what mischief he could get into when he caught sight of Reddy Fox running as hard as ever he could. "It must be that Bowser, the hound, is after Reddy Fox," said Peter Rabbit to himself. "I must watch out that he don't find me."

Just then he caught sight of Johnny Chuck with every little hair standing up on end and running after Reddy Fox as fast as his short legs could go.

"Ho! ho! ho!" shouted Peter Rabbit. "Reddy Fox afraid of Johnny Chuck! Ho! ho! ho!"

Then Peter Rabbit scampered away to find Jimmy Skunk and Bobby Coon and Happy Jack Squirrel to tell them all about how Reddy Fox had run away from Johnny Chuck, for you see they were all a little afraid of Reddy Fox.

Straight home ran Reddy Fox as fast as he could go, and going home he passed the house of Johnny Chuck. Now Johnny couldn't run so fast as Reddy Fox and he was puffing and blowing as only a fat little woodchuck can puff and blow when he has to run hard. Moreover, he had lost his ill temper now and he thought it was the best joke ever was to think that he had actually frightened Reddy Fox. When he came to his own house he stopped and sat on his hind-legs once more. Then he shrilled out after Reddy Fox: "Reddy Fox is a 'fraid-cat, 'fraid-cat! Reddy Fox is a 'fraid-cat!"

And all the Merry Little Breezes of Old Mother West Wind, who were playing on the Green Meadows, shouted: "Reddy Fox is a 'fraid-cat, 'fraid-cat!"

And this is the way that Reddy Fox was surprised and that Johnny Chuck found his way home.

IV. Why Jimmy Skunk Wears Stripes

Jimmy Skunk, as everybody knows, wears a striped suit, a suit of black and white. There was a time, long, long ago, when all the Skunk family wore black. Very handsome their coats were, too, a beautiful, glossy black. They were very, very proud of them and took the greatest care of them, brushing them carefully ever so many times a day.

There was a Jimmy Skunk then, just as there is now, and he was head of all the Skunk family. Now this Jimmy Skunk was very proud and thought himself very much of a gentleman. He was very independent and cared for no one. Like a great many other independent people, he did not always consider the rights of others. Indeed, it was hinted in the wood and on the Green Meadows that not all of Jimmy Skunk's doings would bear the light of day. It was openly said that he was altogether too fond of prowling about at night, but no one could prove that he was responsible for mischief done in the night, for no one saw him. You see his coat was so black that in the darkness of the night it was not visible at all.

Now about this time of which I am telling you Mrs. Ruffed Grouse made a nest at the foot of the Great Pine and in it she laid fifteen beautiful buff eggs. Mrs. Grouse was very happy, very happy indeed, and all the little meadow folks who knew of her happiness were happy too, for they all loved shy, demure, little Mrs. Grouse. Every morning when Peter Rabbit trotted down the Lone Little Path through the wood past the Great Pine he would stop for a few minutes to chat with Mrs. Grouse. Happy Jack Squirrel would bring her the news every afternoon. The Merry Little Breezes of Old Mother West Wind would run up a dozen times a day to see how she was getting along.

One morning Peter Rabbit, coming down the Lone Little Path for his usual morning call, found a terrible state of affairs. Poor little Mrs. Grouse was heartbroken. All about the foot of the Great Pine lay the empty shells of her beautiful eggs. They had been broken and scattered this way and that.

"How did it happen?" asked Peter Rabbit.

"I don't know," sobbed poor little Mrs. Grouse. "In the night when I was fast asleep something pounced upon me. I managed to get away and fly up in the top of the Great Pine. In the morning I found all my eggs broken, just as you see them here."

Peter Rabbit looked the ground over very carefully. He hunted around behind the Great Pine, he looked under the bushes, he studied the ground with a very wise air. Then he hopped off down the Lone Little Path to the Green Meadows. He stopped at the house of Johnny Chuck.

"What makes your eyes so big and round?" asked Johnny Chuck.

Peter Rabbit came very close so as to whisper in Johnny Chuck's ear, and told him all that he had seen. Together they went to Jimmy Skunk's house. Jimmy Skunk was in bed. He was very sleepy and very cross when he came to the door. Peter Rabbit told him what he had seen.

"Too bad! Too bad!" said Jimmy Skunk, and yawned sleepily.

"Won't you join us in trying to find out who did it?" asked Johnny Chuck.

Jimmy Skunk said he would be delighted to come but that he had some other business that morning and that he would join them in the afternoon. Peter Rabbit and Johnny Chuck went on. Pretty soon they met the Merry Little Breezes and told them the dreadful story.

"What shall we do?" asked Johnny Chuck.

"We'll hurry over and tell Old Dame Nature," cried the Merry Little Breezes, "and ask her what to do."

So away flew the Merry Little Breezes to Old Dame Nature and told her all the dreadful story. Old Dame Nature listened very attentively. Then she sent the Merry Little Breezes to all the little meadow folks to tell everyone to be at the Great Pine that afternoon. Now whatever Old Dame Nature commanded all the little meadow folks were obliged to do. They did not dare to disobey her. Promptly at four o'clock that afternoon all the little meadow folks were gathered around the foot of the Great Pine. Broken-hearted little Mrs. Ruffed Grouse sat beside her empty nest, with all the broken shells about her.

Reddy Fox, Peter Rabbit, Johnny Chuck, Billy Mink, Little Joe Otter, Jerry Muskrat, Hooty the Owl, Bobby Coon, Sammy Jay, Blacky the Crow, Grandfather Frog, Mr. Toad, Spotty the Turtle, the Merry Little Breezes, all were there. Last of all came Jimmy Skunk. Very handsome he looked in his shining black coat and very sorry he appeared that such a dreadful thing should have happened. He told Mrs. Grouse how badly he felt, and he loudly demanded that the culprit should be found out and severely punished.

Old Dame Nature has the most smiling face in the world, but this time it was very, very grave indeed. First she asked little Mrs. Grouse to tell her story all over again that all might hear. Then each in turn was asked to tell where he had been the night before. Johnny Chuck, Happy Jack Squirrel, Striped Chipmunk, Sammy Jay and Blacky the Crow, had gone to bed when Mr. Sun went down behind the Purple Hills. Jerry Muskrat, Billy Mink, Little Joe Otter, Grandfather Frog and Spotty the Turtle, had not left the Smiling Pool. Bobby Coon had been down in Farmer Brown's cornfield. Hooty the Owl had been hunting in the lower end of the Green Meadows. Peter Rabbit had been down in the berry patch. Mr. Toad had been under the big piece of bark which he called a house. Old Dame Nature called on Jimmy Skunk last of all. Jimmy protested that he had been very, very tired and had gone to bed very early indeed, and had slept the whole night through.

Then Old Dame Nature asked Peter Rabbit what he had found among the egg shells that morning.

Peter Rabbit hopped out and laid three long black hairs before Old Dame Nature. "These," said Peter Rabbit, "are what I found among the egg shells."

Then Old Dame Nature called Johnny Chuck. "Tell us, Johnny Chuck," said she, "what you saw when you called at Jimmy Skunk's house this morning."

"I saw Jimmy Skunk," said Johnny Chuck, "and Jimmy seemed very, very sleepy. It seemed to me that his whiskers were yellow."

"That will do," said Old Dame Nature, and then she called Old Mother West Wind.

"What time did you come down on the Green Meadows this morning?" asked Old Dame Nature.

"Just at the break of day," said Old Mother West Wind, "as Mr. Sun was coming up from behind the Purple Hills."

"And whom did you see so early in the morning?" asked Old Dame Nature.

"I saw Bobby Coon going home from old Farmer Brown's cornfield," said Old Mother West Wind. "I saw Hooty the Owl coming back from the lower end of the Green Meadows. I saw Peter Rabbit down in the berry patch. Last of all I saw something like a black shadow coming down the Lone Little Path toward the house of Jimmy Skunk."

Everyone was looking very hard at Jimmy Skunk. Jimmy began to look very unhappy and very uneasy.

"Who wears a black coat?" asked Dame Nature.

"Jimmy Skunk!" shouted all the little meadow folks.

"What *might* make whiskers yellow?" asked Old Dame Nature.

No one seemed to know at first. Then Peter Rabbit spoke up. "It *might* be the yolk of an egg," said Peter Rabbit.

"Who are likely to be sleepy on a bright sunny morning?" asked Old Dame Nature.

"People who have been out all night," said Johnny Chuck, who himself always goes to bed with the sun.

"Jimmy Skunk," said Old Dame Nature, and her voice was very stern, very stern indeed, and her face was very grave, "Jimmy Skunk, I accuse you of having broken and eaten the eggs of Mrs. Grouse. What have you to say for yourself?"

Jimmy Skunk hung his head. He hadn't a word to say. He just wanted to sneak away by himself.

"Jimmy Skunk," said Old Dame Nature, "because your handsome black coat of which you are so proud has made it possible for you to move about in the night without being seen, and because we can no longer trust you upon your honor, henceforth you and your descendants shall wear a striped coat, which is the sign that you cannot be trusted. Your coat hereafter shall be black and white, that when you move about in the night you will always be visible."

And this is why that to this day Jimmy Skunk wears a striped suit of black and white.

V. The Wilful Little Breeze

Old Mother West Wind was tired—tired and just a wee bit cross—cross because she was tired. She had had a very busy day. Ever since early morning she had been puffing out the white sails of the ships on the big ocean that they might go faster; she had kept all the big and little wind mills whirling and whirling to pump water for thirsty folks and grind corn for hungry folks; she had blown away all the smoke from tall chimneys and engines and steamboats. Yes, indeed, Old Mother West Wind had been very, very busy.

Now she was coming across the Green Meadows on her way to her home behind the Purple Hills, and as she came she opened the big bag she carried and called to her children, the Merry Little Breezes, who had been playing hard on the Green Meadows all the long day. One by one they crept into the big bag, for they were tired, too, and ready to go to their home behind the Purple Hills.

Pretty soon all were in the bag but one, a wilful little Breeze, who was not quite ready to go home; he wanted to play just a little longer. He danced ahead of Old Mother West Wind. He kissed the sleepy daisies. He shook the nodding buttercups. He set all the little poplar leaves a dancing, too, and he wouldn't come into the big bag.

So Old Mother West Wind closed the big bag and slung it over her shoulder. Then she started on towards her home behind the Purple Hills.

When she had gone the wilful little Breeze left behind suddenly felt very lonely—very lonely indeed! The sleepy daisies didn't want to play. The nodding buttercups were cross. Great round bright Mr. Sun, who had been shining and shining all day long, went to bed and put on his night cap of golden clouds. Black shadows came creeping, creeping out into the Green Meadows.

The wilful little Breeze began to wish that he was safe in Old Mother West Wind's big bag with all the other Merry Little Breezes.

So he started across the Green Meadows to find the Purple Hills. But all the hills were black now and he could not tell which he should look behind to find his home with Old Mother West Wind and the Merry Little Breezes. How he did wish that he had minded Old Mother West Wind.

By and by he curled up under a bayberry bush and tried to go to sleep, but he was lonely, oh, so lonely!

and he couldn't go to sleep. Old Mother Moon came up and flooded all the Green Meadows with light, but it wasn't like the bright light of jolly round Mr. Sun, for it was cold and white and it made many black shadows.

Pretty soon the wilful little Breeze heard Hooty the Owl out hunting for a meadow mouse for his dinner. Then down the Lone Little Path which ran close to the bayberry bush trotted Reddy Fox. He was trotting very softly and every minute or so he turned his head and looked behind him to see if he was followed. It was plain to see that Reddy Fox was bent on mischief.

When he reached the bayberry bush Reddy Fox sat down and barked twice. Hooty the Owl answered him at once and flew over to join him. They didn't see the wilful little Breeze curled up under the bayberry bush, so intent were these two rogues in plotting mischief. They were planning to steal down across the Green Meadows to the edge of the Brown Pasture where Mr. Bob White and pretty Mrs. Bob White and a dozen little Bob Whites had their home.

"When they run along the ground I'll catch 'em, and when they fly up in the air you'll catch 'em and we'll gobble 'em all up," said Reddy Fox to Hooty the Owl. Then he licked his chops and Hooty the Owl snapped his bill, just as if they were tasting tender little Bob Whites that very minute. It made the wilful little Breeze shiver to see them. Pretty soon they started on towards the Brown Pasture.

When they were out of sight the wilful little Breeze jumped up and shook himself. Then away he sped across the Green Meadows to the Brown Pasture.

And because he could go faster and because he went a shorter way he got there first. He had to hunt and hunt to find Mrs. and Mr. Bob White and all the little Bob Whites, but finally he did find them, all with their heads tucked under their wings fast asleep. The wilful little Breeze shook Mr. Bob White very gently. In an instant he was wide awake.

"Sh-h-h," said the wilful little Breeze. "Reddy Fox and Hooty the Owl are coming to the Brown Pasture to gobble up you and Mrs. Bob White and all the little Bob Whites."

"Thank you, little Breeze," said Mr. Bob White, "I think I'll move my family."

Then he woke Mrs. Bob White and all the little Bob Whites. With Mr. Bob White in the lead away they all flew to the far side of the Brown Pasture where they were soon safely hidden under a juniper tree.

The wilful little Breeze saw them safely there, and when they were nicely hidden hurried back to the place where the Bob Whites had been sleeping. Reddy Fox was stealing up through the grass very, very softly. Hooty the Owl was flying as silently as a shadow. When Reddy Fox thought he was near enough he drew himself together, made a quick spring and landed right in Mr. Bob White's empty bed. Reddy Fox and Hooty the Owl looked so surprised and foolish when they found that the Bob Whites were not there that the wilful little Breeze nearly laughed out loud.

Then Reddy Fox and Hooty the Owl hunted here and hunted there, all over the Brown Pasture, but they couldn't find the Bob Whites.

And the wilful little Breeze went back to the juniper

tree and curled himself up beside Mr. Bob White to sleep, for he was lonely no longer.

VI. Reddy Fox Goes Fishing

One morning when Mr. Sun was very, very bright and it was very, very warm, down on the Green Meadows Reddy Fox came hopping and skipping down the Lone Little Path that leads to the Laughing Brook. Hoppity, skip, skippity hop! Reddy felt very much pleased with himself that sunny morning. Pretty soon he saw Johnny Chuck sitting up very straight close by the little house where he lives.

"Johnny Chuck, Chuck, Chuck! Johnny Chuck, Chuck, Chuck! Johnny Woodchuck!" called Reddy Fox.

Johnny Chuck pretended not to hear. His mother had told him not to play with Reddy Fox, for Reddy Fox was a bad boy.

"Johnny Chuck, Chuck, Chuck! Johnny Wood-chuck!" called Reddy again.

This time Johnny turned and looked. He could see Reddy Fox turning somersaults and chasing his tail and rolling over and over in the little path.

"Come on!" said Reddy Fox. "Let's go fishing!"

"Can't," said Johnny Chuck, because, you know, his mother had told him not to play with Reddy Fox.

"I'll show you how to catch a fish," said Reddy Fox, and tried to jump over his own shadow.

"Can't," said good little Johnny Chuck again, and turned away so that he couldn't see Reddy Fox chasing Butterflies and playing catch with the Field Mice children.

So Reddy Fox went down to the Laughing Brook all alone. The Brook was laughing and singing on its way to join the Big River. The sky was blue and the sun was bright. Reddy Fox jumped on the Big Rock in the middle of the Laughing Brook and peeped over the other side. What do you think he saw? Why, right down below in a Dear Little Pool were Mr. and Mrs. Trout and all the little Trouts.

Reddy Fox wanted some of those little Trouts to take home for his dinner, but he didn't know how to catch them. He lay flat down on the Big Rock and reached way down into the Dear Little Pool, but all the little Trouts laughed at Reddy Fox and not one came within reach. Then Mr. Trout swam up so quickly that Reddy Fox didn't see him coming and bit Reddy's little black paw hard.

"Ouch!" cried Reddy Fox, pulling his little black paw out of the water. And all the little Trouts laughed at Reddy Fox.

Just then along came Billy Mink.

"Hello, Reddy Fox!" said Billy Mink. "What are you doing here?"

"I'm trying to catch a fish," said Reddy Fox.

"Pooh! That's easy!" said Billy Mink. "I'll show you how."

So Billy Mink lay down on the Big Rock side of Reddy Fox and peeped over into the Dear Little Pool where all the little Trouts were laughing at Reddy Fox and having such a good time. But Billy Mink took care, such very great care, that Mr. Trout and Mrs. Trout should not see him peeping over into the Dear Little Pool.

When Billy Mink saw all those little Trouts playing in the Dear Little Pool he laughed. "You count three, Reddy Fox," said he, "and I'll show you how to catch a fish."

"One!" said Reddy Fox, "Two! Three!"

Splash! Billy Mink had dived head first into the Dear Little Pool. He spattered water way up onto Reddy Fox, and he frightened old Mr. Frog so that he fell over backwards off the lily-pad where he was taking a morning nap right into the water. In a minute Billy Mink climbed out on the other side of the Dear Little Pool and sure enough, he had caught one of the little Trouts.

"Give it to me," cried Reddy Fox.

"Catch one yourself," said Billy Mink. "Old Grandpa Mink wants a fish for his dinner, so I'm going to take this home. You're afraid, Reddy Fox! Fraid-cat! Fraid-cat!"

Billy Mink shook the water off of his little brown coat, picked up the little Trout and ran off home.

Reddy Fox lay down again on the Big Rock and peeped into the Dear Little Pool. Not a single Trout could he see. They were all hiding safely with Mr. and Mrs. Trout. Reddy Fox watched and watched. The sun was warm, the Laughing Brook was singing a lullaby and—what do you think? Why, Reddy Fox went fast asleep right on the edge of the great Big Rock.

By and by Reddy Fox began to dream. He dreamed that he had a nice little brown coat that was waterproof, just like the little brown coat that Billy Mink wore. Yes, and he dreamed that he had learned to swim and to catch fish just as Billy Mink did. He dreamed that the Dear Little Pool was full of little

Trouts and that he was just going to catch one when—splash! Reddy Fox had rolled right off of the Big Rock into the Dear Little Pool.

The water went into the eyes of Reddy Fox, and it went up his nose and he swallowed so much that he felt as if he never, never would want another drink of water. And his beautiful red coat, which old Mother Fox had told him to be very, very careful of because he couldn't have another for a whole year, was oh so wet! And his pants were wet and his beautiful bushy tail, of which he was so proud, was so full of water that he couldn't hold it up, but had to drag it up the bank after him as he crawled out of the Dear Little Pool.

"Ha! Ha! Ha!" laughed Mr. Kingfisher, sitting on a tree.

"Ho! Ho! Ho!" laughed old Mr. Frog, who had climbed back on his lily-pad.

"He! He! He!" laughed all the little Trouts and Mr. Trout and Mrs. Trout, swimming round and round in the Dear Little Pool.

"Ha! Ha! Ha! Ho! Ho! Ho! He! He! He!" laughed Billy Mink, who had come back to the Big Rock just in time to see Reddy Fox tumble in.

Reddy Fox didn't say a word, he was so ashamed. He just crept up the Lone Little Path to his home, dragging his tail, all wet and muddy, behind him, and dripping water all the way.

Johnny Chuck was still sitting by his door as his mother had told him to. Reddy Fox tried to go past without being seen, but Johnny Chuck's bright little eyes saw him.

"Where are your fish, Reddy Fox?" called Johnny Chuck.

Reddy Fox said never a word, but walked faster. "Why don't you turn somersaults, and jump over your shadow and chase Butterflies and play with the little Field Mice, Reddy Fox?" called Johnny Chuck. But Reddy Fox just walked faster. When he got most home he saw old Mother Fox sitting in the doorway with a great big switch across her lap, for Mother Fox had told Reddy Fox not to go near the Laughing Brook.

And this is all I am going to tell you about how Reddy Fox went fishing.

VII. Jimmy Skunk Looks for Beetles

Jimmy Skunk opened his eyes very early one morning and peeped out of his snug little house on the hill. Big, round Mr. Sun, with a very red, smiling face, had just begun to climb up into the sky. Old Mother West Wind was just starting down to the Green Meadows with her big bag over her shoulder. In that bag Jimmy Skunk knew she carried all her children, the Merry Little Breezes, whom she was taking down to the Green Meadows to play and frolic all day.

"Good morning, Mother West Wind," said Jimmy Skunk, politely. "Did you see any beetles as you came down the hill?"

Old Mother West Wind said, no, she hadn't seen any beetles as she came down the hill.

"Thank you," said Jimmy Skunk, politely. "I guess I'll have to go look myself, for I'm very, very hungry."

So Jimmy Skunk brushed his handsome black and

white coat, and washed his face and hands, and started out to try to find some beetles for his breakfast.
First he went down to the Green Meadows and
stopped at Johnny Chuck's house. But Johnny Chuck
was still in bed and fast asleep. Then Jimmy Skunk
went over to see if Reddy Fox would go with him to
help find some beetles for his breakfast. But Reddy
Fox had been out very, very late the night before and
he was still in bed fast asleep, too.

So Jimmy Skunk set out all alone along the Crooked
Little Path up the hill to find some beetles for his
breakfast. He walked very slowly, for Jimmy Skunk
never hurries. He stopped and peeped under every
old log to see if there were any beetles. By and by he
came to a big piece of bark beside the Crooked Little
Path. Jimmy Skunk took hold of the piece of bark
with his two little black paws and pulled and pulled.
All of a sudden, the big piece of bark turned over so
quickly that Jimmy Skunk fell flat on his back.

When Jimmy Skunk had rolled over onto his feet
again, there sat old Mr. Toad right in the path, and
old Mr. Toad was very, very cross indeed. He swelled
and he puffed and he puffed and he swelled, till he
was twice as big as Jimmy Skunk had ever seen him
before.

"Good morning, Mr. Toad," said Jimmy Skunk.
"Have you seen any beetles?"

But Mr. Toad blinked his great round goggly eyes
and he said:

"What do you mean, Jimmy Skunk, by pulling the
roof off my house?"

"Is that the roof of your house?" asked Jimmy
Skunk politely. "I won't do it again."

Then Jimmy Skunk stepped right over old Mr. Toad, and went on up the Crooked Little Path to look for some beetles.

By and by he came to an old stump of a tree which was hollow and had the nicest little round hole in one side. Jimmy Skunk took hold of one edge with his two little black paws and pulled and pulled. All of a sudden the whole side of the old stump tore open and Jimmy Skunk fell flat on his back.

When Jimmy Skunk had rolled over onto his feet again there was Striped Chipmunk hopping up and down right in the middle of the path, he was so angry.

"Good morning, Striped Chipmunk," said Jimmy Skunk. "Have you seen any beetles?"

But Striped Chipmunk hopped faster than ever and he said:

"What do you mean, Jimmy Skunk, by pulling the side off my house?"

"Is that the side of your house?" asked Jimmy Skunk, politely. "I won't do it again."

Then Jimmy Skunk stepped right over Striped Chipmunk, and went on up the Crooked Little Path to look for some beetles.

Pretty soon he met Peter Rabbit hopping along down the Crooked Little Path. "Good morning, Jimmy Skunk, where are you going so early in the morning?" said Peter Rabbit.

"Good morning, Peter Rabbit. Have you seen any beetles?" asked Jimmy Skunk, politely.

"No, I haven't seen any beetles, but I'll help you find some," said Peter Rabbit. So he turned about and hopped ahead of Jimmy Skunk up the Crooked Little Path.

Now because Peter Rabbit's legs are long and he is always in a hurry, he got to the top of the hill first. When Jimmy Skunk reached the end of the Crooked Little Path on the top of the hill he found Peter Rabbit sitting up very straight and looking and looking very hard at a great flat stone.

"What are you looking at, Peter Rabbit?" asked Jimmy Skunk.

"Sh-h-h!" said Peter Rabbit, "I think there are some beetles under that great flat stone where that little black string is sticking out. Now when I count three you grab that string and pull hard; perhaps you'll find a beetle at the other end."

So Jimmy Skunk got ready and Peter Rabbit began to count.

"One!" said Peter. "Two!" said Peter. "Three!"

Jimmy Skunk grabbed the black string and pulled as hard as ever he could and out came—Mr. Black Snake! The string Jimmy Skunk had pulled was Mr. Black Snake's tail, and Mr. Black Snake was very, very angry indeed.

"Ha! Ha! Ha!" laughed Peter Rabbit.

"What do you mean, Jimmy Skunk," said Mr. Black Snake, "by pulling my tail?"

"Was that your tail?" said Jimmy Skunk, politely. "I won't do it again. Have you seen any beetles?"

But Mr. Black Snake hadn't seen any beetles and he was so cross that Jimmy Skunk went on over the hill to look for some beetles.

Peter Rabbit was still laughing and laughing and laughing. And the more he laughed the angrier grew Mr. Black Snake, till finally he started after Peter Rabbit to teach him a lesson.

Then Peter Rabbit stopped laughing, for Mr. Black Snake can run very fast. Away went Peter Rabbit down the Crooked Little Path as fast as he could go, and away went Mr. Black Snake after him.

But Jimmy Skunk didn't even look once to see if Mr. Black Snake had caught Peter Rabbit, for Jimmy Skunk had found some beetles and was eating his breakfast.

VIII. Billy Mink's Swimming Party

Billy Mink was coming down the bank of the Laughing Brook. Billy Mink was feeling very good indeed. He had had a good breakfast, the sun was warm, little white cloud ships were sailing across the blue sky and their shadows were sailing across the Green Meadows, the birds were singing and the bees were humming. Billy Mink felt like singing too, but Billy Mink's voice was not meant for singing.

By and by Billy Mink came to the Smiling Pool. Here the Laughing Brook stopped and rested on its way to join the Big River. It stopped its noisy laughing and singing and just lay smiling and smiling in the warm sunshine. The little flowers on the bank leaned over and nodded to it. The beech tree, which was very old, sometimes dropped a leaf into it. The cattails kept their feet cool in the edge of it.

Billy Mink jumped out on the Big Rock and looked down into the Smiling Pool. Over on a green lily-pad he saw old Grandfather Frog.

"Hello, Grandfather Frog," said Billy Mink.

"Hello, Billy Mink," said Grandfather Frog. "What mischief are you up to this fine sunny morning?"

Just then Billy Mink saw a little brown head swimming along one edge of the Smiling Pool.

"Hello, Jerry Muskrat!" shouted Billy Mink.

"Hello your own self, Billy Mink," shouted Jerry Muskrat, "Come in and have a swim; the water's fine!"

"Good," said Billy Mink. "We'll have a swimming party."

So Billy Mink called all the Merry Little Breezes of Old Mother West Wind, who were playing with the flowers on the bank, and sent them to find Little Joe Otter and invite him to come to the swimming party. Pretty soon back came the Little Breezes and with them came Little Joe Otter.

"Hello, Billy Mink," said Little Joe Otter. "Here I am!"

"Hello, Little Joe Otter," said Billy Mink. "Come up here on the Big Rock and see who can dive the deepest into the Smiling Pool."

So Little Joe Otter and Jerry Muskrat climbed up on the Big Rock side of Billy Mink and they all stood side by side in their little brown bathing suits looking down into the Smiling Pool.

"Now when I count three we'll all dive into the Smiling Pool together and see who can dive the deepest. One!" said Billy Mink. "Two!" said Billy Mink. "Three!" said Billy Mink.

And when he said "Three" in they all went head first. My, such a splash as they did make! They upset old Grandfather Frog so that he fell off his lily-pad. They frightened Mr. and Mrs. Trout so that they jumped right out of the water. Tiny Tadpole had such a scare that he hid way, way down in the mud with only the tip of his funny little nose sticking out.

"Chug-a-rum," said old Grandfather Frog, climbing out on his lily-pad. "If I wasn't so old I would show you how to dive."

"Come on, Grandfather Frog!" cried Billy Mink. "Show us how to dive."

And what do you think? Why, old Grandfather Frog actually got so excited that he climbed up on the Big Rock to show them how to dive. Splash! went Grandfather Frog into the Smiling Pool. Splash! went Billy Mink right behind him. Splash! Splash! went Little Joe Otter and Jerry Muskrat, right at Billy Mink's heels.

"Hurrah!" shouted Mr. Kingfisher, sitting on a branch of the old beech tree. And then just to show them that he could dive, too, splash! he went into the Smiling Pool.

Such a noise as they did make! All the Little Breezes of Old Mother West Wind danced for joy on the bank. Blacky the Crow and Sammy Jay flew over to see what was going on.

"Now, let's see who can swim the farthest under water," cried Billy Mink.

So they all stood side by side on one edge of the Smiling Pool.

"Go!" shouted Mr. Kingfisher, and in they all plunged. Little ripples ran across the Smiling Pool and then the water became as smooth and smiling as if nothing had gone into it with a plunge.

Now old Grandfather Frog began to realize that he wasn't as young as he used to be, and he couldn't swim as fast as the others anyway. He began to get short of breath, so he swam up to the top and stuck just the tip of his nose out to get some more air. Sammy Jay's sharp eyes saw him.

"There's Grandfather Frog!" he shouted.

So then Grandfather Frog popped his head out and swam over to his green lily-pad to rest.

Way over beyond the Big Rock little bubbles in three long rows kept coming up to the top of the Smiling Pool. They showed just where Billy Mink, Little Joe Otter and Jerry Muskrat were swimming way down out of sight. It was the air from their lungs making the bubbles. Straight across the Smiling Pool went the lines of little bubbles and then way out on the farther side two little heads bobbed out of water close together. They were Billy Mink and Little Joe Otter. A moment later Jerry Muskrat bobbed up beside them.

You see they had swum clear across the Smiling Pool and of course they could swim no farther.

So Billy Mink's swimming party was a great success.

IX. Peter Rabbit Plays a Joke

One morning when big round Mr. Sun was climbing up in the sky and Old Mother West Wind had sent all her Merry Little Breezes to play in the Green Meadows, Johnny Chuck started out for a walk. First he sat up very straight and looked and looked all around to see if Reddy Fox was anywhere about, for you know Reddy Fox liked to tease Johnny Chuck.

But Reddy Fox was nowhere to be seen, so Johnny

Chuck trotted down the Lone Little Path to the wood. Mr. Sun was shining as brightly as ever he could and Johnny Chuck, who was very, very fat, grew very, very warm. By and by he sat down on the end of a log under a big tree to rest.

Thump! Something hit Johnny Chuck right on the top of his round little head. It made Johnny Chuck jump.

"Hello, Johnny Chuck!" said a voice that seemed to come right out of the sky. Johnny Chuck tipped his head way, way back and looked up. He was just in time to see Happy Jack Squirrel drop a nut. Down it came and hit Johnny Chuck right on the tip of his funny, black, little nose.

"Oh!" said Johnny Chuck, and tumbled right over back off the log. But Johnny Chuck was so round and so fat and so roly-poly that it didn't hurt him a bit.

"Ha! Ha! Ha!" laughed Happy Jack up in the tree.

"Ha! Ha! Ha!" laughed Johnny Chuck, picking himself up. Then they both laughed together, it was such a good joke.

"What are you laughing at?" asked a voice so close to Johnny Chuck that he rolled over three times he was so surprised. It was Peter Rabbit.

"What are you doing in my wood?" asked Peter Rabbit.

"I'm taking a walk," said Johnny Chuck.

"Good," said Peter Rabbit, "I'll come along too."

So Johnny Chuck and Peter Rabbit set out along the Lone Little Path through the wood. Peter Rabbit hopped along with great big jumps, for Peter's legs are long and meant for jumping, but Johnny Chuck couldn't keep up though he tried very hard, for

Johnny's legs are short. Pretty soon Peter Rabbit came back, walking very softly. He whispered in Johnny Chuck's ear.

"I've found something," said Peter Rabbit.

"What is it?" asked Johnny Chuck.

"I'll show you," said Peter Rabbit, "but you must be very, very still, and not make the least little bit of noise."

Johnny Chuck promised to be very, very still for he wanted very much to see what Peter Rabbit had found. Peter Rabbit tip-toed down the Lone Little Path through the wood, his funny long ears pointing right up to the sky. And behind him tip-toed Johnny Chuck, wondering and wondering what it could be that Peter Rabbit had found.

Pretty soon they came to a nice mossy green log right across the Lone Little Path. Peter Rabbit stopped and sat up very straight. He looked this way and looked that way. Johnny Chuck stopped too and he sat up very straight and looked this way and looked that way, but all he could see was the mossy green log across the Lone Little Path.

"What is it, Peter Rabbit?" whispered Johnny Chuck.

"You can't see it yet," whispered Peter Rabbit, "for first we have to jump over that mossy green log. Now I'll jump first, and then you jump just the way I do, and then you'll see what it is I've found," said Peter Rabbit.

So Peter Rabbit jumped first, and because his legs are long and meant for jumping, he jumped way, way over the mossy green log. Then he turned around and sat up to see Johnny Chuck jump over the mossy green log, too.

Johnny Chuck tried to jump very high and very far, just as he had seen Peter Rabbit jump, but Johnny Chuck's legs are very short and not meant for jumping. Besides, Johnny Chuck was very, very fat. So though he tried very hard indeed to jump just like Peter Rabbit, he stubbed his toes on the top of the mossy green log and over he tumbled, head first, and landed with a great big thump right on Reddy Fox, who was lying fast asleep on the other side of the mossy green log.

Peter Rabbit laughed and laughed until he had to hold his sides.

My, how frightened Johnny Chuck was when he saw what he had done! Before he could get on his feet he had rolled right over behind a little bush, and there he lay very, very still.

Reddy Fox awoke with a grunt when Johnny Chuck fell on him so hard, and the first thing he saw was Peter Rabbit laughing so that he had to hold his sides. Reddy Fox didn't stop to look around. He thought that Peter Rabbit had jumped on him. Up jumped Reddy Fox and away ran Peter Rabbit. Away went Reddy Fox after Peter Rabbit. Peter dodged behind the trees, and jumped over the bushes, and ran this way and ran that way, just as hard as ever he could, for Peter Rabbit was very much afraid of Reddy Fox. And Reddy Fox followed Peter Rabbit behind the trees and over the bushes this way and that way, but he couldn't catch Peter Rabbit. Pretty soon Peter Rabbit came to the house of Jimmy Skunk. He knew that Jimmy Skunk was over in the pasture, so he popped right in and then he was safe, for the door of Jimmy Skunk's house was too small for Reddy Fox to squeeze in. Reddy Fox sat down and waited, but Peter Rabbit didn't come out. By and by Reddy Fox gave it up and trotted off home where old Mother Fox was waiting for him.

All this time Johnny Chuck had sat very still, watching Reddy Fox try to catch Peter Rabbit. And when he saw Peter Rabbit pop into the house of Jimmy Skunk and Reddy Fox trot away home, Johnny Chuck stood up and brushed his little coat very clean and then he trotted back up the Lone Little Path through the wood to his own dear little path through the Green Meadows where the Merry Little Breezes of Old Mother West Wind were still playing, till he was safe in his own snug little home once more.

X. How Sammy Jay Was Found Out

Sammy Jay was very busy, very busy indeed. When anyone happened that way Sammy Jay pretended to be doing nothing at all, for Sammy Jay thought himself a very fine gentleman. He was very proud of his handsome blue coat with white trimmings and his high cap, and he would sit on a fence post and make fun of Johnny Chuck working at a new door for his snug little home in the Green Meadows, and of Striped Chipmunk storing up heaps of corn and nuts for the winter, for most of the time Sammy Jay was an idle fellow. And when Sammy Jay *was* busy, he was pretty sure to be doing something he ought not to do, for idle people almost always get into mischief.

The door of the house was too small
for Reddy Fox to squeeze in.
See page 38.

Sammy Jay was in mischief now, and that is why he pretended to be doing nothing when he thought anyone was looking.

Old Mother West Wind had come down from her home behind the Purple Hills very early that morning. Indeed, jolly, round, red Mr. Sun had hardly gotten out of bed when she crossed the Green Meadows on her way to help the big ships across the ocean. Old Mother West Wind's eyes were sharp, and she saw Sammy Jay before Sammy Jay saw her.

"Now what can Sammy Jay be so busy about, and why is he so very, very quiet?" thought Old Mother West Wind. "He must be up to some mischief."

So when she opened her big bag and turned out all her Merry Little Breezes to play on the Green Meadows she sent one of them to see what Sammy Jay was doing in the old chestnut tree. The Merry Little Breeze danced along over the tree tops just as if he hadn't a thought in the world but to wake up all the little leaves and set them to dancing too, and Sammy Jay, watching Old Mother West Wind and the other Merry Little Breezes, didn't see this Merry Little Breeze at all.

Pretty soon it danced back to Old Mother West Wind and whispered in her ear: "Sammy Jay is stealing the nuts Happy Jack Squirrel had hidden in the hollow of the old chestnut tree, and is hiding them for himself in the tumble down nest that Blacky the Crow built in the Great Pine last year." "Aha!" said Old Mother West Wind. Then she went on across the Green Meadows.

"Good morning, Old Mother West Wind," said Sammy Jay as she passed the fence post where he was sitting.

"Good morning, Sammy Jay," said Old Mother West Wind. "What brings you out so early in the morning?"

"I'm out for my health, Old Mother West Wind," said Sammy Jay politely. "The doctor has ordered me to take a bath in the dew at sunrise every morning."

Old Mother West Wind said nothing, but went on her way across the Green Meadows to blow the ships across the ocean. When she had passed Sammy Jay hurried to take the last of Happy Jack's nuts to the old nest in the Great Pine.

Poor Happy Jack! Soon he came dancing along with another nut to put in the hollow of the old chestnut tree. When he peeped in and saw that all his big store of nuts had disappeared he couldn't believe his own eyes. He put in one paw and felt all around but not a nut could he feel. Then he climbed in and sure enough, the hollow was empty.

Poor Happy Jack! There were tears in his eyes when he crept out again. He looked all around but no one was to be seen but handsome Sammy Jay, very busy brushing his beautiful blue coat.

"Good morning, Sammy Jay, have you seen anyone pass this way?" asked Happy Jack. "Someone has stolen my store of nuts from the hollow in the old chestnut tree."

Sammy Jay pretended to feel very badly indeed, and in his sweetest voice, for his voice was very sweet in those days, he offered to help Happy Jack try to catch the thief who had stolen the store of nuts from the hollow in the old chestnut tree.

Together they went down across the Green

Meadows asking everyone whom they met if they had seen the thief who had stolen Happy Jack's store of nuts from the hollow in the old chestnut tree. All the Merry Little Breezes joined in the search, and soon everyone who lived in the Green Meadows or in the wood knew that someone had stolen all of Happy Jack Squirrel's store of nuts from the hollow in the old chestnut tree. And because everyone liked Happy Jack, everyone felt very sorry indeed for him.

The next morning all the Merry Little Breezes of Old Mother West Wind were turned out of the big bag into the Green Meadows very early indeed, for they had a lot of errands to do. All over the Green Meadows they hurried, all through the wood, up and down the Laughing Brook and all around the Smiling Pool, inviting everybody to meet at the Great Pine on the hill at nine o'clock to form a committee of the whole—that's what Old Mother West Wind called it—a committee of the whole— to try to find the thief who stole Happy Jack's nuts from the hollow in the old chestnut tree.

And because everyone liked Happy Jack every- one went to the Great Pine on the hill—Reddy Fox, Bobby Coon, Jimmy Skunk, Striped Chipmunk, who is Happy Jack's cousin you know, Billy Mink, Little Joe Otter, Jerry Muskrat, Hooty the Owl, who was almost too sleepy to keep his eyes open, Blacky the Crow, Johnny Chuck, Peter Rabbit, even old Grandfather Frog. Of course Sammy Jay was there, looking his handsomest.

When they had all gathered around the Great Pine, Old Mother West Wind pointed to the old nest way up in the top of it. "Is that your nest?" she asked Blacky the Crow.

"It was, but I gave it to my cousin, Sammy Jay," said Blacky the Crow.

"Is that your nest, and may I have a stick out of it?" asked Old Mother West Wind of Sammy Jay.

"It is," said Sammy Jay, with his politest bow, "and you are welcome to a stick out of it." To himself he thought, "She will only take one from the top and that won't matter."

Old Mother West Wind suddenly puffed out her cheeks and blew so hard that she blew a big stick right out of the bottom of the old nest. Down it fell bumpity-bump on the branches of the Great Pine. After it fell—what do you think? Why, hickory nuts and chestnuts and acorns and hazel nuts, such a lot of them!

"Why! Why-e-e!" cried Happy Jack. "There are all my stolen nuts!"

Everybody turned to look at Sammy Jay, but he was flying off through the wood as fast as he could go. "Stop thief!" cried Old Mother West Wind. "Stop thief!" cried all the Merry Little Breezes and Johnny Chuck and Billy Mink and all the rest. But Sammy Jay didn't stop.

Then all began to pick up the nuts that had fallen from the old nest where Sammy Jay had hidden them. By and by, with Happy Jack leading the way, they all marched back to the old chestnut tree and there Happy Jack stored all the nuts away in his snug little hollow once more.

And ever since that day, Sammy Jay, whenever he tries to call, just screams: "Thief!" "Thief!" "Thief!"

XI. Jerry Muskrat's Party

All the Merry Little Breezes of Old Mother West Wind were hurrying over the Green Meadows. Some flew this way and some ran that way and some danced the other way. You see Jerry Muskrat had asked them to carry his invitations to a party at the Big Rock in the Smiling Pool.

Of course everyone said that they would be delighted to go to Jerry Muskrat's party. Round Mr. Sun shone his very brightest. The sky was its bluest and the little birds had promised to be there to sing for Jerry Muskrat, so of course all the little folks in the Green Meadows and in the wood wanted to go.

There were Johnny Chuck and Reddy Fox and Jimmy Skunk and Bobby Coon and Happy Jack Squirrel and Striped Chipmunk and Billy Mink and Little Joe Otter and Grandfather Frog and old Mr. Toad and Mr. Black Snake—all going to Jerry Muskrat's party.

When they reached the Smiling Pool they found Jerry Muskrat all ready. His brothers and his sisters, his aunts and his uncles and his cousins were all there. Such a merry, merry time as there was in the Smiling Pool! How the water did splash! Billy Mink and Little Joe Otter and Grandfather Frog jumped right in as soon as they got there. They played tag in the water and hide and seek behind the Big Rock. They turned somersaults down the slippery slide and they had such a good time!

But Reddy Fox and Peter Rabbit and Bobby Coon and Johnny Chuck and Jimmy Skunk and Happy Jack and Striped Chipmunk couldn't swim, so of course they couldn't play tag in the water or hide and seek or go down the slippery slide; all they could do was sit around to look on and wish that they knew how to swim, too. So of course they didn't have a good time. Soon they began to wish that they hadn't come to Jerry Muskrat's party. When he found that they were not having a good time, poor Jerry Muskrat felt very badly indeed. You see he lives in the water so much that he had quite forgotten that there was any one who couldn't swim, or he never, never would have invited all the little meadow folks who live on dry land.

"Let's go home," said Peter Rabbit to Johnny Chuck.

"We can have more fun up on the hill," said Jimmy Skunk.

Just then Little Joe Otter came pushing a great big log across the Smiling Pool.

"Here's a ship, Bobby Coon. You get on one end and I'll give you a sail across the Smiling Pool," shouted Little Joe Otter.

So Bobby Coon crawled out on the big log and held on very tight, while Little Joe Otter swam behind and pushed the big log. Across the Smiling Pool they went and back again. Bobby Coon had such a good ride that he wanted to go again, but Jimmy Skunk wanted a ride. So Bobby Coon hopped off of the big log and Jimmy Skunk hopped on and away he went across the Smiling Pool with Little Joe Otter pushing behind.

Then Jerry Muskrat found another log and gave Peter Rabbit a ride. Jerry Muskrat's brothers and sisters and aunts and uncles and cousins found logs and took Reddy Fox and Johnny Chuck and even Mr. Toad back and forth across the Smiling Pool.

Happy Jack Squirrel sat up very straight on the end of his log and spread his great bushy tail for a sail. All the little Breezes blew and blew and Happy Jack Squirrel sailed round and round the Smiling Pool.

Sometimes some one would fall off into the water and get wet, but Jerry Muskrat or Billy Mink always pulled them out again, and no one cared the tiniest bit for a wetting.

In the bushes around the Smiling Pool the little birds sang and sang. Reddy Fox barked his loudest. Happy Jack Squirrel chattered and chir-r-r-ed. All the muskrats squealed and squeaked, for Jerry Muskrat's party was such fun!

By and by when Mr. Sun went down behind the Purple Hills to his home and Old Mother West Wind with all her Merry Little Breezes went after him, and the little stars came out to twinkle and twinkle, the Smiling Pool lay all quiet and still, but smiling and smiling to think what a good time everyone had had at Jerry Muskrat's party.

XII. Bobby Coon and Reddy Fox Play Tricks

It was night. All the little stars were looking down and twinkling and twinkling. Mother Moon was doing her best to make the Green Meadows as light as Mr. Sun did in the daytime. All the little birds except Hooty the Owl and Boomer the Night Hawk, and noisy Mr. Whip-poor-will were fast asleep in their little nests. Old Mother West Wind's Merry Little Breezes had all gone to sleep, too. It was oh so still! Indeed it was so very still that Bobby Coon, coming down the Lone Little Path through the wood, began to talk to himself.

"I don't see what people want to play all day and sleep all night for," said Bobby Coon. "Night's the best time to be about. Now Reddy Fox—"

"Be careful what you say about Reddy Fox," said a voice right behind Bobby Coon.

Bobby Coon turned around very quickly indeed, for he had thought he was all alone. There was Reddy Fox himself, trotting down the Lone Little Path through the wood.

"I thought you were home and fast asleep, Reddy Fox," said Bobby Coon.

"You were mistaken," said Reddy Fox, "for you see I'm out to take a walk in the moonlight."

So Bobby Coon and Reddy Fox walked together down the Lone Little Path through the wood to the Green Meadows. They met Jimmy Skunk, who had dreamed that there were a lot of beetles up on the hill, and was just going to climb the Crooked Little Path to see.

"Hello, Jimmy Skunk!" said Bobby Coon and Reddy Fox. "Come down to the Green Meadows with us."

Jimmy Skunk said he would, so they all went down on the Green Meadows together, Bobby Coon first, Reddy Fox next and Jimmy Skunk last of all, for Jimmy Skunk never hurries. Pretty soon they came to the house of Johnny Chuck.

"Listen," said Bobby Coon, "Johnny Chuck is fast asleep."

They all listened and they could hear Johnny Chuck snoring away down in his snug little bed.

"Let's give Johnny Chuck a surprise," said Reddy Fox.

"What shall it be?" asked Bobby Coon.

"I know," said Reddy Fox. "Let's roll that big stone right over Johnny Chuck's doorway; then he'll have to dig his way out in the morning."

So Bobby Coon and Reddy Fox pulled and tugged and tugged and pulled at the big stone till they had rolled it over Johnny Chuck's doorway. Jimmy Skunk pretended not to see what they were doing.

"Now let's go down to the Laughing Brook and wake up old Grandfather Frog and hear him say 'Chug-a-rum,'" said Bobby Coon.

"Come on!" cried Reddy Fox, "I'll get there first!"

Away raced Reddy Fox down the Lone Little Path and after him ran Bobby Coon, going to wake old Grandfather Frog from a nice comfortable sleep on his green lily-pad.

But Jimmy Skunk didn't go. He watched Reddy Fox and Bobby Coon until they were nearly to the Laughing Brook. Then he began to dig at one side of the big stone which filled the doorway of Johnny Chuck's house. My, how he made the dirt fly! Pretty soon he had made a hole big enough to call through to Johnny Chuck, who was snoring away, fast asleep in his snug little bed below.

"Johnny Chuck, Chuck, Chuck! Johnny Woodchuck!" called Jimmy Skunk.

But Johnny Chuck just snored.

"Johnny Chuck, Chuck, Chuck! Johnny Woodchuck!" called Jimmy Skunk once more.

But Johnny Chuck just snored. Then Jimmy Skunk called again, this time louder than before.

"Who is it?" asked a very sleepy voice.

"It's Jimmy Skunk. Put your coat on and come up here!" called Jimmy Skunk.

"Go away, Jimmy Skunk. I want to sleep!" said Johnny Chuck.

"I've got a surprise for you, Johnny Chuck. You'd better come!" called Jimmy Skunk through the little hole he had made. When Johnny Chuck heard that Jimmy Skunk had a surprise for him he wanted to know right away what it could be, so though he was very, very sleepy, he put on his coat and started up for his door to see what the surprise was that Jimmy Skunk had. And there he found the big stone Reddy Fox and Bobby Coon had put there, and of course he was very much surprised indeed. He thought Jimmy Skunk had played him a mean trick and for a few minutes he was very mad. But Jimmy Skunk soon told him who had filled up his doorway with the big stone.

"Now you push from that side, Johnny Chuck, and I'll pull from this side, and we'll soon have this big stone out of your doorway," said Jimmy Skunk.

So Johnny Chuck pushed and Jimmy Skunk pulled, and sure enough they soon had the big stone out of Johnny Chuck's doorway.

"Now," said Jimmy Skunk, "we'll roll this big stone down the Lone Little Path to Reddy's Fox's house and we'll give Reddy Fox a surprise."

So Johnny Chuck and Jimmy Skunk tugged and pulled and rolled the big stone down to the house of Reddy Fox, and sure enough, it filled his doorway.

"Good night, Jimmy Skunk," said Johnny Chuck, and trotted down the Lone Little Path toward home, chuckling to himself all the way.

Jimmy Skunk walked slowly up the Lone Little Path to the wood, for Jimmy Skunk never hurries. Pretty soon he came to the big hollow tree where Bobby Coon lives, and there he met Hooty the Owl.

"Hello, Jimmy Skunk, where have you been?" asked Hooty the Owl.

"Just for a walk," said Jimmy Skunk. "Who lives in this big hollow tree?"

Now of course Jimmy Skunk knew all the time, but he pretended he didn't.

"Oh, this is Bobby Coon's house," said Hooty the Owl.

"Let's give Bobby Coon a surprise," said Jimmy Skunk.

"How?" asked Hooty the Owl.

"We'll fill his house full of sticks and leaves," said Jimmy Skunk.

Hooty the Owl thought that would be a good joke, so while Jimmy Skunk gathered all the old sticks and leaves he could find, Hooty the Owl stuffed them into the old hollow tree, which was Bobby Coon's house, until he couldn't get in another one.

"Good night," said Jimmy Skunk as he began to climb the Crooked Little Path up the hill to his own snug little house.

"Good night," said Hooty the Owl, as he flew like a big soft shadow over to the Great Pine.

By and by when old Mother Moon was just going to bed and all the little stars were too sleepy to twinkle any longer, Reddy Fox and Bobby Coon, very tired and very wet from playing in the Laughing Brook, came up the Lone Little Path, ready to tumble into their snug little beds. They were chuckling over the trick they had played on Johnny Chuck, and the way they had waked up old Grandfather Frog, and all the other mischief they had done. What do you suppose they said when they reached their homes and found that someone else had been playing jokes, too?

I'm sure I don't know, but round, red Mr. Sun was laughing very hard as he peeped over the hill at Reddy Fox and Bobby Coon, and he won't tell why.

XIII. Johnny Chuck Finds the Best Thing in the World

Old Mother West Wind had stopped to talk with the Slender Fir Tree.

"I've just come across the Green Meadows," said Old Mother West Wind, "and there I saw the Best Thing in the World."

Striped Chipmunk was sitting under the Slender Fir Tree and he couldn't help hearing what Old Mother West Wind said. "The Best Thing in the World—now what can that be?" thought Striped Chipmunk. "Why, it must be heaps and heaps of nuts and acorns! I'll go and find it."

So Striped Chipmunk started down the Lone Little Path through the wood as fast as he could run. Pretty soon he met Peter Rabbit.

"Where are you going in such a hurry, Striped Chipmunk?" asked Peter Rabbit.

"Down in the Green Meadows to find the Best

Thing in the World," replied Striped Chipmunk, and ran faster.

"The Best Thing in the World," said Peter Rabbit, "why, that must be a great pile of carrots and cabbage! I think I'll go and find it."

So Peter Rabbit started down the Lone Little Path through the wood as fast as he could go after Striped Chipmunk.

As they passed the great hollow tree Bobby Coon put his head out. "Where are you going in such a hurry?" asked Bobby Coon.

"Down in the Green Meadows to find the Best Thing in the World!" shouted Striped Chipmunk and Peter Rabbit, and both began to run faster.

"The Best Thing in the World," said Bobby Coon to himself, "why, that must be a whole field of sweet milky corn. I think I'll go and find it."

So Bobby Coon climbed down out of the great hollow tree and started down the Lone Little Path through the wood as fast as he could go after Striped Chipmunk and Peter Rabbit, for there is nothing that Bobby Coon likes to eat so well as sweet milky corn.

At the edge of the wood they met Jimmy Skunk.

"Where are you going in such a hurry?" asked Jimmy Skunk.

"Down in the Green Meadows to find the Best Thing in the World!" shouted Striped Chipmunk and Peter Rabbit and Bobby Coon. Then they all tried to run faster.

"The Best Thing in the World," said Jimmy Skunk. "Why, that must be packs and packs of beetles!" And for once in his life Jimmy Skunk began to hurry down the Lone Little Path after Striped Chipmunk and Peter Rabbit and Bobby Coon.

They were all running so fast that they didn't see Reddy Fox until he jumped out of the long grass and asked:

"Where are you going in such a hurry?"

"To find the Best Thing in the World!" shouted Striped Chipmunk and Peter Rabbit and Bobby Coon and Jimmy Skunk, and each did his best to run faster.

"The Best Thing in the World," said Reddy Fox to himself, "Why, that must be a whole pen full of tender young chickens, and I must have them."

So away went Reddy Fox as fast as he could run down the Lone Little Path after Striped Chipmunk, Peter Rabbit, Bobby Coon and Jimmy Skunk.

By and by they all came to the house of Johnny Chuck.

"Where are you going in such a hurry?" asked Johnny Chuck.

"To find the Best Thing in the World," shouted Striped Chipmunk and Peter Rabbit and Bobby Coon and Jimmy Skunk and Reddy Fox.

"The Best Thing in the World," said Johnny Chuck. "Why, I don't know of anything better than my own little home and the warm sunshine and the beautiful blue sky."

So Johnny Chuck stayed at home and played all day among the flowers with the Merry Little Breezes of Old Mother West Wind and was as happy as could be.

But all day long Striped Chipmunk and Peter Rabbit and Bobby Coon and Jimmy Skunk and Reddy Fox ran this way and ran that way over the Green

Meadows trying to find the Best Thing in the World. The sun was very, very warm and they ran so far and they ran so fast that they were very, very hot and tired, and still they hadn't found the Best Thing in the World.

When the long day was over they started up the Lone Little Path past Johnny Chuck's house to their own homes. They didn't hurry now for they were so very, very tired! And they were cross—oh so cross! Striped Chipmunk hadn't found a single nut. Peter Rabbit hadn't found so much as the leaf of a cabbage. Bobby Coon hadn't found the tiniest bit of sweet milky corn. Jimmy Skunk hadn't seen a single beetle. Reddy Fox hadn't heard so much as the peep of a chicken. And all were as hungry as hungry could be.

Half way up the Lone Little Path they met Old Mother West Wind going to her home behind the hill. "Did you find the Best Thing in the World?" asked Old Mother West Wind.

"No!" shouted Striped Chipmunk and Peter Rabbit and Bobby Coon and Jimmy Skunk and Reddy Fox all together.

"Johnny Chuck has it," said Old Mother West Wind. "It is being happy with the things you have and not wanting things which some one else has. And it is called Con-tent-ment."

XIV. Little Joe Otter's Slippery Slide

Little Joe Otter and Billy Mink had been playing together around the Smiling Pool all one sunshiny morning. They had been fishing and had taken home

"Johnny Chuck has it," said Old Mother West Wind.
See page 54.

a fine dinner of Trout for old Grandfather Mink and blind old Granny Otter. They had played tag with the Merry Little Breezes. They had been in all kinds of mischief and now they just didn't know what to do.

They were sitting side by side on the Big Rock trying to push each other off into the Smiling Pool. Round, smiling, red Mr. Sun made the Green Meadows very warm indeed, and Reddy Fox, over in the tall grass, heard them splashing and shouting and having such a good time that he wished he liked the nice cool water and could swim, too.

"I've thought of something!" cried Little Joe Otter.

"What is it?" asked Billy Mink.

Little Joe Otter just looked wise and said nothing.

"Something to eat?" asked Billy Mink.

"No," said Little Joe Otter.

"I don't believe you've thought of anything at all," said Billy Mink.

"I have too!" said Little Joe Otter. "It's something to do."

"What?" demanded Billy Mink.

Just then Little Joe Otter spied Jerry Muskrat. "Hi, Jerry Muskrat! Come over here!" he called.

Jerry Muskrat swam across to the Big Rock and climbed up beside Billy Mink and Little Joe Otter.

"What are you fellows doing?" asked Jerry Muskrat.

"Having some fun," said Billy Mink. "Little Joe Otter has thought of something to do, but I don't know what it is."

"Let's make a slide," cried Little Joe Otter.

"You show us how," said Billy Mink.

So Little Joe Otter found a nice smooth place on

the bank, and Billy Mink and Jerry Muskrat brought mud and helped him pat it down smooth until they had the loveliest slippery slide in the world. Then Little Joe Otter climbed up the bank to the top of the slippery slide and lay down flat on his stomach. Billy Mink gave him a push and away he went down, down the slippery slide, splash into the Smiling Pool. Then Jerry Muskrat tried it and after him Billy Mink. Then all did it over again. Sometimes they went down the slippery slide on their backs, sometimes flat on their stomachs, sometimes head first, sometimes feet first. Oh such fun as they did have! Even Grandfather Frog came over and tried the slippery slide.

Johnny Chuck, over in the Green Meadows, heard the noise and stole down the Lone Little Path to see. Jimmy Skunk, looking for beetles up on the hill, heard the noise and forgot that he hadn't had his breakfast. Reddy Fox, taking a nap, woke up and hurried over to watch the fun. Last of all came Peter Rabbit.

Little Joe Otter saw him coming. "Hello, Peter Rabbit!" he shouted. "Come and try the slippery slide."

Now Peter Rabbit couldn't swim, but he pretended that he didn't want to.

"I've left my bathing suit at home," said Peter Rabbit.

"Never mind," said Billy Mink. "Mr. Sun will dry you off."

"And we'll help," said all the Merry Little Breezes of Old Mother West Wind.

But Peter Rabbit shook his head and said, "No."

Faster and faster went Billy Mink and Little Joe

Otter and Jerry Muskrat and old Grandfather Frog
down the slippery slide into the Smiling Pool.

Peter Rabbit kept coming near and nearer until
finally he stood right at the top of the slippery slide.
Billy Mink crept up behind him very softly and gave
him a push. Peter Rabbit's long legs flew out from
under him and down he sat with a thump on the slippery slide. "Oh," cried Peter Rabbit, and tried to
stop himself. But he couldn't do it and so away he
went down the slippery slide, splash into the Smiling
Pool.

"Ha! ha! ha!" laughed Billy Mink.

"Ho! ho! ho!" shouted Little Joe Otter.

"He! he! he!" laughed Jerry Muskrat and old
Grandfather Frog and Sammy Jay and Jimmy Skunk
and Reddy Fox and Blacky the Crow and Mr.
Kingfisher, for you know Peter Rabbit was forever
playing jokes on them.

Poor Peter Rabbit! The water got in his eyes and up
his nose and into his mouth and made him choke and
splutter, and then he couldn't get back on the bank,
for you know Peter Rabbit couldn't swim.

When Little Joe Otter saw what a dreadful time
Peter Rabbit was having he dove into the Smiling
Pool and took hold of one of Peter Rabbit's long ears.
Billy Mink swam out and took hold of the other long
ear. Jerry Muskrat swam right under Peter Rabbit
and took him on his back. Then with old Grandfather
Frog swimming ahead they took Peter Rabbit right
across the Smiling Pool and pulled him out on the
grassy bank, where it was nice and warm. All the
Merry Little Breezes of Old Mother West Wind came
over and helped Mr. Sun dry Peter Rabbit off.

Away he went down the slippery slide.
See page 58.

Then they all sat down together and watched Little Joe Otter turn a somersault down the slippery slide.

XV. The Tale of Tommy Trout Who Didn't Mind

In the Laughing Brook, which ripples and sings all day long, lived Mr. Trout and Mrs. Trout, and a whole lot of little Trouts. There were so many little Trouts that Mr. Trout and Mrs. Trout were kept very busy indeed getting breakfast and dinner and supper for them, and watching out for them and teaching them how to swim and how to catch foolish little flies that sometimes fell on the water and how to keep out of the way of big hungry fish and sharp eyed Mr. Kingfisher and big men and little boys who came fishing with hooks and lines.

Now all the little Trouts were very, very good and minded just what Mrs. Trout told them—all but Tommy Trout, for Tommy Trout—oh, dear, dear! Tommy Trout never could mind right away. He always had to wait a little instead of minding when he was spoken to.

Tommy Trout didn't mean to be bad. Oh dear, no! He just wanted to have his own way, and because Tommy Trout had his own way and didn't mind Mrs. Trout there isn't any Tommy Trout now. No sir, there isn't as much as one little blue spot of his beautiful little coat left because—why, just because Tommy Trout didn't mind.

One day when round, red Mr. Sun was shining and the Laughing Brook was singing on its way to join the

Big River, Mrs. Trout started out to get some nice plump flies for dinner. All the little Trouts were playing in their dear little pool, safe behind the Big Rock. Before she started Mrs. Trout called all the little Trouts around her and told them not to leave their little pool while she was gone, "For," said she, "something dreadful might happen to you."

All the little Trouts, except Tommy Trout, promised that they would surely, surely stay inside their dear little pool. Then they all began to jump and chase each other and play as happy as could be, all but Tommy Trout.

As soon as Mrs. Trout had started Tommy Trout swam off by himself to the edge of the pool. "I wonder what is on the other side of the Big Rock," said Tommy Trout. "The sun is shining and the brook is laughing and nothing could happen if I go just a little speck of a ways."

So, when no one was looking, Tommy Trout slipped out of the safe little pool where all the other little Trouts were playing. He swam just a little speck of a ways. But he couldn't see around the Big Rock. So he swam just a little speck of a ways farther still. Now he could see almost around the Big Rock. Then he swam just a little speck of a ways farther and—oh dear, dear! he looked right into the mouth of a great big, big fish called Mr. Pickerel, who is very fond of little Trouts and would like to eat one for breakfast every day.

"Ah ha!" said Mr. Pickerel, opening his big, big mouth very, very wide.

Tommy Trout turned to run back to the dear, dear safe little pool where all the other little Trouts were

Mrs. Trout started out to get some
nice plump flies for dinner.
See page 61.

playing so happily, but he was too late. Into that great big, big mouth he went instead, and Mr. Pickerel swallowed him whole.

"Ah ha," said Mr. Pickerel, "I like little Trouts."

And nothing more was ever heard of Tommy Trout, who didn't mind.

XVI. Spotty the Turtle Wins a Race

All the little people who live on the Green Meadows and in the Smiling Pool and along the Laughing Brook were to have a holiday. The Merry Little Breezes of Old Mother West Wind had been very busy, oh, very busy indeed, in sending word to all the little meadow folks. You see, Peter Rabbit had been boasting of how fast he could run. Reddy Fox was quite sure that he could run faster than Peter Rabbit. Billy Mink, who can move so quickly you hardly can see him, was quite sure that neither Peter Rabbit nor Reddy Fox could run as fast as he. They all met one day beside the Smiling Pool and agreed that old Grandfather Frog should decide who was the swiftest.

Now Grandfather Frog was accounted very wise. You see he had lived a long time, oh, very much longer than any of the others, and therefore, because of the wisdom of age, Grandfather Frog was always called on to decide all disputes. He sat on his green lily-pad while Billy Mink sat on the Big Rock, and Peter Rabbit and Reddy Fox sat on the bank. Each in turn told why he thought he was the fastest. Old Grandfather Frog listened and listened and said never a word until they were all through. When they had finished, he stopped to catch a foolish green fly and then he said:

"The best way to decide who is the swiftest is to have a race."

So it was agreed that Peter Rabbit and Reddy Fox and Billy Mink should start together from the old butternut tree on one edge of the Green Meadows, race away across the Green Meadows to the little hill on the other side and each bring back a nut from the big hickory which grew there. The one who first reached the old butternut tree with a hickory nut would be declared the winner. The Merry Little Breezes flew about over the Green Meadows telling everyone about the race and everyone planned to be there.

It was a beautiful summer day. Mr. Sun smiled and smiled, and the more he smiled the warmer it grew. Everyone was there to see the race—Striped Chipmunk, Happy Jack Squirrel, Sammy Jay, Blacky the Crow, Hooty the Owl and Bobby Coon all sat up in the old butternut tree where it was cool and shady. Johnny Chuck, Jerry Muskrat, Jimmy Skunk, Little Joe Otter, Grandfather Frog and even old Mr. Toad, were there. Last of all came Spotty the Turtle. Now Spotty the Turtle is a very slow walker and he cannot run at all. When Peter Rabbit saw him coming up towards the old butternut tree he shouted: "Come, Spotty, don't you want to race with us?"

Everybody laughed because you know Spotty is so very, very slow; but Spotty didn't laugh and he didn't get cross because everyone else laughed.

"There is a wise old saying, Peter Rabbit," said

Spotty the Turtle, "which shows that those who run fastest do not always reach a place first. I think I *will* enter this race."

Everyone thought that that was the best joke they had heard for a long time, and all laughed harder than ever. They all agreed that Spotty the Turtle should start in the race too.

So they all stood in a row, Peter Rabbit first, then Billy Mink, then Reddy Fox, and right side of Reddy Fox Spotty the Turtle.

"Are you ready?" asked Grandfather Frog. "Go!"

Away went Peter Rabbit with great big jumps. After him went Billy Mink so fast that he was just a little brown streak going through the tall grass, and side by side with him ran Reddy Fox. Now just as they started Spotty the Turtle reached up and grabbed the long hair on the end of Reddy's big tail. Of course Reddy couldn't have stopped to shake him off, because Peter Rabbit and Billy Mink were running so fast that he had to run his very best to keep up with them. But he didn't even know that Spotty the Turtle was there. You see Spotty is not very heavy and Reddy Fox was so excited that he did not notice that his big tail was heavier than usual.

The Merry Little Breezes flew along, too, to see that the race was fair. Peter Rabbit went with great big jumps. Whenever he came to a little bush he jumped right over it, for Peter Rabbit's legs are long and meant for jumping. Billy Mink is so slim that he slipped between the bushes and through the long grass like a little brown streak. Reddy Fox, who is bigger than either Peter Rabbit or Billy Mink, had no trouble in keeping up with them. Not one of them noticed that Spotty the Turtle was hanging fast to the end of Reddy's tail.

Now just at the foot of the little hill on which the big hickory tree grew was a little pond. It wasn't very wide but it was quite long. Billy Mink remembered this pond and he chuckled to himself as he raced along, for he knew that Peter Rabbit couldn't swim and he knew that Reddy Fox does not like the water, so therefore both would have to run around it. He himself can swim even faster than he can run. The more he thought of this, the more foolish it seemed that he should hurry so on such a warm day. "For," said Billy Mink to himself, "even if they reach the pond first, they will have to run around it, while I can swim across it and cool off while I am swimming. I will surely get there first." So Billy Mink ran slower and slower, and pretty soon he had dropped behind.

Mr. Sun, round and red, looking down, smiled and smiled to see the race. The more he smiled the warmer it grew. Now Peter Rabbit had a thick gray coat and Reddy Fox had a thick red coat, and they both began to get very, very warm. Peter Rabbit did not make such long jumps as when he first started. Reddy Fox began to feel very thirsty, and his tongue hung out. Now that Billy Mink was behind them they thought they did not need to hurry so.

Peter Rabbit reached the little pond first. He had not thought of that pond when he agreed to enter the race. He stopped right on the edge of it and sat up on his hind-legs. Right across he could see the big hickory tree, so near and yet so far, for he knew that he must run around the pond and then back again, and it was a long, long way. In just a moment Reddy Fox ran out of the bushes and Reddy felt very much as Peter Rabbit did. Way, way behind them was Billy Mink, trotting along comfortably and chuckling to himself. Peter Rabbit looked at Reddy Fox in dismay, and Reddy Fox looked at Peter Rabbit in dismay. Then they both looked at Billy Mink and remembered that Billy Mink could swim right across.

Then off Peter Rabbit started as fast as he could go around the pond one way, and Reddy Fox started around the pond the other way. They were so excited that neither noticed a little splash in the pond. That was Spotty the Turtle who had let go of Reddy's tail and now was swimming across the pond, for you know that Spotty is a splendid swimmer. Only once or twice he stuck his little black nose up to get some air. The rest of the time he swam under water and no one but the Merry Little Breezes saw him. Right across he swam, and climbed up the bank right under the big hickory tree.

Now there were just three nuts left under the hickory tree. Two of these Spotty took down to the edge of the pond and buried in the mud. The other he took in his mouth and started back across the pond. Just as he reached the other shore up trotted Billy Mink, but Billy Mink didn't see Spotty. He was too intent watching Reddy Fox and Peter Rabbit, who were now half way around the pond. In he jumped with a splash. My! How good that cool water did feel! He didn't have to hurry now, because he felt sure that the race was his. So he swam round and round and chased some fish and had a beautiful time in the water. By and by he looked up and saw that Peter Rabbit was almost around the pond one way and Reddy Fox was almost around the pond the other way. They both looked tired and hot and discouraged.

Then Billy Mink swam slowly across and climbed out on the bank under the big hickory tree. But where were the nuts? Look as he would, he could not see a nut anywhere, yet the Merry Little Breezes had said there were three nuts lying under the hickory tree. Billy Mink ran this way and ran that way. He was still running around, poking over the leaves and looking under the twigs and pieces of bark when Peter Rabbit and Reddy Fox came up.

Then they, too, began to look under the leaves and under the bark. They pawed around in the grass, they hunted in every nook and cranny, but not a nut could they find. They were tired and cross and hot and they accused Billy Mink of having hidden the nuts. Billy Mink stoutly insisted that he had not hidden the nuts, that he had not found the nuts, and when they saw how hard he was hunting they believed him.

All the afternoon they hunted and hunted and hunted, and all the afternoon Spotty the Turtle, with the nut in his mouth, was slowly, oh, so slowly, crawling straight back across the Green Meadows towards the old butternut tree. Round, red Mr. Sun was getting very close to the Purple Hills, where he goes to bed every night, and all the little meadow folks were getting ready to go to their homes. They were wondering and wondering what could have happened to the racers, when Sammy Jay spied the Merry Little Breezes dancing across the Green Meadows.

"Here come the Merry Little Breezes; they'll tell us who wins the race," cried Sammy Jay.

When the Merry Little Breezes reached the old butternut tree, all the little meadow folks crowded around them, but the Merry Little Breezes just laughed and laughed and wouldn't say a word. Then all of a sudden, out of the tall meadow grass crept Spotty the Turtle and laid the hickory nut at the feet of old Grandfather Frog. Old Grandfather Frog was so surprised that he actually let a great green fly buzz right past his nose.

"Where did you get that hickory nut?" asked Grandfather Frog.

"Under the big hickory tree on the hill on the other side of the Green Meadows," said Spotty.

Then all the Merry Little Breezes clapped their hands and shouted: "He did! He did! Spotty wins the race!"

Then they told how Spotty reached the pond by clinging to the tip of Reddy Fox's tail, and had hidden the other two nuts, and then how he had patiently crawled home while Billy Mink and Reddy Fox and Peter Rabbit were hunting and hunting for the nuts they could not find.

And so Spotty the Turtle was awarded the race, and to this day Peter Rabbit and Reddy Fox and Billy Mink can't bear the sight of a hickory nut.

THE END

The Adventures of
Peter Cottontail

by
Thornton W. Burgess

*"Cottontail, Peter Cottontail! How much better
sounding that is than Peter Rabbit!"*
See page 76.

I. Peter Rabbit Decides to Change His Name

"Peter Rabbit! Peter Rabbit! I don't see what Mother Nature ever gave me such a common sounding name as that for. People laugh at me, but if I had a fine sounding name they wouldn't laugh. Some folks say that a name doesn't amount to anything, but it does. If I should do some wonderful thing, nobody would think anything of it. No, Sir, nobody would think anything of it at all just because—why just because it was done by Peter Rabbit."

Peter was talking out loud, but he was talking to himself. He sat in the dear Old Briar-patch with an ugly scowl on his usually happy face. The sun was shining, the Merry Little Breezes of Old Mother West Wind were dancing over the Green Meadows, the birds were singing, and happiness, the glad, joyous happiness of springtime, was everywhere but in Peter Rabbit's heart. There there seemed to be no room for anything but discontent. And such foolish discontent—discontent with his name! And yet, do you know, there are lots of people just as foolish as Peter Rabbit.

"Well, what are you going to do about it?"

The voice made Peter Rabbit jump and turn around hastily. There was Jimmy Skunk poking his head in at the opening of one of Peter's private little paths. He was grinning, and Peter knew by that grin that Jimmy had heard what he had said. Peter didn't

73

know what to say. He hung his head in a very shame-
faced way.

"You've got something to learn," said Jimmy Skunk.

"What is it?" asked Peter.

"It's just this," replied Jimmy.

> "There's nothing in a name except
>   Just what we choose to make it.
> It lies with us and no one else
>   How other folks shall take it.
> It's what we do and what we say
> And how we live each passing day
> That makes it big or makes it small
> Or even worse than none at all.
> A name just stands for what we are;
>   It's what we choose to make it.
> And that's the way and only way
>   That other folks will take it."

Peter Rabbit made a face at Jimmy Skunk. "I don't
like being preached to."

"I'm not preaching; I'm just telling you what you
ought to know without being told," replied Jimmy
Skunk. "If you don't like your name, why don't you
change it?"

"What's that?" cried Peter sharply.

"If you don't like your name, why don't you change
it?" repeated Jimmy.

Peter sat up and the disagreeable frown had left
his face. "I—I—hadn't thought of that," he said slowly. "Do you suppose I could, Jimmy Skunk?"

"Easiest thing in the world," replied Jimmy Skunk.
"Just decide what name you like and then ask all
your friends to call you by it."

"I believe I will!" cried Peter Rabbit.

"Well, let me know what it is when you have decided," said Jimmy, as he started for home. And all the way up the Crooked Little Path, Jimmy chuckled to himself as he thought of foolish Peter Rabbit trying to change his name.

II. Peter Finds a Name

Peter Rabbit had quite lost his appetite. When Peter forgets to eat you may make up your mind that Peter has something very important to think about. At least he has something on his mind that he thinks is important. The fact is Peter had fully made up his mind to change his name. He thought Peter Rabbit too common a name. But when he tried to think of a better one, he found that no name that he could think of really pleased him any more. So he thought and he thought and he thought and he thought. And the more he thought the less appetite he had.

Now Jimmy Skunk was the only one to whom Peter had told how discontented he was with his name, and it was Jimmy who had suggested to Peter that he change it. Jimmy thought it a great joke, and he straightway passed the word along among all the little meadow and forest people that Peter Rabbit was going to change his name. Everybody laughed and chuckled over the thought of Peter Rabbit's foolishness, and they planned to have a great deal of fun with Peter as soon as he should tell them his new name.

Peter was sitting on the edge of the Old Briar-patch

one morning when Ol' Mistah Buzzard passed, flying low. "Good mo'ning, Brer Cottontail," said Ol' Mistah Buzzard, with a twinkle in his eye.

At first Peter didn't understand that Ol' Mistah Buzzard was speaking to him, and by the time he did it was too late to reply, for Ol' Mistah Buzzard was way, way up in the blue, blue sky. "Cottontail, Cottontail," said Peter over and over to himself and began to smile. Every time he said it he liked it better.

"Cottontail, Peter Cottontail! How much better sounding that is than Peter Rabbit! That sounds as if I really was somebody. Yes, Sir, that's the very name I want. Now I must send word to all my friends that hereafter I am no longer Peter Rabbit, but Peter Cottontail."

Peter kicked up his heels in just the funny way he always does when he is pleased. Suddenly he remembered that such a fine, long, high-sounding name as Peter Cottontail demanded dignity. So he stopped kicking up his heels and began to practice putting on airs. But first he called the Merry Little Breezes and told them about his change of name and asked them to tell all his friends that in the future he would not answer to the name of Peter Rabbit, but only to the name of Peter Cottontail. He was very grave and earnest and important as he explained it to the Merry Little Breezes. The Merry Little Breezes kept their faces straight while he was talking, but as soon as they had left him to carry his message they burst out laughing. It was such a joke!

And they giggled as they delivered this message to each of the little forest and meadow people:

"Peter Rabbit's changed his name.
   In the future without fail
You must call him, if you please,
   Mr. Peter Cottontail."

While they were doing this, Peter was back in the Old Briar-patch practicing new airs and trying to look very high and mighty and important, as became one with such a fine-sounding name as Peter Cottontail.

III. There's Nothing Like the Old Name After All

Bobby Coon and Jimmy Skunk had their heads together. Now when these two put their heads together, you may make up your mind that they are planning mischief. Yes, Sir, there is sure to be mischief afoot when Bobby Coon and Jimmy Skunk put their heads together as they were doing now. Had Peter Rabbit seen them, he might not have felt so easy in his mind as he did. But Peter didn't see them. He was too much taken up with trying to look as important as his new name sounded. He was putting on airs and holding his head very high as he went down to the Smiling Pool to call on Jerry Muskrat.

Whenever any one called him by his old name, Peter pretended not to hear. He pretended that he had never heard that name and didn't know that he was being spoken to. Bobby Coon and Jimmy Skunk thought it a great joke and they made up their minds that they would have some fun with Peter and perhaps make him see how very foolish he was. Yes, Sir, they planned to teach Peter a lesson. Bobby Coon hurried away to find Reddy Fox and tell him that Peter had gone down to the Smiling Pool, and that if he hid beside the path, he might catch Peter on the way back.

Jimmy Skunk hunted up Blacky the Crow and Sammy Jay and told them of his plan and what he wanted them to do to help. Of course they promised that they would. Then he went to Ol' Mistah Buzzard and told him. Ol' Mistah Buzzard grinned and promised that he would do his share. Then Bobby Coon and Jimmy Skunk hid where they could see all that would happen.

Peter had reached the Smiling Pool and now sat on the bank admiring his own reflection in the water and talking to Jerry Muskrat. He had just told Jerry that when his old name was called out he didn't hear it any more when along came Blacky the Crow.

"Hello, Peter Rabbit! You're just the fellow I am looking for; I've a very important message for you," shouted Blacky.

Peter kept right on talking with Jerry Muskrat just as if he didn't hear, although he was burning with curiosity to know what the message was.

"I say, Peter Rabbit, are you deaf?" shouted Blacky the Crow.

Jerry Muskrat looked up at Blacky and winked. "Peter Rabbit isn't here," said he. "This is Peter Cottontail."

"Oh!" said Blacky. "My message is for Peter Rabbit, and it's something he really ought to know. I'm sorry he isn't here." And with that, away flew Blacky the Crow, chuckling to himself.

Peter looked quite as uncomfortable as he felt, but of course he couldn't say a word after boasting that he didn't hear people who called him Peter Rabbit. Pretty soon along came Sammy Jay. Sammy seemed very much excited.

"Oh, Peter Rabbit, I'm so glad I've found you!" he cried. "I've some very important news for you."

Peter had all he could do to sit still and pretend not to hear, but he did.

"This is Peter Cottontail," said Jerry Muskrat, winking at Sammy Jay.

"Oh," replied Sammy, "My news is for Peter Rabbit!" and off he flew, chuckling to himself.

Peter looked and felt more uncomfortable than ever. He bade Jerry Muskrat good-by and started for the dear Old Briar-patch to think things over. When he was half way there, Ol' Mistah Buzzard came sailing down out of the sky.

"Brer Cottontail," said he, "if yo' see anything of Brer Rabbit, yo' can tell him that Brer Fox am hiding behind that big bunch of grass just ahead."

Peter stopped short, and his heart gave a great leap. There, behind the clump of grass, was something red, sure enough. Peter didn't wait to see more. He started for a hiding-place he knew of in the Green Forest as fast as he could go, and behind him raced Reddy Fox. As he ran, he heard Blacky the Crow and Sammy Jay laughing, and then he knew that this was the news that they had had for him.

"I—I—guess that Peter Rabbit is a good enough name, after all," he panted.

IV. Peter Rabbit Fools Jimmy Skunk

Peter Rabbit came hopping and skipping down the Crooked Little Path. Unc' Billy Possum always calls him Brer Rabbit, but everybody else calls him Peter. Peter was feeling very fine that morning, very fine indeed. Every few minutes he jumped up in the air, and kicked his heels together, just for fun. Presently he met Jimmy Skunk.

Jimmy was on his way back from Farmer Brown's cornfield, where he had been helping Blacky the Crow get free from a snare. Jimmy was still tickling and laughing over the way Blacky the Crow had been caught. He had to tell Peter Rabbit all about it.

Peter thought it just as good a joke as did Jimmy, and the two trotted along side by side, planning how they would spread the news all over the Green Meadows that Blacky the Crow, who thinks himself so smart, had been caught.

"That reminds me," said Jimmy Skunk suddenly, "I haven't had my breakfast yet. Have you seen any beetles this morning, Peter Rabbit?"

Peter Rabbit stopped and scratched his long left ear with his long left hind foot.

"Now you speak of it, it seems to me that I did," said Peter Rabbit.

"Where?" asked Jimmy Skunk eagerly.

Peter pretended to think very hard.

"It seems to me that it was back at the top of the Crooked Little Path up the hill," said Peter.

"I think I will go look for them at once," replied Jimmy.

"All right," replied Peter, "I'll show you the way."

So up the Crooked Little Path hopped Peter Rabbit, and right behind him trotted Jimmy Skunk. By and by they came to an old pine stump. Peter Rabbit stopped. He put one hand on his lips.

"Hush!" whispered Peter. "I think there is a whole family of beetles on the other side of this stump. You creep around the other side, and I'll creep around this side. When I thump the ground, you spring right around and grab them before they can run away."

So Jimmy Skunk crept around one side of the stump, and Peter Rabbit crept around the other side. Suddenly Peter thumped the ground hard, twice. Jimmy Skunk was waiting and all ready to spring. When he heard those thumps, he just sprang as quickly as he could. What do you think happened?

Why, Jimmy Skunk landed *thump!* right on Reddy Fox, who was taking a sun nap on the other side of the pine stump!

"Ha, ha, ha," shouted Peter Rabbit, and started down the Crooked Little Path as fast as his long legs could take him.

V. Reddy Fox Gets into Trouble

Reddy Fox, curled up behind the big pine stump, was dreaming of a coop full of chickens, where there was no Bowser the Hound to watch over them. Suddenly something landed on him with a thump that knocked all his breath out. For an instant it frightened Reddy so that he just shook and shook. Then he got his senses together and discovered that it was Jimmy Skunk who had jumped on him.

Jimmy was very polite. He begged Reddy's pardon. He protested that it was all a mistake. He explained how Peter Rabbit had played a trick on both of them, and how he himself was just looking for beetles for breakfast.

Now, Reddy Fox is very quick-tempered, and as soon as he realized that he had been made the victim of a joke, he lost his temper completely. He glared at Jimmy Skunk. He was so angry that he stuttered.

"Y-y-you, y-y-y-you, y-y-y-you did that on p-p-purpose," said Reddy Fox.

"No such thing!" declared Jimmy Skunk. "I tell you it was a joke on the part of Peter Rabbit, and if you don't believe me, just look down there on the Green Meadows."

Reddy Fox looked. There sat Peter, his hands on his hips, his long ears pointed straight up to the blue sky, and his mouth wide open, as he laughed at the results of his joke.

Reddy shook his fist.

"Ha, ha, ha," shouted Peter Rabbit.

Reddy Fox looked hard at Jimmy Skunk, but like all the other little meadow and forest people, he has a very great respect for Jimmy Skunk, and though he would have liked to quarrel with Jimmy, he thought it wisest not to. Instead, he started after Peter Rabbit as fast as his legs could go.

Now, Reddy Fox can run very fast, and when

Peter saw him coming, Peter knew that he would have to use his own long legs to the very best of his ability. Away they went across the Green Meadows. Jimmy Skunk, sitting on top of the hill, could see the white patch on the seat of Peter Rabbit's trousers bobbing this way and that way, and right behind him was Reddy Fox. Now, Peter Rabbit could run fast enough to keep away from Reddy for a while. You remember that Peter's eyes are so placed that he can see behind him without turning his head. So he knew when Reddy was getting too near.

In and out among the bushes along the edge of the Green Meadows they dodged, and the more he had to run, the angrier Reddy Fox grew. He paid no attention to where they were going; his whole thought was of catching Peter Rabbit.

Now, when Peter began to grow tired he began to work over towards Farmer Brown's cornfield, where he knew that Farmer Brown's boy was hiding, with Bowser the Hound. Dodging this way and that way, Peter worked over to the fence corner, where Jimmy Skunk had watched Blacky the Crow get caught in a snare. He let Reddy almost catch him, then he dodged out into the open cornfield, and Reddy, of course, followed him.

"Bow-wow, bow-wow-wow!"

Reddy did not need to turn to know what had happened. Bowser the Hound had seen him and was after him. Peter just ducked behind a big bunch of grass and sat down to get his breath, while Reddy started off as hard as he could go, with Bowser the Hound behind him.

VI. Reddy Fools Bowser the Hound

Away across the Green Meadows and up the hill through the Green Forest raced Reddy Fox at the top of his speed. Behind him, nose to the ground, came Bowser the Hound, baying at the top of his lungs. Reddy ran along an old stone wall and jumped as far out into the field as he could.

"I guess that will fool him for a while," panted Reddy, as he sat down to get his breath.

When Bowser came to the place where Reddy had jumped on the stone wall, he just grinned.

"That's too old a trick to fool me one minute," said Bowser to himself, and he just made a big circle, so that in a few minutes he had found Reddy's tracks again.

Every trick that Reddy had heard old Granny Fox tell about he tried, in order to fool Bowser the Hound, but it was of no use at all. Bowser seemed to know exactly what Reddy was doing, and wasted no time.

Reddy was beginning to get worried. He was getting dreadfully out of breath. His legs ached. His big, plumey tail, of which he is very, very proud, had become dreadfully heavy. Granny Fox had warned him never, never to run into the snug house they had dug unless he was obliged to save his life, for that would tell Bowser the Hound where they lived, and then they would have to move.

How Reddy did wish that wise old Granny Fox would come to his relief. He was running along the back of Farmer Brown's pasture, and he could hear

Bowser the Hound altogether too near for comfort. He looked this way and he looked that way for a chance to escape. Just ahead of him he saw a lot of woolly friends. They were Farmer Brown's sheep. Reddy had a bright idea. Like a flash he sprang on the back of one of the sheep. It frightened the sheep as badly as Reddy had been frightened, when Jimmy Skunk had landed on him that morning.

"Baa, baa, baa!" cried the sheep and started to run. Reddy hung on tightly, and away they raced across the pasture.

Now Bowser the Hound trusts wholly to his nose to follow Reddy Fox or Peter Rabbit or his master, Farmer Brown's boy. So he did not see Reddy jump on the back of the sheep, and, of course, when he reached the place where Reddy had found his strange horse, he was puzzled. Round and round, and round and round Bowser worked in a circle, but no trace of Reddy could he find.

And all the time Reddy sat behind the stone wall on the far side of the pasture, getting his wind and laughing and laughing at the smart way in which he had fooled Bowser the Hound.

VII. Reddy Invites Peter Rabbit to Take a Walk

Old Granny Fox was not feeling well. For three days she had been unable to go out hunting, and for three days Reddy Fox had tried to find something to tempt Granny's appetite. He had brought in a tender young chicken from Farmer Brown's hen yard, and he had stolen a plump trout from Billy

Mink's storehouse, but Granny had just turned up her nose.

"What I need," said Granny Fox, "is a tender young rabbit."

Now, Reddy Fox is very fond of Granny Fox, and when she said that she needed a tender young rabbit, Reddy made up his mind that he would get it for her, though how he was going to do it he didn't know. Dozens of times he had tried to catch Peter Rabbit, and every time Peter's long legs had taken him to a place of safety. "I'll just have to fool Peter Rabbit," said Reddy Fox, as he sat on his door-step and looked over the Green Meadows.

Reddy Fox is very sly. He is so sly that it is hard work to be sure when he is honest and when he is playing a trick. As he sat on his door-step, looking across the Green Meadows, he saw the Merry Little Breezes coming his way. Reddy smiled to himself. When they got near enough, he shouted to them.

"Will you do something for me?" he asked.

"Of course we will," shouted the Merry Little Breezes, who are always delighted to do something for others.

"I wish you would find Peter Rabbit and tell him that I have found a new bed of tender young carrots in Farmer Brown's garden, and invite him to go there with me to-morrow morning at sun-up," said Reddy Fox.

Away raced the Merry Little Breezes to find Peter Rabbit and give him the invitation of Reddy Fox. Pretty soon back they came to tell Reddy that Peter Rabbit would be delighted to meet Reddy on the edge of the Old Briar-patch at sun-up the next morning, and go with him to get some tender young carrots.

Reddy smiled to himself, for now he was sure that he would get Peter Rabbit for Granny's breakfast.

Early the next morning, just before sun-up, Reddy Fox started down the Lone Little Path and hurried across the Green Meadows to the Old Briar-patch. Reddy was dressed in his very best suit of clothes, and very smart and handsome he looked. When he reached the Old Briar-patch he could see nothing of Peter Rabbit. He waited and waited and waited, but still Peter Rabbit did not come. Finally he gave it up and decided that he would go over and have a look at the young carrots in Farmer Brown's garden. When he got there, what do you think he saw? Why, all around that bed of tender young carrots were footprints, and the footprints were Peter Rabbit's!

Reddy Fox ground his teeth and snarled wickedly, for he knew then that instead of fooling Peter Rabbit, Peter Rabbit had fooled him. Just then up came one of the Merry Little Breezes of Old Mother West Wind.

"Good morning, Reddy Fox," said the Merry Little Breeze.

"Good morning," replied Reddy Fox, and if you could have seen him and heard him, you would never have suspected how ill-tempered he was feeling.

"Peter Rabbit asked me to come and tell you that he is very sorry that he could not meet you at the Briar-patch this morning, but that he grew so hungry thinking of those tender young carrots that he just had to come and get some before sun-up, and he is very much obliged to you for telling him about them.

He says they are the finest young carrots that he has ever tasted," said the Merry Little Breeze.

The heart of Reddy Fox was filled with rage, but he did not let the Merry Little Breeze know it. He just smiled and sent the Merry Little Breeze back to Peter Rabbit to tell him how glad he was that Peter enjoyed the carrots, and to invite Peter to meet him the next morning on the edge of the Old Briar-patch at sun-up, to go with him to a patch of sweet clover which he had just found near the old hickory-tree.

The Merry Little Breeze danced off with the message. Pretty soon he was back to say that Peter Rabbit would be delighted to go to the sweet clover patch the next morning.

Reddy grinned as he trudged off home. "I'll just be at the clover patch an hour before sun-up to-morrow morning, and then we'll see!" he said to himself.

VIII. Peter Rabbit Gets an Early Breakfast

Peter Rabbit crept out of his snug little bed in the middle of the Old Briar-patch two hours before sun-up and hurried over to the big hickory-tree. Sure enough, close by, he found a beautiful bed of sweet clover, just as Reddy Fox had said was there. Peter chuckled to himself as he ate and ate and ate, until his little round stomach was so full that he could hardly hop.

When he had eaten all that he could, he hurried back to the Old Briar-patch to finish his morning nap, and all the time he kept chuckling to himself. You see, Peter was suspicious of Reddy Fox, and so he had gone over to the sweet clover bed alone two hours before sun-up.

Peter Rabbit had hardly left the sweet clover bed when Reddy Fox arrived. Reddy lay down in the long meadow grass and grinned to himself as he waited. Slowly the minutes went by, until up from behind the Purple Hills came jolly, round, red Mr. Sun—but no Peter Rabbit. Reddy stopped grinning.

"Perhaps," said he to himself, "Peter is waiting for me on the edge of the Old Briar-patch and wasn't going to try to fool me."

So Reddy hurried over to the Old Briar-patch, and sure enough there was Peter Rabbit sitting on the edge of it. When Peter saw him coming, he dodged in behind a big clump of friendly old brambles. Reddy came up with his broadest smile.

"Good morning, Peter Rabbit," said Reddy. "Shall we go over to that sweet clover bed?"

Peter put one hand over his mouth to hide a smile. "Oh," said he, "I was so dreadfully hungry for sweet clover that I couldn't wait until sun-up, and so I went over two hours ago. I hope you will excuse me, Reddy Fox. I certainly do appreciate your kindness in telling me of that new, sweet clover bed and I hope I have not put you out."

"Certainly not," replied Reddy Fox, in his pleasantest manner, and you know Reddy Fox can be very pleasant indeed when he wants to be. "It is a very great pleasure to be able to give you pleasure. There is nothing I so like to do as to give pleasure to others. By the way, I have just heard that Farmer Brown has a new planting of young cabbage in the corner of his garden. Will you meet me

"Good morning, Peter Rabbit," said Reddy.
"Shall we go over to that sweet clover bed?"
See page 89.

here at sun-up to-morrow morning to go over there?"

"I will be delighted to, I will indeed!" replied Peter Rabbit, and all the time he smiled to himself behind his hand.

Reddy Fox bade Peter Rabbit good-by in the pleasantest way you can imagine, yet all the time, down in his heart, Reddy was so angry that he hardly knew what to do, for you see he had got to go back to Granny Fox without the tender young rabbit which he had promised her.

"This time I will be there two hours before sun-up, and then we will see, Peter Rabbit, who is the smartest!" said Reddy Fox to himself.

IX. Reddy Fox Gets a Scare

Peter Rabbit looked up at the silvery moon and laughed aloud. Then he kicked up his heels and laughed again as he started out across the Green Meadows towards Farmer Brown's garden. You see, Peter was suspicious, very suspicious indeed of Reddy Fox. So, as it was a beautiful night for a walk, he thought he would just run over to Farmer Brown's garden and see if he could find that bed of newly planted cabbage, about which Reddy Fox had told him.

So Peter hopped and skipped across the Green Meadows, singing as he went:

> "Hold, ol' Miss Moon, hold up your light!
>   Show the way! show the way!
> The little stars are shining bright;
>   Night folks all are out to play."

When Peter reached Farmer Brown's garden, he had no trouble in finding the new planting of cabbage. It was tender. It was good. My, how good it was! Peter started in to fill his little round stomach. He ate and ate and ate and ate! By and by, just when he thought he couldn't eat another mouthful, he happened to look over to a patch of moonlight. For just a second Peter's heart stopped beating. There was Reddy Fox coming straight over to the new cabbage bed!

Peter Rabbit didn't know what to do. Reddy Fox hadn't seen him yet, but he would in a minute or two, unless Peter could hide. He was too far from the dear Old Briar-patch to run there. Peter looked this way and looked that way. Ha! ha! There lay Farmer Brown's boy's old straw hat, just where he had left it when the supper horn blew. Peter crawled under it. It covered him completely.

Peter peeped out from under one edge. He saw Reddy Fox standing in the moonlight, looking at the bed of newly set cabbage. Reddy was smiling as if his thoughts were very pleasant. Peter shivered. He could just guess what Reddy was thinking—how he would gobble up Peter, when once he got him away from the safety of the Old Briar-patch.

The thought made Peter so indignant that he forgot that he was hiding, and he sat up on his hind-legs. Of course, he lifted the straw hat with him. Then he remembered and sat down again in a hurry. Of course, the straw hat went down quite as quickly.

Presently Peter peeped out. Reddy Fox was staring and staring at the old straw hat, and he wasn't smiling now. He actually looked frightened. It gave Peter an idea. He made three long hops straight towards Reddy Fox, all the time keeping the old straw hat over him. Of course the hat went along with him, and, because it covered Peter all up, it looked for all the world as if the hat was alive.

Reddy Fox gave one more long look at the strange thing coming towards him through the cabbage bed, and then he started for home as fast as he could go, his tail between his legs.

Peter Rabbit just lay down right where he was and laughed and laughed and laughed. And it almost seemed as if the old straw hat laughed too.

X. Peter Has Another Great Laugh

It was just sun-up as Reddy Fox started down the Lone Little Path to the Green Meadows. Reddy was late. He should be over at the Old Briar-patch by this time. He was afraid now that Peter Rabbit would not be there. When he came in sight of the Old Briar-patch, there sat Peter on the edge of it.

"Good morning, Peter Rabbit," said Reddy Fox, in his politest manner. "I am sorry to have kept you waiting; it is all because I had a terrible fright last night."

"Is that so? What was it?" asked Peter, ducking down behind a big bramble bush to hide his smile.

"Why, I went over to Farmer Brown's garden to see if that new planting of young cabbage was all right, and there I met a terrible monster. It frightened me so that I did not dare to come out this morning until jolly, round Mr. Sun had begun to climb up in the sky, and so I am a little late. Are you ready, Peter Rabbit, to go up to the new planting of young cabbage with me?" asked Reddy, in his pleasantest manner.

Now, what do you think Peter Rabbit did? Why, Peter just began to laugh. He laughed and laughed and shouted! He lay down on his back and kicked his heels for very joy! But all the time he took care to keep behind a big, friendly bramble bush.

Reddy Fox stared at Peter Rabbit. He just didn't know what to make of it. He began to think that Peter had gone crazy. He couldn't see a thing to laugh at, yet here was Peter laughing fit to kill himself. Finally Peter stopped and sat up.

"Did—did—the monster catch you, Reddy Fox?" he asked, wiping his eyes.

"No," replied Reddy, "it didn't catch me, because I could run faster than it could, but it chased me all the way home."

"In that case, I think I'll not go up to the cabbage bed this morning, for you know I cannot run as fast as you can, Reddy, and the monster might catch me," replied Peter, very gravely. "Besides," he added, "I have had my fill of tender young cabbage, and it was very nice indeed."

"What!" shouted Reddy Fox.

"Yes," continued Peter Rabbit, "I just couldn't wait till morning, so I went up there early last night. I'm much obliged to you for telling me of it, Reddy Fox; I am indeed."

For just a little minute an ugly look crept into Reddy's face, for now he knew that once more Peter Rabbit had fooled him. But he kept his temper and managed to smile, as he said:

"Oh, don't mention it, Peter Rabbit, don't mention it. But tell me, didn't you meet the monster?"

"No," replied Peter Rabbit. And then, do what he would, he couldn't keep sober another minute, but began to laugh just as he had before.

"What's the joke, Peter Rabbit? Tell me so that I can laugh too," begged Reddy Fox.

"Why," said Peter Rabbit, when he could get his breath, "the joke is that the monster that frightened you so was the old straw hat of Farmer Brown's boy, and I was underneath it, Ha, ha, ha! Ho, ho, ho!"

Then Reddy Fox knew just how badly Peter Rabbit had fooled him. With a snarl he sprang right over the bramble bush at Peter Rabbit, but Peter was watching and darted away along one of his own special little paths through the Old Briar-patch. Reddy tried to follow, but the brambles tore his clothes and scratched his face and stuck to his feet. Finally he had to give it up. Torn and bleeding and angry, he turned back home, and as he left the Old Briar-patch, he could still hear Peter Rabbit laughing.

XI. Shadow the Weasel Gets Lost

All the Green Meadows had heard how Peter Rabbit had frightened Reddy Fox with an old straw hat, and everywhere that Reddy went some one was sure to shout after him:

> "Reddy Fox is fine to see;
> He's as brave as brave can be
> 'Til he meets an old straw hat,
> Then he don't know where he's at!"

Then Reddy would lose his temper and chase his tormentors. Most of all, he wanted to catch Peter Rabbit. He lay in wait for Peter in fence corners and behind bushes and trees, but somehow Peter seemed always to know that Reddy was there.

In the Old Briar-patch Peter was safe. Reddy had tried to follow him there, but he had found that it was of no use at all. Peter's paths were so narrow, and the brambles tore Reddy's clothes and scratched him so, that he had to give it up.

Reddy was thinking of this one day as he sat on his door-step, scowling over at the Old Briar-patch, and then all of a sudden he thought of Shadow the Weasel. Shadow is so slim that he can go almost anywhere that any one else can, and he is so fierce that nearly all of the Little Meadow people are terribly afraid of him. Reddy smiled. It was a mean, wicked, crafty smile. Then he hopped up and hurried to find Shadow the Weasel and tell him his plan.

Shadow listened, and then he too began to smile. "It's easy, Reddy Fox, the easiest thing in the world! We'll get Peter Rabbit just as sure as fat hens are good eating," said he, as they started for the Old Briar-patch.

Reddy's plan was very simple. Shadow the Weasel was to follow Peter Rabbit along Peter's narrow little paths and drive Peter out of the Old Briar-patch on to the Green Meadows, where Reddy Fox could surely catch him.

So Reddy Fox sat down to wait while Shadow started into the Old Briar-patch. Peter Rabbit heard him coming and, of course, Peter began to run. Now, when Peter first made his home in the Old Briar-patch, he had foreseen that some day Shadow the Weasel might come to hunt him there, so Peter had made dozens and dozens of little paths, twisting and turning and crossing and recrossing in the most puzzling way. Of course, Peter himself knew every twist and turn of every one of them, but Shadow had not gone very far before he was all mixed up. He kept his sharp little nose to the ground to smell Peter's footsteps, but Peter kept crossing his own tracks so often that pretty soon Shadow could not tell which path Peter had last taken.

Peter led him farther and farther into the middle of the Old Briar-patch. Right there Shadow came to a great big puddle of water. Peter had jumped clear across it, for you know Peter's legs are long and meant for jumping.

Now, Shadow hates to get his feet wet, and when he reached the puddle, he stopped. He glared with fierce little red eyes across at Peter Rabbit, sitting on the other side. Then he started around the edge.

Peter waited until Shadow was almost around, and then he jumped back across the puddle. There was nothing for Shadow to do but go back around, which he did. Of course, Peter just did the same thing over again, all the time laughing in his sleeve, for Shadow the Weasel was growing angrier and angrier. Finally he grew so angry that he tried to jump the puddle himself, and in he fell with a great splash!

When Shadow crawled out, wet and muddy, Peter had disappeared, and Shadow couldn't tell which path he had taken. Worse still, he didn't know which path to take to get out himself. He tried one after another, but after a little while he would find himself back at the puddle in the middle of the Old Briar-patch. Shadow the Weasel was lost! Yes, Sir, Shadow the Weasel was lost in the Old Briar-patch.

Outside, Reddy Fox waited and watched, but no frightened Peter Rabbit came jumping out as he expected. What could it mean? After a long, long time he saw some one very muddy and very wet and very tired crawl out of one of Peter Rabbit's little paths. It was Shadow the Weasel.

Reddy took one good look at him and then he hurried away. He didn't want to hear what Shadow the Weasel would say. And as he hurried across the Green Meadows, he heard Peter Rabbit's voice from the middle of the Old Briar-patch.

"If at first you don't succeed, try, try again!" shouted Peter Rabbit.

Reddy Fox ground his teeth.

XII. The Plot of Two Scamps

Sammy Jay, looking around for mischief, found Reddy Fox sitting on his door-step with his chin in both hands and looking as if he hadn't a friend in the world.

"What are you doing?" asked Sammy Jay.

"I'm just a-studying," replied Reddy Fox.

"What are you studying? Perhaps I can help you," said Sammy Jay.

Reddy Fox heaved a long sigh. "I'm a-studying how I can catch Peter Rabbit," replied Reddy.

Sammy Jay scratched his head thoughtfully. Reddy Fox still sat with his chin in his hands and thought and thought and thought. Sammy Jay sat on one foot and scratched and scratched and scratched his head with the other. Suddenly Sammy looked up.

"I have it!" said he. "You remember the hollow log over beyond the old hickory-tree?"

Reddy nodded his head.

"Well, I'll go down and invite Peter Rabbit to come over there and see the strangest thing in the world. You know what great curiosity Peter Rabbit has. Now, you be hiding in the hollow log, and when you hear me say to Peter Rabbit, 'the strangest thing in the world is waiting for you over there, Peter,' you spring out, and you'll have Peter."

Reddy Fox brightened up. This plan certainly did look good to Reddy. Peter had fooled him so many times that he was almost in despair. He knew that if he sent another invitation to Peter, Peter would suspect right away that it meant mischief. But Peter wouldn't think that Sammy Jay was planning mischief, because he knew that Sammy is the greatest news teller in the Green Forest.

So Reddy Fox trotted off to the hollow log down by the big hickory-tree and crept inside. Sammy Jay flew over to the Old Briar-patch to look for Peter Rabbit. He found him sitting under a big bramble bush.

"Good morning, Peter Rabbit," said Sammy Jay, with his finest manner.

Peter looked at Sammy sharply as he returned his greeting. Sammy Jay wasn't in the habit of being so polite to Peter, and Peter began to study just what it could mean.

"I saw the strangest thing in the world this morning," said Sammy Jay.

Peter pricked up his ears. In spite of himself, he began to grow curious. "What was it, Sammy Jay?" he asked.

Sammy looked very mysterious. "I really don't know what it is," he replied, "but I can show it to you, if you want to see for yourself, Peter Rabbit."

Of course Peter wanted to see it, so he started out across the Green Meadows with Sammy Jay. Now the farther he went, the more time he had to think, and by the time he had nearly reached the old hickory-tree, Peter began to suspect a trick.

Sammy Jay motioned Peter to approach very carefully. "It's right over there, in that hollow log, Peter," he whispered. "You go peep in, and you'll see it." Then Sammy prepared to give the signal to Reddy Fox.

Peter hopped a couple of steps nearer, and then he sat up very straight and gazed at the hollow log. Somehow he didn't just like the looks of it. He didn't know why, but he just didn't. Then along came one of Old Mother West Wind's Merry Little Breezes, dancing right past the hollow log and up to Peter Rabbit, and with him he brought a funny smell.

Peter's little wobbly nose wrinkled. That funny smell certainly reminded Peter of Reddy Fox. He wrinkled his nose again. Then he suddenly whirled about. "Excuse me, Sammy Jay," he exclaimed. "I just remembered something very important!" And before Sammy Jay could open his mouth, Peter had started like a little brown streak for the Old Briar-patch.

XIII. Reddy Fox Comes to Life

Reddy Fox lay on the side hill. Bobby Coon found him there, and when Bobby spoke to him, Reddy made no reply. Bobby went over and looked at him. Reddy's eyes were closed. Bobby grinned to himself, then he tip-toed a little nearer and shouted "boo" right in one of Reddy's little black ears. Still Reddy did not move. Bobby Coon's face grew sober. He poked Reddy with his foot, but still Reddy did not move. Then he pulled Reddy's tail, and still Reddy did not move. "It must be that Reddy Fox is dead," thought Bobby Coon, and he hurried away to tell the news.

There was great excitement on the Green Meadows and in the Green Forest when the little people there heard that Reddy Fox was dead. Of course, every one wanted to see Reddy, and soon there was a procession of little meadow and forest people hurrying across the Green Meadows to the hillside where Reddy Fox lay. Jimmy Skunk, Johnny Chuck, Billy Mink, Little Joe Otter, Unc' Billy Possum, Danny Meadow Mouse, Spotty the Turtle, old Mr. Toad, Grandfather Frog, Jerry Muskrat, Sammy Jay, Blacky the Crow, Happy Jack Squirrel, Striped Chipmunk, Jumper the Hare, Prickly Porky, all were there. They formed a big circle around Reddy Fox.

Then they began to talk about Reddy. Some told of the good things that Reddy had done and what a fine gentleman he was. Others told of the mean things that Reddy Fox had done and how glad they were that they would no longer have to watch out for him.

Soon there was a procession of little meadow and forest people hurrying across the Green Meadows.

See page 101.

It was surprising the number of bad things that were said. But then, they felt safe in saying them, for was not Reddy lying right there before them, stone dead?

Now, Peter Rabbit had not heard the news until late in the day, and when he did hear it, he started as fast as his long legs could take him to have a last look at Reddy. Half way there he suddenly stopped and scratched one of his long ears. Peter was thinking. It was mighty funny that Reddy Fox should have died without any one having heard that he was sick. Peter started on again, but this time he did not hurry. Presently he cut a long twig, which he carried along with him. When he reached the circle around Reddy Fox, he stole up behind Prickly Porky the Porcupine and whispered in his ear.

Prickly Porky took the long twig which Peter handed to him, while Peter went off at a little distance and climbed up on an old stump where he could see. Prickly Porky reached over and tickled one of Reddy's black ears. For a minute nothing happened. Then the black ear twitched. Prickly Porky tickled the end of Reddy's little black nose; then he tickled it again. What do you think happened? Why, Reddy Fox sneezed!

My, my, my! How that circle around Reddy Fox did disappear! All the little people who were afraid of Reddy Fox scampered away as fast as they could run, while all the other little people who were not afraid of Reddy Fox began to laugh, and the one who laughed loudest of all was Peter Rabbit, as he started back to the Old Briar-patch.

Of course, Reddy Fox knew then that it was of no use at all to pretend that he was dead, so he sprang to his feet and started after Peter Rabbit at the top of his speed, but when he reached the Old Briar-patch, Peter was safely inside, and Reddy could hear him laughing as if he would split his sides.

"If at first you don't succeed, try, try again!" shouted Peter Rabbit.

XIV. Peter Rabbit in a Tight Place

"Hop along, skip along,
　　The sun is shining bright;
Hum a song, sing a song,
　　My heart is always light."

It is true, Peter Rabbit always is light-hearted. For days and days Reddy Fox had been trying to catch Peter, and Peter had had to keep his wits very sharp indeed in order to keep out of Reddy's way. Still, it didn't seem to worry Peter much. Just now he was hopping and skipping down the Lone Little Path without a care in the world.

Presently Peter found a nice, shady spot close by a big rock. Underneath one edge of the rock was a place just big enough for Peter to crawl in—it was just the place for a nap. Peter was beginning to feel sleepy, so he crawled in there and soon was fast asleep.

By and by Peter began to dream. He dreamed that he had gone for a long walk, way, way off from the safe Old Briar-patch, and that out from behind a big bush had sprung Reddy Fox. Just as Reddy's teeth were about to close on Peter, Peter woke up. It was such a relief to find that he was really snug and safe under the big rock that he almost shouted aloud. But he didn't, and a minute later he was, oh, so glad he hadn't, for he heard a voice that seemed as if it was right in his ear. It was the voice of Reddy Fox. Yes, Sir, it was the voice of Reddy Fox.

Peter hardly dared to breathe, and you may be sure that he did not make even the smallest sound, for Reddy Fox was sitting on the very rock under which Peter was resting. Reddy Fox was talking to Blacky the Crow. Peter listened with all his might, for what do you think Reddy Fox was saying? Why, he was telling Blacky the Crow of a new plan to catch Peter Rabbit and was asking Blacky to help him.

Peter had never been so frightened in his life, for here was Reddy Fox so close to him that Peter could have reached out and touched one of Reddy's legs, as he kicked his heels over the edge of the big rock. By and by Blacky the Crow spoke.

"I saw Peter Rabbit coming down this way early this morning," said Blacky, "and I don't think he has gone home. Why don't you go over and hide near the Old Briar-patch and catch Peter when he comes back? I will watch out, and if I see Peter, I will tell him that you have gone hunting your breakfast way over beyond the big hill. Then he will not be on the watch."

"The very thing," exclaimed Reddy Fox, "and if I catch him, I will surely do something for you, Blacky. I believe that I will go right away."

Then the two rascals planned, and chuckled as they thought how they would outwit Peter Rabbit.

"I'm getting hungry," said Reddy Fox, as he arose and stretched. "I wonder if there is a field mouse hiding under this old rock. I believe I'll look and see."

Peter's heart almost stood still as he heard Reddy Fox slide down off the big rock. He wriggled himself still further under the rock and held his breath. Just then Blacky the Crow gave a sharp "Caw, caw, caw!" That meant that Blacky saw something, and almost at once Peter heard a sound that sometimes filled his heart with fear but which now filled it with great joy. It was the voice of Bowser the Hound. Reddy Fox heard it, too, and he didn't stop to look under the big rock.

A little later Peter very cautiously crawled out of his resting place and climbed up where he could look over the Green Meadows. Way over on the far side he could see Reddy Fox running at the top of his speed, and behind him was Bowser the Hound.

"My! but that was a tight place," said Peter Rabbit, as he stretched himself.

XV. Johnny Chuck Helps Peter

Johnny Chuck had watched Reddy Fox try to fool and catch Peter Rabbit, and sometimes Johnny had been very much afraid that Reddy would succeed. But Peter had been too smart for Reddy every time, and Johnny had laughed with the other little people of the Green Meadows whenever the Merry Little Breezes had brought a new story of how Peter had outwitted Reddy.

"Peter'll have to watch out sharper than ever now, for Granny Fox is almost well, and she is very angry because Reddy could not catch Peter Rabbit for her when she was ill. She says that she is going to show that stupid Reddy how to do it and do it quickly," said Jimmy Skunk, when he stopped to chat with Johnny Chuck one fine morning.

Johnny had just been laughing very hard over one of Peter Rabbit's tricks, but now his face grew very sober, very sober indeed. "It won't do to let old Granny Fox catch Peter. It won't do at all. We must all turn in and help Peter," said Johnny. "Why, what would the Green Meadows and the Green Forest be like with no Peter Rabbit?" he added.

Late that afternoon Johnny Chuck happened to find Peter Rabbit taking a nap. Yes, Sir, Peter had actually gone to sleep outside the dear Old Briar-patch. At first Johnny thought that he would waken him and tell him that Reddy Fox was hunting right near. But just then Johnny's bright eyes saw something that made him chuckle. It was the home of some hot-tempered friends of his, a beautiful home made of what looked like gray paper. It was fastened to a bush just above a little patch leading to the very spot where Peter lay fast asleep. Johnny chuckled again, then off he hurried. He sat down on top of a little hill. Pretty soon Reddy Fox came along through the hollow below.

"Hello, Reddy Fox! Do you want to know how you can catch Peter Rabbit?" asked Johnny.

Reddy looked up. He didn't know just what to say. He knew that Johnny Chuck and Peter had always been the very best of friends. Still, friends fall out sometimes, and perhaps Johnny and Peter had. Reddy decided that he would be polite.

"I certainly do, Johnny Chuck," he replied. "Can you tell me how to do it?"

"Yes," said Johnny. "Peter is fast asleep over yonder behind that little bunch of huckleberry bushes. There is a little path through them. All you have to do is to hurry up that little path as fast and as still as you can."

Reddy Fox waited to hear no more. His eyes glistened as he started off at the top of his speed up the little path. Just as Johnny had expected, Reddy went in such a hurry that he didn't use his eyes for anything but signs of Peter Rabbit.

Bang! Reddy had run head first into the paper house of Johnny Chuck's hot-tempered friends. In fact he had smashed the whole side in. Out poured old Mrs. Hornet and all her family, and they had their little needles with them. Reddy forgot all about Peter Rabbit. He yelled at the top of his lungs and started for home, slapping at old Mrs. Hornet, whom he never could hit, and stopping every few minutes to roll over and over.

Of course when he yelled, Peter Rabbit awoke and sat up to see what all the fuss was about. He saw Reddy running as if his life depended upon it. Over on the little hill he saw Johnny Chuck laughing so that the tears ran down his face. Then Peter began to laugh, too, and ran over to ask Johnny Chuck to tell him all about it.

XVI. Reddy Fox Tells a Wrong Story

Reddy Fox was a sight! There was no doubt about that. When he started down on to the Green Meadows that morning he limped like an old, old man. Yes indeed, Reddy was a sorry looking sight.

His head was swelled so that one eye was closed, and he could hardly see out of the other. Reddy never would have ventured out but that he just had to have some fresh mud from the Smiling Pool.

Reddy had waited until most of the little meadow people were out of the way. Then he had tried to hurry so as to get back again as quickly as possible.

But Johnny Chuck's sharp eyes had spied Reddy, and Johnny had guessed right away what the trouble was. He hurried over to tell Peter Rabbit. Then the two little scalawags hunted up Jimmy Skunk and Bobby Coon to tell them, and the four hid near the Lone Little Path to wait for Reddy's return.

Pretty soon Reddy came limping along. Even Johnny Chuck was surprised at the way Reddy's face had swelled. It was plastered all over with mud, and he was a sorry sight indeed.

Bobby Coon appeared very much astonished to see Reddy in such condition, though of course Johnny Chuck had told him all about how Reddy had run head first into the home of old Mrs. Hornet and her family the day before.

Bobby stepped out in the Lone Little Path.

"Why, Reddy Fox, what has happened to you?" he exclaimed.

Reddy didn't see the others hiding in the long grass. He didn't want Bobby Coon to know that he had been so careless as to run his head into a hornets' nest, so he told a wrong story. He put on a long face. That is, it was as long as he could make it, considering that it was so swelled.

"I've had a most terrible accident, Bobby Coon," said Reddy, sighing pitifully. "It happened yesterday as I was returning from an errand over beyond the hill. Just as I was coming through the deepest part of the wood I heard some one crying. Of course I stopped to find out what the matter was."

"Of course!" interrupted Bobby Coon. "Certainly! To be sure! Of course!"

Reddy looked at him suspiciously, but went on with his tale. "Right down in the thickest, blackest place I found one of Unc' Billy Possum's children being worried to death by Digger the Badger. I couldn't see that little Possum hurt."

"Of course not!" broke in Bobby Coon.

"So I jumped in and tackled old man Badger, and I had him almost whipped, when I slipped over the edge of a big rock on the side of the hill. It took the skin off my face and bruised me something terrible. But I don't care, so long as I saved that little Possum child," concluded Reddy as he started on.

Johnny Chuck stole up behind him and thrust a sharp brier into the seat of Reddy's pants. At the same time Johnny made a noise like a whole family of hornets. Reddy Fox forgot his limp. He never even turned his head to look behind. Instead, he started off at his best speed, and it wasn't until he heard a roar of laughter behind him that he realized that he had been fooled again.

XVII. Reddy Almost Gets Peter Rabbit

Reddy Fox really was almost ill from the effects of the stings which old Mrs. Hornet and her family had given him when he knocked in the side of their house.

For several days he limped around, his head badly swollen. Yes, Sir, Reddy Fox was in a dreadful bad way. The worst of it was that none of the other little meadow and forest people seemed to be the least bit sorry for him. Some of them actually laughed at him. Peter Rabbit did. Reddy Fox had made life very uncomfortable for Peter for a long time, and now Peter was actually enjoying Reddy's discomfort.

Now, while he was laid up this way, Reddy had plenty of time to think. He noticed that when he went out to walk, all those who kept at a safe distance when he was well now hardly got out of his way. They knew that he felt too sore and mean to try to catch them. Peter Rabbit hardly turned out of his path. A bright idea came to Reddy. He would continue to appear to feel badly, even after he was well. He would keep his head bound up and would limp down to the Smiling Pool for some mud every day. Then, when Peter Rabbit came near enough, Reddy would catch him.

So day after day Reddy limped down to the Smiling Pool. He kept his head tied up as if it was as bad as ever, and as he walked, he groaned as if in great pain. Even some of those who hated him most began to feel a little bit sorry for Reddy Fox. Peter has a very soft heart, and although he knew that Reddy Fox would like nothing better than to gobble him up, he began to feel sorry for Reddy.

One morning Peter sat just outside the Old Briarpatch, when Reddy came limping along. He looked more miserable than usual. Just as it had been for several days, one of Reddy's eyes was closed.

"It must be hard work to see with only one eye," said Peter Rabbit.

"It is," replied Reddy, with a great sigh. "It is very hard work, indeed."

"I don't see how you manage to get enough to eat," continued Peter, in his most sympathetic voice.

Reddy sighed again. "I don't, Peter Rabbit. I don't get enough to eat, and I'm nearly starved this very minute."

When he said this such a note of longing crept into his voice that Peter instantly grew suspicious. While he was sorry for Reddy, he had no desire to make Reddy feel better by furnishing himself for a meal. Peter hopped around to the blind side of Reddy and turned his back to him, as he inquired for the health of old Granny Fox.

Now, you know that Peter's eyes are so placed in his head that he can see behind him without turning his head. Reddy Fox did not know this, or if he did he had forgotten it. Very slowly and craftily the closed eye opened a wee bit, and in that line of yellow was a hungry look. Peter Rabbit saw it and with a great jump landed behind a friendly bramble bush in the Old Briarpatch.

"Ha! ha!" shouted Peter, "I'd rather talk with you, Reddy Fox, when you haven't got a closed eye with such a hungry look in it. Ta, ta!"

Reddy Fox just shook his fist at Peter Rabbit, and started off home, pulling the bandage from his head as he went.

XVIII. Johnny Chuck Prepares for Winter

There was something in the air that Peter Rabbit couldn't understand. It made him feel frisky and happy and ready to run a race or have a frolic with

any one who might happen along. He couldn't understand why it didn't make all his friends and neighbors on the Green Meadows and in the Green Forest
feel the same way. But it didn't. No, Sir, it didn't.
Some of those with whom he best liked to play
wouldn't play at all, not even for a few minutes; said
they hadn't time. Peter was puzzling over it as he
scampered down the Lone Little Path, kicking his
heels and trying to jump over his own shadow. Just
ahead of him, sitting on his own door-step, sat
Johnny Chuck.

"My goodness, how fat Johnny Chuck is getting!"
thought Peter Rabbit. Then he shouted: "Come on
and play hide and seek, Johnny Chuck!"

But Johnny Chuck shook his head. "Can't!" said he.
"I've got to get ready for winter."

Peter Rabbit sat down and looked at Johnny Chuck
curiously. He couldn't understand why anybody
should take the trouble to get ready for winter. He
didn't, excepting that he put on a warmer coat. So he
couldn't imagine why Johnny Chuck should have to
get ready for winter.

"How do you do it?" he asked.

"Do what?" Johnny Chuck looked up in surprise.

"Why, get ready for winter, of course," Peter
replied, just a wee bit impatiently.

Johnny Chuck looked at Peter as if he thought
Peter very stupid indeed.

"Why, I eat, of course," said he shortly, and began
to stuff himself as if he hadn't had anything to eat for
a week, when all the time he was so fat and roly-poly
that he could hardly waddle.

Peter's eyes twinkled. "I should think you did!" he

exclaimed. "I wouldn't mind getting ready for winter that way myself." You know Peter thinks a very great deal of his stomach. Then he added: "I should think you were trying to eat enough to last you all winter."

Johnny Chuck yawned sleepily and then once more began to eat. "I am," he said briefly, talking with his mouth full.

"What's that?" cried Peter Rabbit, his big eyes popping out.

"I said I'm trying to eat enough to last me all winter! That's the way I get ready for winter," replied Johnny Chuck, just a wee bit crossly. "I think I've got enough now," he added. "How cool it is getting! I think I'll go down and go to sleep. I'll see you in the spring, Peter Rabbit."

"Wha— what's that?" exclaimed Peter Rabbit, looking as if he thought he hadn't heard aright. But Johnny Chuck had disappeared inside his house.

XIX. Peter Rabbit Gets Another Surprise

Peter Rabbit sat on Johnny Chuck's door-step for five long minutes, scratching his head first with one hand, then with the other.

"Now, what did Johnny Chuck mean by saying that he would see me in the spring?" said Peter Rabbit to himself. "Here it isn't winter yet, and it will be a long, long time before spring, yet Johnny Chuck spoke just as if he didn't expect to see me until winter has passed. Is he going away somewhere? If he isn't, why won't I see him all winter, just as I have all summer?"

The more Peter thought about it, the more puzzled

he became. At last he had a happy thought. "I'll just run down to the Smiling Pool and ask Grandfather Frog. He is very old and very wise, and he will surely know what Johnny Chuck meant."

So, kicking up his heels, Peter Rabbit started down the Lone Little Path, lipperty-lipperty-lip, across the Green Meadows to the Smiling Pool. There he found Grandfather Frog sitting as usual on his big lily-pad, but the lily-pad wasn't as green as it used to be, and Grandfather Frog didn't look as smart as usual. His big, goggly eyes looked heavy and dull, just as if they didn't see much of anything at all. Grandfather Frog nodded sleepily and once nearly fell off the big lily-pad.

"Good morning, Grandfather Frog!" shouted Peter Rabbit.

"Eh? What?" said Grandfather Frog, blinking his eyes and putting one hand behind an ear, as if he was hard of hearing.

"I said good morning, Grandfather Frog!" shouted Peter Rabbit, a little louder than before.

"No," replied Grandfather Frog grumpily, "it isn't a good morning; it's too chilly." He shivered as he spoke.

Peter Rabbit pretended not to notice how grumpy Grandfather Frog was. In his most polite way he asked: "Can you tell me, Grandfather Frog, where Johnny Chuck spends the winter?"

"Spends it at home, of course. Don't bother me with such foolish questions!" snapped Grandfather Frog.

"But if he is going to spend the winter at home, what did he mean by saying that he would see me in

"No," replied Grandfather Frog grumpily,
"it isn't a good morning."
See page 115.

the spring, just as if he didn't expect to see me before then?" persisted Peter Rabbit.

Grandfather Frog yawned, shook himself, yawned again, and said:

"Johnny Chuck probably meant just what he said, and I think I'll follow his example. It's getting too cold for an old fellow like me. I begin to feel it in my bones. I'm getting so sleepy that I guess the sooner I hunt up my bed in the mud at the bottom of the Smiling Pool the better. Chugarum! Johnny Chuck is wise. I'll see you in the spring, Peter Rabbit, and tell you all about it."

And with that, Grandfather Frog dived with a great splash into the Smiling Pool.

XX. Peter Tries Ol' Mistah Buzzard

Peter Rabbit sat on the edge of the Smiling Pool and stared at the place where Grandfather Frog had disappeared with a great splash. He watched the tiny waves spread out in rings that grew bigger and bigger and then finally disappeared too. Now what did Grandfather Frog mean when he said: "I'll see you in the spring, Peter Rabbit?" Johnny Chuck had said that very same thing as he had gone down the long hall of his snug house, yet it would be a long, long time before spring, for it was not winter yet. Where did they expect to be all winter, and what did they expect to do? The more Peter puzzled over it, the less he could understand it.

> "My head is whirling round and round,
>   So many funny things I've found;
>   Folks say it grows too cold to stay,

　　　　Yet do not seem to go away.
　　　　They talk of meeting in the spring
　　　　But don't explain a single thing.

"They just go into their houses and say good-by. I don't understand it at all, at all," said Peter Rabbit, staring at the big lily-pad on which Grandfather Frog had sat all summer, watching for foolish green flies to come his way. Somehow that big lily-pad made Peter Rabbit feel terribly lonely. Then he had a happy thought.

"I'll just run over and ask Ol' Mistah Buzzard what it all means; he'll be sure to know," said Peter Rabbit, and off he started, lipperty-lipperty-lip, for the Green Forest.

When Peter got where he could see the tall dead tree that Ol' Mistah Buzzard had made his favorite resting-place, he could see Ol' Mistah Buzzard stretching his big wings, as if he was getting ready to fly. Peter hurried faster. He didn't want Mistah Buzzard to get away before he could ask him what Johnny Chuck and Grandfather Frog had meant. Peter couldn't shout, because he hasn't much of a voice, you know, and then he was out of breath, anyway. So he just made those long legs of his go as fast as ever they could, which is very fast indeed.

Just as Peter Rabbit almost reached the tall dead tree, Ol' Mistah Buzzard jumped off the branch he had been sitting on, gave two or three flaps with his great wings, and then, spreading them out wide, began to sail round and round and up and up, as only Ol' Mistah Buzzard can.

"Wait! Wait! Please wait!" panted Peter Rabbit, but his voice was so weak that Ol' Mistah Buzzard didn't hear him. He saw Peter, however, but of course he didn't know that Peter wanted to talk with him. With a long swoop, Ol' Mistah Buzzard sailed off right over Peter's head.

"Good-by, Brer Rabbit; Ah'll see yo' in the spring!" said Ol' Mistah Buzzard, and before Peter could say a word, he was out of hearing up in the sky.

Peter watched him go up and up until he was just a speck in the blue, blue sky.

"Now what did he mean by that? Is he going to stay up in the sky until spring?" asked Peter Rabbit of himself. But not knowing, of course he couldn't answer.

XXI. Happy Jack Squirrel Is Too Busy to Talk

Peter Rabbit sat with his mouth wide open staring up into the blue, blue sky, where Ol' Mistah Buzzard was growing smaller and smaller. Finally he was just a teeny, weeny speck, and then Peter couldn't see him at all. Peter hitched up his trousers and sat for a long time, looking very thoughtful. He was troubled in his mind, was Peter Rabbit. First Johnny Chuck had said: "I'll see you in the spring," and had disappeared underground; then Grandfather Frog had said: "I'll see you in the spring," and had disappeared in the Smiling Pool; now Ol' Mistah Buzzard had said: "Ah'll see yo' in the spring," and had disappeared up in the blue, blue sky.

"And they all spoke just as if they meant it," said Peter to himself. "I believe I'll go over and see Happy Jack Squirrel. Perhaps he can tell me what it all means."

So off started Peter Rabbit, lipperty-lipperty-lip, through the Green Forest, looking for Happy Jack Squirrel. Pretty soon he caught a glimpse of Happy Jack's gray coat.

"Hi, Happy Jack!" called Peter, hurrying as fast as he could.

"Hello, Peter Rabbit! Don't bother me this morning. I've got too much to do to be bothered," said Happy Jack, digging a little hole in the ground while he talked.

Peter grew curious at once, so curious that he forgot all about what he was going to ask Happy Jack. He sat down and watched Happy Jack put a nut in the hole and cover it up. Then Happy Jack hurried to dig another hole and do the same thing over again.

"What are you doing that for?" asked Peter Rabbit.

"Doing it for? Why, I'm getting ready for winter, of course, stupid!" said Happy Jack, as he paused for breath.

"But I thought you stored your nuts and corn in a hollow tree!" exclaimed Peter Rabbit.

"So I do," replied Happy Jack, "but I would be foolish to put all my supplies in one place, so I bury some of them."

"But how do you remember where you bury them?" persisted Peter.

"I don't always, but when I forget, my nose helps me out. Then I just dig down and get them," said Happy Jack. "Now I can't stop to talk any more, for I am late this year, and the first thing I know winter will be here."

Then Peter remembered what he had come for. "Oh, Happy Jack, what did Johnny Chuck and

Grandfather Frog and Ol' Mistah Buzzard mean by saying that they would see me in the spring?" he cried.

"Can't stop to tell you now!" replied Happy Jack, running this way and that way, and pulling over the fallen leaves to hunt for another nut. "Winter's coming, and I've got to be ready for it. Can't stop to talk."

And that was all Peter Rabbit could get out of him, although he followed Happy Jack about and bothered him with questions until Happy Jack quite lost his temper. Peter sighed. He saw Chatterer the Red Squirrel and Striped Chipmunk both quite as busy as Happy Jack.

"It's of no use to ask them, for they are doing the same thing that Happy Jack is," thought Peter. "I don't see the use of all this fuss about winter, anyway. I don't have to get ready for it. I believe I'll go down to the Smiling Pool again and see if maybe Grandfather Frog has come up."

XXII. Unc' Billy Possum Explains Things

Peter Rabbit had sat still all day long in his safe hiding-place in the middle of the dear Old Briar-patch. Jolly, round, red Mr. Sun had gone to bed behind the Purple Hills, and the black shadows had raced out across the Green Meadows and into the Green Forest. Now the moonlight was driving them back a little way. Peter hopped out of the Old Briar-patch into the moonlight and stretched first one leg and then another. Then he jumped up and down three or four times to get the kinks out of his long hind-legs, and finally started off up the Lone Little Path, lipperty-lipperty-lip.

Half way up the Lone Little Path Peter almost ran headlong into Unc' Billy Possum.

"Mah goodness, Brer Rabbit, yo'all done give me a powerful start!" exclaimed Unc' Billy. "What yo'all in such a right smart hurry fo'?"

Peter Rabbit grinned as he stopped running. "I didn't mean to frighten you, Uncle Billy. The fact is, I was on my way up to your house to see how you and old Mrs. Possum and all the children do this fine fall weather," said Peter Rabbit.

Unc' Billy Possum looked at Peter Rabbit sharply. "Seems to me that yo'all have taken a powerful sudden interest in we-alls. Ah don' remember seeing yo' up our way fo' a long time, Brer Rabbit," said he.

Peter looked a little foolish, for it was true that he hadn't been near Unc' Billy's hollow tree for a long time. "You see, I've been very busy getting ready for winter," said Peter, by way of an excuse.

Unc' Billy began to chuckle and then to laugh. He rested both hands on his knees and laughed and laughed.

Peter Rabbit couldn't see anything to laugh at and he began to get just a wee bit provoked.

"What's the joke?" he demanded.

"The very idea of Brer Rabbit getting ready for winter or of being busy about anything but other people's affairs!" cried Unc' Billy, wiping his eyes.

Peter tried to feel and to look very angry, but he couldn't. No, Sir, he couldn't. The very twinkle in Unc' Billy Possum's eyes made Peter want to laugh, too. In fact Peter just had to laugh. Finally both stopped laughing, and Peter told Unc' Billy all about the things that had troubled him.

"Johnny Chuck disappeared down in his house and said he would see me in the spring; what did he mean by that?" asked Peter.

"Just what he said," replied Unc' Billy. "He done gone down to his bed and gone to sleep, and he's gwine to stay asleep until next spring."

Peter's eyes looked as if they would pop right out of his head. "And Grandfather Frog, what has become of him?" he asked.

"Oh, Grandfather Frog, he done gone to sleep, too, down in the mud at the bottom of the Smiling Pool. Ah reckon yo' will see Grandfather Frog come up right pert in the spring," said Unc' Billy.

"And Ol' Mistah Buzzard—he shouted down from the blue, blue sky that he would see me in the spring; has he gone to sleep up there?" asked Peter.

Unc' Billy Possum threw back his head and laughed fit to kill himself.

"Bless yo' long ears, no, Brer Rabbit! No indeed! Oh my, no! Brer Buzzard done fly away down Souf to ol' Virginny to stay through the cold winter. And Ah most wish Ah was right along with him," added Unc' Billy, suddenly growing sober.

Then Peter Rabbit had a sudden thought. "You aren't going away to sleep all winter, are you, Uncle Billy?" he asked anxiously.

The grin came back to Unc' Billy's face. "No, Brer Rabbit. Ah reckons yo'all can find me right in mah hollow tree most any time this winter, if yo' knock loud enough. But Ah don' reckon on going out much, and Ah do reckon Ah'm going to have a right smart lot of sleep," replied Unc' Billy.

XXIII. Peter Rabbit Has a Bright Idea

Peter Rabbit had a bright idea. At least Peter thought it was, and he chuckled over it a great deal. The more he thought about it, the better it seemed. What was it? Why, to follow the plan of Johnny Chuck and Grandfather Frog to avoid the cold, stormy weather by sleeping all winter. Yes, Sir, that was Peter Rabbit's bright idea.

> "If Johnny Chuck can sleep and sleep
>   The whole long, stormy winter through,
>   It ought to be, it seems to me,
>   The very thing for me to do."

Peter Rabbit said this to himself, as he sat in the middle of the Old Briar-patch, chewing the end of a straw. If Johnny Chuck could do it, of course he could do it. All he would have to do would be to find a snug, warm house which nobody else was using, fix himself a comfortable bed, curl up, and go to sleep. Peter tried to picture himself sleeping away while the snow lay deep all over the Green Meadows and the Smiling Pool could smile no more because the ice, the hard, black ice, would not let it.

Finally Peter could sit still no longer. He just had to tell some one about his bright idea and—and—well, he wasn't quite sure of just the way to go to sleep and sleep so long, for never in his life had Peter Rabbit slept more than a very, very short time without waking to see that no danger was near.

"I'll just run up and see Uncle Billy Possum!" said Peter.

Unc' Billy Possum was sitting in his doorway in his big, hollow tree in the Green Forest, when Peter Rabbit came hurrying up, lipperty-lipperty-lip. Peter hardly waited to say good morning before he began to tell Unc' Billy all about his bright idea. Unc' Billy listened gravely, although there was a twinkle in his eyes.

"The first thing yo' must do is to find a warm place to sleep, Brer Rabbit," said Unc' Billy.

"Oh, that's easy enough!" said Peter.

"And then yo' must get fat, Brer Rabbit," continued Unc' Billy.

"What's that?" exclaimed Peter Rabbit, looking very much puzzled.

"Ah say yo' must get fat," repeated Unc' Billy, slapping his own fat sides.

"What for?" asked Peter.

"To keep yo' warm while yo' are asleep," replied Unc' Billy.

"Must I get very fat?" Peter asked.

"Yes, Sah, yo' must get very fat indeed," said Unc' Billy, and smiled, for it was hard to think of Peter Rabbit as very fat.

"How—how can I get fat?" asked Peter, and looked just a little bit worried.

"By eating and eating and eating, and between times sitting still," replied Unc' Billy Possum.

"That's easy, at least the eating is!" said Peter, who, you know, thinks a great deal of his stomach. "Is that all, Uncle Billy?"

"The first thing yo' must do is to find a warm place to sleep, Brer Rabbit," said Unc' Billy.
See page 125.

"That's about all, excepting yo' mustn't have anything on yo' mind when yo' try to go to sleep, Brer Rabbit. Yo' mustn't get to worrying fo' fear Brer Fox gwine to find yo' while yo' are asleep," said Unc' Billy, and grinned when Peter happened to turn his head.

Peter thanked Unc' Billy and hurried back to the Old Briar-patch to think over all that Unc' Billy had told him.

"I certainly will try it," said Peter.

XXIV. Peter Prepares for a Long Sleep

Day after day Peter Rabbit ran about this way and that over the Green Meadows and through the Green Forest, as if he had something on his mind. Jimmy Skunk noticed it. So did Billy Mink and Bobby Coon. But Peter wouldn't stop to explain. Indeed, he was always in such a hurry that he wouldn't stop at all, but when he met them would shout "Hello!" over his shoulder and keep right on running, lipperty-lipperty-lip. Unc' Possum was the only one who guessed what it meant.

Unc' Billy grinned as he watched Peter running about with such a serious and important air. "Brer Rabbit is trying dreadful hard to fool his-self. Ah reckon he's looking fo' a place to curl up and try to sleep all winter," said Unc' Billy.

Unc' Billy had guessed just right. Peter was looking for a place to curl up to sleep all winter. Peter was too lazy to dig a new house for himself. Then it was too late in the fall, anyway. He would just find some old, deserted house that some of Jimmy Skunk's relatives or Johnny Chuck's relations had given up using. So Peter went poking into every old house he knew of, trying to find one that wasn't so tumble-down that it wouldn't do. At last he found one that he thought would be just the place, and Peter chuckled to himself as he planned how he would curl up in the bedchamber, way down at the end of the long hall.

"Nobody'll ever guess where I am!" he said to himself and laughed aloud.

Then Peter remembered that Unc' Billy Possum had told him that it was necessary to eat a great deal so as to be very fat before going to sleep, for that was the way to keep warm all winter. So Peter started out to grow fat. This would be fun, the very best kind of fun, for there is nothing Peter Rabbit loves more than to fill his stomach, unless it is to satisfy his curiosity.

> "Peter Rabbit's stomach is
>   A thing that's most amazing;
> It takes so long to fill it up
>   His time is short for lazing."

Perhaps this is the reason why, when Peter isn't eating, he wants to loaf around and watch other people work. Anyway, Peter is a tremendous eater, and now that he wanted to grow fat, he felt that he must eat more than ever. So he began at once to eat and eat and eat. But there was one very important thing that Peter had forgotten. He had quite forgotten that it was now late in the fall, and the tender, young, green things which Peter dearly loves to eat were gone. He could no longer go down to the sweet clover patch and fill himself full to bursting. Farmer Brown had taken away all the cabbages and carrots and turnips that had made his garden so attractive to Peter.

So now Peter had to hunt for what he had to eat. That made a great deal of running about, and it is very hard work to grow fat when one runs about. The more Peter ate, the more he had to hunt for his food; and the more he had to hunt for his food, the more he had to run about; and the more he had to run about, the more he hurried and the faster he ran. Now, of course running takes fat off.

"Oh, dear!" cried Peter Rabbit. "Getting fat is not as easy as I thought!"

XXV. Unc' Billy Possum Plays a Joke

> "Some folks never seem to be
> Satisfied or quite content;
> Always wanting something more
> That fo' them was never meant."

Unc' Billy Possum said this to himself as he watched Peter Rabbit hurrying about through the Green Forest and over the Green Meadows, eating as fast as ever he could so as to grow fat that he might keep warm while he slept all winter. Now Unc' Billy Possum knew perfectly well that Peter Rabbit couldn't sleep all winter as Johnny Chuck does, for Old Mother Nature had never planned that Peter should. But Unc' Billy knew that it was of no use to tell Peter that, for Peter wouldn't believe him. So he chuckled as he watched Peter rush around hunting for food and actually running off what little fat he did have, instead of putting on more.

Of course it just happened that Unc' Billy Possum was right over near the old house built by Grandfather Skunk a long time ago, which Peter Rabbit had decided to sleep in all winter. It just happened that he saw Peter when he finally went down to the little bedchamber at the end of the long hall to curl up and try to go to sleep.

Unc' Billy grinned. Then he chuckled. Finally he laughed until his fat sides shook.

"Ah reckon Ah'm gwine to have some fun with Brer Rabbit," said Unc' Billy, still chuckling, as he trotted off through the Green Forest. He went over to Bobby Coon's house and found Bobby, who had been out all night, just getting ready for bed. But Bobby is always ready to play a joke, and when Unc' Billy told him about Peter Rabbit and what fun it would be to give Peter a scare, Bobby scrambled down from his hollow tree right away. Then they hunted up Jimmy Skunk, and the three started for the old house of Grandfather Skunk, where Peter Rabbit was trying to go to sleep for the winter.

"Ah done tell Peter that when he tried to go to sleep he mustn't get to thinking about what would happen if Brer Fox should jes' happen along and find him asleep. Ah reckons that that is the very first thing Peter did think of, as soon as he curled himself up and that he's thinking of it more'n ever right this blessed minute. Yo'alls wait while Ah listen at the door."

Unc' Billy stole very softly to the door of the old house. Then he began to grin and beckoned to Bobby Coon and Jimmy Skunk to come listen. They could hear long sighs from way down in the bedchamber at the end of the long hall. They heard Peter twist and turn, as he tried to make himself comfortable. But when they heard him saying a verse over and over to try to make himself go to sleep, they had to clap their hands over their mouths to keep from laughing out loud.

When they grew tired of listening, Unc' Billy whispered to Jimmy Skunk. Jimmy Skunk grinned, and then he crept a little way down the long hall and began to scratch with his stout claws, as if he were digging. When he stopped, Unc' Billy put his mouth down close to the doorway and barked as nearly like Reddy Fox as he could. Then Jimmy began to dig again, and pretty soon Unc' Billy barked again. Then all three stole softly away and hid behind some bushes.

"Ah reckon Brer Rabbit is right smart wide-awake instead of going to sleep fo' the winter!" chuckled Unc' Billy.

XXVI. Peter Rabbit Learns His Lesson

Peter Rabbit, curled up in the little bedchamber at the end of the long hall in the old house made a long time ago by Grandfather Skunk, twisted and turned and tried to make himself feel sleepy. But the harder he tried, the more wide-awake he seemed to feel. Then he began to think of Reddy and Granny Fox and what would happen if by any chance they should find him there fast asleep, and right while he was thinking about it, he heard a noise that made him jump so that he bumped his head.

Peter didn't think anything about the bump on his

head! No, Sir, Peter didn't even notice it. He was too frightened. He held his breath and listened, while his heart went pit-a-pat, pit-a-pat. There it was again, that noise he had heard before! Some one was in the long, dark hall! There was no doubt about it. He could hear claws scratching. Whoever it was, was digging. Digging! The very thought made every hair on Peter Rabbit stand on end. He knew that Johnny Chuck had gone to sleep for the winter. He knew that Jimmy Skunk could walk right in without any trouble, and that Jimmy never takes any trouble that he can avoid. He knew that Bobby Coon and Unc' Billy Possum don't go into houses underground unless they have to, to get away from danger, and very seldom then.

If some one was digging in the long, dark hall, it could mean but one thing—that it must be some one too big to get in without making the hall larger; and the only ones he could think of were Bowser the Hound and Reddy and Granny Fox! Peter shivered and shook, for unlike Johnny Chuck's house, this one had no back door.

"If it's Bowser the Hound, he may get tired and go away. Anyway, I can soon tell, for he will sniff and snuff and blow the sand out of his nose," thought Peter, and strained his ears to hear the first sniff.

But there were no sniffs or snuffs. Instead, Peter heard a sound that made his heart almost stop beating again. It was a bark, a bark that sounded very much like the bark of Reddy Fox, and it came from just outside the door! That could mean but one thing— that old Granny Fox was digging her way in to the little bedchamber, while Reddy kept watch outside.

"Oh, dear! Oh, dear! Why wasn't I content to live as I always have lived? Whatever did I try to do something I never was intended to do for?" cried Peter to himself, and shook with fright harder than ever.

There was nothing to do but to sit still and wait. Peter sat as still as ever he could. After a little while, the noise in the long, dark hall stopped. Peter waited and waited, but all was still, and he began to feel better. Perhaps old Granny Fox didn't know that he was there at all and had grown tired of digging and had gone away. Peter waited a long time and then peeped out into the long hall. Way up at the end he could see light where the doorway was, and by this he knew that no one was in the hall.

Little by little, his heart going pit-a-pat, Peter crept up until he could peep outside. No one was to be seen. With his heart almost in his mouth, Peter sprang out and started for the dear Old Briar-patch as fast as his long legs could take him. And then he heard a sound that made him stop suddenly and sit up.

"Ha, ha, ha! Ho, ho, ho! Hee, hee, hee!"

There, behind some bushes, Unc' Billy Possum, Bobby Coon, and Jimmy Skunk were laughing fit to kill themselves.

Then Peter knew that they had played a joke on him, and he shook his fist at them. But down in his heart he was glad, for he knew that he had learned his lesson—that he had no business to try to do what Old Mother Nature had never intended that he should do.

THE END

The Adventures of Grandfather Frog

by

Thornton W. Burgess

"Have a nice nap?" inquired Jerry, with a broad grin.
See page 138.

I. Billy Mink Finds Little Joe Otter

Billy Mink ran around the edge of the Smiling Pool and turned down by the Laughing Brook. His eyes twinkled with mischief, and he hurried as only Billy can. As he passed Jerry Muskrat's house, Jerry saw him.

"Hi, Billy Mink! Where are you going in such a hurry this fine morning?" he called.

"To find Little Joe Otter. Have you seen anything of him?" replied Billy.

"No," said Jerry. "He's probably down to the Big River fishing. I heard him say last night that he was going."

"Thanks," said Billy Mink, and without waiting to say more he was off like a little brown flash.

Jerry watched him out of sight. "Hump!" exclaimed Jerry. "Billy Mink is in a terrible hurry this morning. Now I wonder what he is so anxious to find Little Joe Otter for. When they get their heads together, it is usually for some mischief."

Jerry climbed to the top of his house and looked over the Smiling Pool in the direction from which Billy Mink had just come. Almost at once he saw Grandfather Frog fast asleep on his big green lily-pad. The legs of a foolish green fly were sticking out of one corner of his big mouth. Jerry couldn't help laughing, for Grandfather Frog certainly did look funny.

137

"He's had a good breakfast this morning, and his full stomach has made him sleepy," thought Jerry. "But he's getting careless in his old age. He certainly is getting careless. The idea of going to sleep right out in plain sight like that!"

Suddenly a new thought popped into his head. "Billy Mink saw him, and that is why he is so anxious to find Little Joe Otter. He is planning to play some trick on Grandfather Frog as sure as pollywogs have tails!" exclaimed Jerry. Then his eyes began to twinkle as he added: "I think I'll have some fun myself."

Without another word Jerry slipped down into the water and swam over to the big green lily-pad of Grandfather Frog. Then he hit the water a smart blow with his tail. Grandfather Frog's big goggly eyes flew open, and he was just about to make a frightened plunge into the Smiling Pool when he saw Jerry.

"Have a nice nap?" inquired Jerry, with a broad grin.

"I wasn't asleep!" protested Grandfather Frog indignantly. "I was just thinking."

"Don't you think it a rather dangerous plan to think so long with your eyes closed?" asked Jerry.

"Well, maybe I did just doze off," admitted Grandfather Frog sheepishly.

"Maybe you did," replied Jerry. "Now listen." Then Jerry whispered in Grandfather Frog's ear, and both chuckled as if they were enjoying some joke, for they are great friends, you know. Afterward Jerry swam back to his house, and Grandfather Frog closed his eyes so as to look just as he did when he was asleep.

Meanwhile Billy Mink had hurried down the Laughing Brook. Half-way to the Big River he met

Little Joe Otter bringing home a big fish, for you know Little Joe is a great fisherman. Billy Mink hastened to tell him how Grandfather Frog had fallen fast asleep on his big green lily-pad.

"It's a splendid chance to have some fun with Grandfather Frog and give him a great scare," concluded Billy.

Little Joe Otter put his fish down and grinned. He likes to play pranks almost as well as he likes to go fishing.

"What can we do?" said he.

"I've thought of a plan," replied Billy. "Do you happen to know where we can find Longlegs the Blue Heron?"

"Yes," said Little Joe. "I saw him fishing not five minutes ago."

Then Billy told Little Joe his plan, and laughing and giggling, the two little scamps hurried off to find Longlegs the Blue Heron.

II. Longlegs the Blue Heron Receives Callers

Longlegs the Blue Heron felt decidedly out of sorts. It was a beautiful morning, too beautiful for any one to be feeling that way. Indeed, it was the same beautiful morning in which Grandfather Frog had caught so many foolish green flies.

Jolly, round, bright Mr. Sun was smiling his broadest. The Merry Little Breezes of Old Mother West Wind were dancing happily here and there over the Green Meadows, looking for some good turn to do for others. The little feathered people to whom Old

Mother Nature has given the great blessing of music in their throats were pouring out their sweetest songs. So it seemed as if there was no good reason why Longlegs should feel out of sorts. The fact is the trouble with Longlegs was an empty stomach. Yes, Sir, that is what ailed Longlegs the Blue Heron that sunshiny morning. You know it is hard work to be hungry and happy at the same time.

So Longlegs stood on the edge of a shallow little pool in the Laughing Brook, grumbling to himself. Just a little while before, he had seen Little Joe Otter carrying home a big fish, and this had made him hungrier and more out of sorts than ever. In the first place it made him envious, and envy, you know, always stirs up bad feelings. He knew perfectly well that Little Joe had got that fish by boldly chasing it until he caught it, for Little Joe can swim even faster than a fish. But Longlegs chose to try to make himself think that it was all luck. Moreover, he wanted to blame some one for his own lack of success, as most people who fail do. So when Little Joe had called out: "Hi, Longlegs, what luck this fine morning?" Longlegs just pretended not to hear. But when Little Joe was out of sight and hearing, he began to grumble to himself.

"No wonder I have no luck with that fellow racing up and down the Laughing Brook," said he. "He isn't content to catch what he wants himself, but frightens the rest of the fish so that an honest fisherman like me has no chance at all. I don't see what Old Mother Nature was thinking of when she gave him a liking for fish. He and Billy Mink are just two worthless little scamps, born to make trouble for other people."

He was still grumbling when these two same little

scamps poked their heads out of the grass on the other side of the little pool. "You look happy, Longlegs. Must be that you have had a good breakfast," said Little Joe, nudging Billy Mink.

Longlegs snapped his great bill angrily. "What are you doing here, spoiling my fishing?" he demanded. "Haven't you got the Big River and all the rest of the Laughing Brook to fool around in? This is my pool, and I'll thank you to keep away!"

Billy Mink chuckled so that Longlegs heard him, and that didn't improve his temper a bit. But before he could say anything more, Little Joe Otter spoke.

"Oh," said he, "we beg your pardon. We just happen to know that Grandfather Frog is sound asleep, and we thought that if you hadn't had good luck this morning, you might like to know about it. As long as you think so ill of us, we'll just run over and tell Blackcap the Night Heron."

Little Joe turned as if to start off in search of Blackcap at once. "Hold on a minute!" called Longlegs, and tried to make his voice sound pleasant, a difficult thing to do, because, you know, his voice is very harsh and disagreeable. "The truth is, I haven't had a mouthful of breakfast and to be hungry is apt to make me cross. Where did you say Grandfather Frog is?"

"I didn't say," replied Little Joe, "but if you really want to know, he is sitting on his big green lily-pad in the Smiling Pool fast asleep right in plain sight."

"Thank you," said Longlegs. "I believe I have an errand up that way, now I think of it. I believe I'll just go over and have a look at him. I have never seen him asleep."

"Thank you," said Longlegs.
"I believe I have an errand up that way."
See page 141.

III. Longlegs Visits the Smiling Pool

Longlegs the Blue Heron watched Billy Mink and Little Joe Otter disappear down the Laughing Brook. As long as they were in sight, he sat without moving, his head drawn down between his shoulders just as if he had nothing more important to think about than a morning nap. But if you had been near enough to have seen his keen eyes, you would never have suspected him of even thinking of a nap. Just as soon as he felt sure that the two little brown-coated scamps were out of sight, he stretched his long neck up until he was almost twice as tall as he had been a minute before. He looked this way and that way to make sure that no danger was near, spread his great wings, flapped heavily up into the air, and then, with his head once more tucked back between his shoulders and his long legs straight out behind him, he flew out over the Green Meadows, and making a big circle, headed straight for the Smiling Pool.

All this time Billy Mink and Little Joe Otter had not been so far away as Longlegs supposed. They had been hiding where they could watch him, and the instant he spread his wings, they started back up the Laughing Brook towards the Smiling Pool to see what would happen there. You see they knew perfectly well that Longlegs was flying up to the Smiling Pool in the hope that he could catch Grandfather Frog for his breakfast. They didn't really mean that any harm should come to Grandfather Frog, but they meant that he should have a great fright. You see, they were like a great many other people, so heedless and thoughtless that they thought it fun to frighten others.

"Of course we'll waken Grandfather Frog in time for him to get away with nothing more than a great scare," said Little Joe Otter, as they hurried along. "It will be such fun to see his big goggly eyes pop out when he opens them and sees Longlegs just ready to gobble him up! And won't Longlegs be hopping mad when we cheat him out of the breakfast he is so sure he is going to have!"

They reached the Smiling Pool before Longlegs, who had taken a roundabout way, and they hid among the bulrushes where they could see and not be seen.

"There's the old fellow just as I left him, fast asleep," whispered Billy Mink.

Sure enough, there on his big green lily-pad sat Grandfather Frog with his eyes shut. At least, they seemed to be shut. And over on top of his big house sat Jerry Muskrat. Jerry seemed to be too busy opening a fresh-water clam to notice anything else; but the truth is he was watching all that was going on. You see, he had suspected that Billy Mink was going to play some trick on Grandfather Frog, so he had warned him. When he had seen Longlegs coming towards the Smiling Pool, he had given Grandfather Frog another warning, and he knew that now he was only pretending to be asleep.

Straight up to the Smiling Pool came Longlegs the Blue Heron, and on the very edge of it, among the bulrushes, he dropped his long legs and stood with his toes in the water, his long neck stretched up so that he could look all over the Smiling Pool. There, just as Little Joe Otter had said, sat Grandfather Frog on his big green lily-pad, fast asleep. At least, he seemed to be fast asleep. The eyes of Longlegs sparkled with hunger and the thought of what a splendid breakfast Grandfather Frog would make. Very slowly, putting each foot down as carefully as he knew how, Longlegs began to walk along the shore so as to get opposite the big green lily-pad where Grandfather Frog was sitting. And over in the bulrushes on the other side, Little Joe Otter and Billy Mink nudged each other and clapped their hands over their mouths to keep from laughing aloud.

IV. The Patience of Longlegs the Blue Heron

> "Patience often wins the day
> When over-haste has lost the way."

If there is one virtue which Longlegs the Heron possesses above another it is patience. Yes, Sir, Longlegs certainly has got patience. He believes that if a thing is worth having, it is worth waiting for, and that if he waits long enough, he is sure to get it. Perhaps that is because he has been a fisherman all his life, and his father and his grandfather were fishermen. You know a fisherman without patience rarely catches anything. Of course Billy Mink and Little Joe Otter laugh at this and say that it isn't so, but the truth is they sometimes go hungry when they wouldn't if they had a little of the patience of Longlegs.

Now Grandfather Frog is another who is very, very patient. He can sit still the longest time waiting for something to come to him. Indeed, he can sit perfectly still so long, and Longlegs can stand perfectly still so long, that Jerry Muskrat and Billy Mink and Little Joe Otter have had many long disputes as to which of the two can keep still the longest.

"He will make a splendid breakfast," thought Longlegs, as very, very carefully he walked along the edge of the Smiling Pool so as to get right opposite Grandfather Frog. There he stopped and looked very hard at Grandfather Frog. Yes, he certainly must be asleep, for his eyes were closed. Longlegs chuckled to himself right down inside without making a sound, and got ready to wade out so as to get within reach.

Now all the time Grandfather Frog was doing some quiet chuckling himself. You see, he wasn't asleep at all. He was just pretending to be asleep, and all the time he was watching Longlegs out of a corner of one of his big goggly eyes. Very, very slowly and carefully, so as not to make the teeniest, weeniest sound, Longlegs lifted one foot to wade out into the Smiling Pool. Grandfather Frog pretended to yawn and opened his big goggly eyes. Longlegs stood on one foot without moving so much as a feather. Grandfather Frog yawned again, nodded as if he were too sleepy to keep awake, and half closed his eyes. Longlegs waited and waited. Then, little by little, so slowly that if you had been there you would hardly have seen him move, he drew his long neck down until his head rested on his shoulders.

"I guess I must wait until he falls sound asleep again," said Longlegs to himself.

But Grandfather Frog didn't go to sleep. He would nod and nod and then, just when Longlegs would make up his mind that this time he really was asleep, open would pop Grandfather Frog's eyes. So all the long morning Longlegs stood on one foot without moving, watching and waiting and growing hungrier and hungrier, and all the long morning Grandfather Frog sat on his big green lily-pad, pretending that he was oh, so sleepy, and all the time having such a comfortable sun-bath and rest, for very early he had had a good breakfast of foolish green flies.

Over in the bulrushes on the other side of the Smiling Pool two little scamps in brown bathing suits waited and watched for the great fright they had planned for Grandfather Frog, when they had sent Longlegs to try to catch him. They were Billy Mink and Little Joe Otter. At first they laughed to themselves and nudged each other at the thought of the trick they had played. Then, as nothing happened, they began to grow tired and uneasy. You see they do not possess patience. Finally they gave up in disgust and stole away to find some more exciting sport. Grandfather Frog saw them go and chuckled harder than ever to himself.

V. Grandfather Frog Jumps Just in Time

Back and forth over the Green Meadows sailed Whitetail the Marsh Hawk. Like Longlegs the Blue Heron, he was hungry. His sharp eyes peered down among the grasses, looking for something to eat, but some good fairy seemed to have warned the very little people who live there that Whitetail was out hunting. Perhaps it was one of Old Mother West

Wind's children, the Merry Little Breezes. You know they are always flitting about trying to do some one a good turn.

> "They love to dance and romp and play
> From dawn to dusk the livelong day,
> But more than this they love to find
> A chance to do some favor kind."

Anyway, little Mr. Green Snake seemed to know that Whitetail was out hunting and managed to keep out of sight. Danny Meadow Mouse wasn't to be found. Only a few foolish grasshoppers rewarded his patient search, and these only served to make him feel hungrier then ever. But old Whitetail has a great deal of persistence, and in spite of his bad luck, he kept at his hunting, back and forth, back and forth, until he had been all over the Green Meadows. At last he made up his mind that he was wasting time there.

"I'll just have to look over at the Smiling Pool, and if there is nothing there, I'll take a turn or two along the Big River," thought he and straightway started for the Smiling Pool. Long before he reached it, his keen eyes saw Longlegs the Blue Heron standing motionless on the edge of it, and he knew by the looks of Longlegs that he was watching something which he hoped to catch.

"If it's a fish," thought Whitetail, "it will do me no good, for I am no fisherman. But if it's a Frog—well, Frogs are not as good eating as fat Meadow Mice, but they are very filling."

With that he hurried a little faster, and then he saw what Longlegs was watching so intently. It was, as you know, Grandfather Frog sitting on his big green

lily-pad. Old Whitetail gave a great sigh of satisfac-
tion. Grandfather Frog certainly would be very filling,
very filling, indeed.

Now Longlegs the Blue Heron was so intently
watching Grandfather Frog that he saw nothing else,
and Grandfather Frog was so busy watching Longlegs
that he quite forgot that there might be other dangers. Besides, his back was toward old Whitetail. Of
course Whitetail saw this, and it made him almost
chuckle aloud. Ever so many times he had tried to
catch Grandfather Frog, but always Grandfather Frog
had seen him long before he could get near him.

Now, with all his keen sight, old Whitetail had
failed to see some one else who was sitting right in
plain sight. He had failed because his mind was so
full of Grandfather Frog and Longlegs that he forgot
to look around, as he usually does. Just skimming the
tops of the bulrushes he sailed swiftly out over the
Smiling Pool and reached down with his great, cruel
claws to clutch Grandfather Frog, who sat there pretending to be asleep, but all the time watching
Longlegs and deep down inside chuckling to think
how he was fooling Longlegs.

Slap! That was the tail of Jerry Muskrat hitting the
water. Grandfather Frog knew what that meant—
danger! He didn't know what the danger was, and he
didn't wait to find out. There would be time enough
for that later. When Jerry Muskrat slapped the water
with his tail that way, danger was very near indeed.
With a frightened "Chugarum!" Grandfather Frog
dived head first into the Smiling Pool, and so close
was old Whitetail that the water was splashed right
in his face. He clutched frantically with his great

claws, but all he got was a piece of the big green lily-pad on which Grandfather Frog had been sitting, and of course this was of no use for an empty stomach.

With a scream of disappointment and anger, he whirled in the air and made straight for Jerry Muskrat. But Jerry just laughed in the most provoking way and ducked under water.

VI. Longlegs and Whitetail Quarrel

"'You did!' 'I didn't! I didn't!' 'You did!'
Such a terrible fuss when Grandfather hid!"

You see Longlegs the Blue Heron had stood very patiently on one foot all the long morning waiting for Grandfather Frog to go to sleep on his big green lily-pad. He had felt sure he was to have Grandfather Frog for his breakfast and lunch, for he had had no breakfast, and it was now lunch time. He was so hungry that it seemed to him that the sides of his stomach certainly would fall in because there was nothing to hold them up, and then, without any warning at all, old Whitetail the Marsh Hawk had glided out across the Smiling Pool with his great claws stretched out to clutch Grandfather Frog, and Grandfather Frog had dived into the Smiling Pool with a great splash just in the very nick of time.

Now is there anything in the world so hard on the temper as to lose a good meal when you are very, very, very hungry? Of course Longlegs didn't really have that good meal, but he had thought that he was surely going to have it. So when Grandfather Frog splashed into the Smiling Pool, of course Longlegs lost his temper altogether. His yellow eyes seemed to grow even more yellow.

"You robber! You thief!" he screamed harshly at old Whitetail.

Now old Whitetail was just as hungry as Longlegs, and he had come even nearer to catching Grandfather Frog. He is even quicker-tempered than Longlegs. He had whirled like a flash on Jerry Muskrat, but Jerry had just laughed in the most provoking manner and ducked under water. This had made old Whitetail angrier than ever, and then to be called bad names—robber and thief! It was more than any self-respecting Hawk could stand. Yes, Sir, it certainly was! He fairly shook with rage as he turned in the air once more and made straight for Longlegs the Blue Heron.

"I'm no more robber and thief than you are!" he shrieked.

"You frightened away my Frog!" screamed Longlegs.

"I didn't!"

"You did!"

"I didn't! It wasn't your Frog; it was mine!"

"Chugarum!" said Grandfather Frog to Jerry Muskrat, as they peeped out from under some lily-pads. "I didn't know I belonged to anybody. I really didn't. Did you?"

"No," replied Jerry, his eyes sparkling with excitement as he watched Longlegs and Whitetail, "it's news to me."

"You're too lazy to hunt like honest people!" taunted old Whitetail, as he wheeled around Longlegs, watching for a chance to strike with his great, cruel claws.

"I'm too honest to take the food out of other people's mouths!" retorted Longlegs, dancing around so as always to face Whitetail, one of his great, broad wings held in front of him like a shield, and his long, strong bill ready to strike.

Every feather on Whitetail's head was standing erect with rage, and he looked very fierce and terrible. At last he saw a chance, or thought he did, and shot down. But all he got was a feather from that great wing which Longlegs kept in front of him, and before he could get away, that long bill had struck him twice, so that he screamed with pain. So they fought and fought, till the ground was covered with feathers, and they were too tired to fight any longer. Then, slowly and painfully, old Whitetail flew away over the Green Meadows, and with torn and ragged wings, Longlegs flew heavily down the Laughing Brook towards the Big River, and both were sore and stiff and still hungry.

"Dear me! Dear me! What a terrible thing and how useless anger is," said Grandfather Frog, as he climbed back on his big green lily-pad in the warm sunshine.

VII. Grandfather Frog's Big Mouth Gets Him in Trouble

Grandfather Frog has a great big mouth. You know that. Everybody does. His friends of the Smiling Pool, the Laughing Brook, and the Green Meadows have teased Grandfather Frog a great deal about the size of his mouth, but he hasn't minded in the least, not the very least. You see, he learned a long time ago that a big mouth is very handy for catching foolish green flies, especially when two happen to come along together. So he is rather proud of his big mouth, just as he is of his goggly eyes.

But once in a while his big mouth gets him into trouble. It's a way big mouths have. It holds so much that it makes him greedy sometimes. He stuffs it full after his stomach already has all that it can hold, and then of course he can't swallow. Then Grandfather Frog looks very foolish and silly and undignified, and everybody calls him a greedy fellow who is old enough to know better and who ought to be ashamed of himself. Perhaps he is, but he never says so, and he is almost sure to do the same thing over again the first chance he has.

Now it happened that one morning when Grandfather Frog had had a very good breakfast of foolish green flies and really didn't need another single thing to eat, who should come along but Little Joe Otter, who had been down to the Big River fishing. He had eaten all he could hold, and he was taking the rest of his catch to a secret hiding-place up the Laughing Brook.

Now Grandfather Frog is very fond of fish for a change, and when he saw those that Little Joe Otter had, his eyes glistened, and in spite of his full stomach his mouth watered.

"Good morning, Grandfather Frog! Have you had your breakfast yet?" called Little Joe Otter.

Grandfather Frog wanted to say no, but he always tells the truth. "Ye-e-s," he replied, "I've had my breakfast, such as it was. Why do you ask?"

"Oh, for no reason in particular. I just thought that if you hadn't, you might like a fish. But as long as you have breakfasted, of course you don't want one," said Little Joe, his bright eyes beginning to twinkle. He held the fish out so that Grandfather Frog could see just how plump and nice they were.

"Chugarum!" exclaimed Grandfather Frog. "Those certainly are very nice fish, very nice fish indeed. It is very nice of you to think of a poor old fellow like me, and I—er—well, I might find room for just a little teeny, weeny one, if you can spare it."

Little Joe Otter knows all about Grandfather Frog's greediness. He looked at Grandfather Frog's white and yellow waistcoat and saw how it was already stuffed full to bursting. The twinkle in his eyes grew more mischievous than ever as he said: "Of course I can. But I wouldn't think of giving such an old friend a teeny, weeny one."

With that, Little Joe picked out the biggest fish he had and tossed it over to Grandfather Frog. It landed close by his nose with a great splash, and it was almost half as big as Grandfather Frog himself. It was plump and looked so tempting that Grandfather Frog forgot all about his full stomach. He even forgot to be polite and thank Little Joe Otter. He just opened his great mouth and seized the fish. Yes, Sir, that is just what he did. Almost before you could wink an eye, the fish had started down Grandfather Frog's throat head first.

Now you know Grandfather Frog has no teeth, and so he cannot bite things in two. He has to swallow them whole. That is just what he started to do with the fish. It went all right until the head reached his stomach. But you can't put anything more into a thing already full, and Grandfather Frog's stomach was packed as full as it could be of foolish green flies. There the fish stuck, and gulp and swallow as hard as he could, Grandfather Frog couldn't make that fish go a bit farther. Then he tried to get it out again, but it had gone so far down his throat that he couldn't get it back. Grandfather Frog began to choke.

VIII. Spotty the Turtle Plays Doctor

"Greed's a dreadful thing to see,
As everybody will agree."

At first Little Joe Otter, sitting on the bank of the Smiling Pool, laughed himself almost sick as he watched Grandfather Frog trying to swallow a fish almost as big as himself, when his white and yellow waistcoat was already stuffed so full of foolish green flies that there wasn't room for anything more. Such greed would have been disgusting, if it hadn't been so very, very funny. At least, it was funny at first, for the fish had stuck, with the tail hanging out of Grandfather Frog's big mouth. Grandfather Frog hitched this way and hitched that way on his big green lily-pad, trying his best to swallow. Twice he tumbled off with a splash into the Smiling Pool. Each time he scrambled back again and rolled his great goggly eyes in silent appeal to Little Joe Otter to come to his aid.

But Little Joe was laughing so that he had to hold his sides, and he didn't understand that Grandfather Frog really was in trouble. Billy Mink and Jerry

Muskrat came along, and as soon as they saw Grandfather Frog, they began to laugh, too. They just laughed and laughed and laughed until the tears came. They rolled over and over on the bank and kicked their heels from sheer enjoyment. It was the funniest thing they had seen for a long, long time.

"Did you ever see such greed?" gasped Billy Mink.

"Why don't you pull it out and start over again?" shouted Little Joe Otter.

Now this is just what Grandfather Frog was trying to do. At least, he was trying to pull the fish out. He hadn't the least desire in the world to try swallowing it again. In fact, he felt just then as if he never, never wanted to see another fish so long as he lived. But Grandfather Frog's hands are not made for grasping slippery things, and the tail of a fish is very slippery indeed. He tried first with one hand, then with the other, and at last with both. It was of no use at all. He just couldn't budge that fish. He couldn't cough it up, because it had gone too far down for that. The more he clawed at that waving tail with his hands, the funnier he looked, and the harder Little Joe Otter and Billy Mink and Jerry Muskrat laughed. They made such a noise that Spotty the Turtle, who had been taking a sun-bath on the end of an old log, slipped into the water and started to see what it was all about.

Now Spotty the Turtle is very, very slow on land, but he is a good swimmer. He hurried now because he didn't want to miss the fun. At first he didn't see Grandfather Frog.

"What's the joke?" he asked.

Little Joe Otter simply pointed to Grandfather

As soon as they saw Grandfather Frog,
they began to laugh, too.
See page 156.

Frog. Little Joe had laughed so much that he couldn't even speak. Spotty looked over to the big green lily-pad and started to laugh too. Then he saw great tears rolling down from Grandfather Frog's eyes and heard little choky sounds. He stopped laughing and started for Grandfather Frog as fast as he could swim. He climbed right up on the big green lily-pad, and reaching out, grabbed the end of the fish tail in his beak-like mouth. Then Spotty the Turtle settled back and pulled, and Grandfather Frog settled back and pulled. Splash! Grandfather Frog had fallen backward into the Smiling Pool on one side of the big green lily-pad. Splash! Spotty the Turtle had fallen backward into the Smiling Pool on the opposite side of the big green lily-pad. And the fish which had caused all the trouble lay floating on the water.

"Thank you! Thank you!" gasped Grandfather Frog, as he feebly crawled back on the lily-pad. "A minute more, and I would have choked to death."

"Don't mention it," replied Spotty the Turtle.

"I never, never will," promised Grandfather Frog.

IX. Old Mr. Toad Visits Grandfather Frog

Grandfather Frog and old Mr. Toad are cousins. Of course you know that without being told. Everybody does. But not everybody knows that they were born in the same place. They were. Yes, Sir, they were. They were born in the Smiling Pool. Both had long tails and for a while no legs, and they played and swam together without ever going on shore. In fact, when they were babies, they couldn't live out of the water. And people who saw them didn't know the difference between them and called them by the same names—tadpoles or pollywogs. But when they grew old enough to have legs and get along without tails, they parted company.

You see, it was this way: Grandfather Frog (of course he wasn't grandfather then) loved the Smiling Pool so well that he couldn't think of leaving it. He heard all about the Great World and what a wonderful place it was, but he couldn't and wouldn't believe that there could be any nicer place than the Smiling Pool, and so he made up his mind that he would live there always.

But Mr. Toad could hardly wait to get rid of his tail before turning his back on the Smiling Pool and starting out to see the Great World. Nothing that Grandfather Frog could say would stop him, and away Mr. Toad went, when he was so small that he could hide under a clover leaf. Grandfather Frog didn't expect ever to see him again. But he did, though it wasn't for a long, long time. And when he did come back, he had grown so that Grandfather Frog hardly knew him at first. And right then and there began a dispute which they have kept up ever since: whether it was best to go out into the Great World or remain in the home of childhood. Each was sure that what he had done was best, and each is sure of it to this day.

So whenever old Mr. Toad visits Grandfather Frog, as he does every once in a while, they are sure to argue and argue on this same old subject. It was so on the day that Grandfather Frog had so nearly choked to death. Old Mr. Toad had heard about it from one of the Merry Little Breezes of Old Mother West Wind and right away had started for the Smiling Pool to pay his respects to Grandfather Frog, and to tell him how glad he was that Spotty the Turtle had come along just in time to pull the fish out of Grandfather Frog's throat.

Now all day long Grandfather Frog had had to listen to unpleasant remarks about his greediness. It was such a splendid chance to tease him that everybody around the Smiling Pool took advantage of it. Grandfather Frog took it good-naturedly at first, but after a while it made him cross, and by the time his cousin, old Mr. Toad, arrived, he was sulky and just grunted when Mr. Toad told him how glad he was to find Grandfather Frog quite recovered.

Old Mr. Toad pretended not to notice how out of sorts Grandfather Frog was but kept right on talking.

"If you had been out in the Great World as much as I have been, you would have known that Little Joe Otter wasn't giving you that fish for nothing," said he.

Grandfather Frog swelled right out with anger. "Chugarum!" he exclaimed in his deepest, gruffest voice. "Chugarum! Go back to your Great World and learn to mind your own affairs, Mr. Toad."

Right away old Mr. Toad began to swell with anger too. For a whole minute he glared at Grandfather Frog, so indignant he couldn't find his tongue. When he did find it, he said some very unpleasant things, and right away they began to dispute.

"What good are you to anybody but yourself, never seeing anything of the Great World and not knowing anything about what is going on or what other people are doing?" asked old Mr. Toad.

"I'm minding my own affairs and not meddling with things that don't concern me, as seems to be the way out in the Great World you are so fond of talking about," retorted Grandfather Frog. "Wise people know enough to be content with what they have. You've been out in the Great World ever since you could hop, and what good has it done you? Tell me that! You haven't even a decent suit of clothes to your back." Grandfather Frog patted his white and yellow waistcoat as he spoke and looked admiringly at the reflection of his handsome green coat in the Smiling Pool.

Old Mr. Toad's eyes snapped, for you know his suit is very plain and rough.

"People who do honest work for their living have no time to sit about in fine clothes admiring themselves," he replied sharply. "I've learned this much out in the Great World, that lazy people come to no good end, and I know enough not to choke myself to death."

Grandfather Frog almost choked again, he was so angry. You see old Mr. Toad's remarks were very personal, and nobody likes personal remarks when they are unpleasant, especially if they happen to be true. Grandfather Frog was trying his best to think of something sharp to say in reply, when Mr. Redwing, sitting in the top of the big hickory-tree, shouted: "Here comes Farmer Brown's boy!"

Grandfather Frog forgot his anger and began to look anxious. He moved about uneasily on his big green lily-pad and got ready to dive into the Smiling Pool, for he was afraid that Farmer Brown's boy had a pocketful of stones as he usually did have when he came over to the Smiling Pool.

Old Mr. Toad didn't look troubled the least bit. He didn't even look around for a hiding-place. He just sat still and grinned.

"You'd better watch out, or you'll never visit the Smiling Pool again," called Grandfather Frog.

"Oh," replied old Mr. Toad, "I'm not afraid. Farmer Brown's boy is a friend of mine. I help him in his garden. How to make friends is one of the things the Great World has taught me."

"Chugarum!" said Grandfather Frog. "I'd have you to know that—"

But what it was that he was to know old Mr. Toad never found out, for just then Grandfather Frog caught sight of Farmer Brown's boy and without waiting even to say good-by he dived into the Smiling Pool.

X. Grandfather Frog Starts Out to See the Great World

Grandfather Frog looked very solemn as he sat on his big green lily-pad in the Smiling Pool. He looked very much as if he had something on his mind. A foolish green fly actually brushed Grandfather Frog's nose and he didn't even notice it. The fact is he did have something on his mind. It had been there ever since his cousin, old Mr. Toad, had called the day before and they had quarreled as usual over the question whether it was best never to leave home or to go out into the Great World.

Right in the midst of their quarrel along had come Farmer Brown's boy. Now Grandfather Frog is afraid of Farmer Brown's boy, so when he appeared, Grandfather Frog stopped arguing with old Mr. Toad and with a great splash dived into the Smiling Pool and hid under a lily-pad. There he stayed and watched his cousin, old Mr. Toad, grinning in the most provoking way, for he wasn't afraid of Farmer Brown's boy. In fact, he had boasted that they were friends. Grandfather Frog had thought that this was just an idle boast, but when he saw Farmer Brown's boy tickle old Mr. Toad under his chin with a straw, while Mr. Toad sat perfectly still and seemed to enjoy it, he knew that it was true.

Grandfather Frog had not come out of his hiding-place until after old Mr. Toad had gone back across the Green Meadows and Farmer Brown's boy had gone home for his supper. Then Grandfather Frog had climbed back on his big green lily-pad and had sat there half the night without once leading the chorus of the Smiling Pool with his great deep bass voice as he usually did. He was thinking, thinking very hard. And now, this bright, sunshiny morning, he was still thinking.

The fact is Grandfather Frog was beginning to wonder if perhaps, after all, Mr. Toad was right. If the Great World had taught him how to make friends with Farmer Brown's boy, there really must be some things worth learning there. Not for the world would Grandfather Frog have admitted to old Mr. Toad or to any one else that there was anything for him to learn, for you know he is very old and by his friends is accounted very wise. But right down in his heart he was beginning to think that perhaps there were some things which he couldn't learn in the Smiling Pool. So he sat and thought and thought. Suddenly he made up his mind.

"Chugarum!" said he. "I'll do it!"

"Do what?" asked Jerry Muskrat, who happened to be swimming past.

"I'll go out and see for myself what this Great World my cousin, old Mr. Toad, is so fond of talking about is like," replied Grandfather Frog.

"Don't you do it," advised Jerry Muskrat. "Don't you do anything so foolish as that. You're too old, much too old, Grandfather Frog, to go out into the Great World."

Now few old people like to be told that they are too old to do what they please, and Grandfather Frog is no different from others. "You just mind your own affairs, Jerry Muskrat," he retorted sharply. "I guess I know what is best for me without being told. If my cousin, old Mr. Toad, can take care of himself out in the Great World, I can. He isn't half so spry as I am. I'm going, and that is all there is about it!"

With that Grandfather Frog dived into the Smiling Pool, swam across to a place where the bank was low, and without once looking back started across the Green Meadows to see the Great World.

XI. Grandfather Frog Is Stubborn

> "Fee, fi, fe, fum!
> Chug, chug, chugarum!"

Grandfather actually had started out to see the Great World. Yes, Sir, he had turned his back on the Smiling Pool, and nothing that Jerry Muskrat could say made the least bit of difference. Grandfather Frog had made up his mind, and when he does that, it is just a waste of time and breath for any one to try to make him change it. You see Grandfather Frog is stubborn. Yes, that is just the word—stubborn. He would see for himself what this Great World was that his cousin, old Mr. Toad, talked so much about and said was so much better than the Smiling Pool where Grandfather Frog had spent his whole life.

"If old Mr. Toad can take care of himself, I can take care of myself out in the Great World," said Grandfather Frog to himself as, with great jumps, he started out on to the Green Meadows. "I guess he isn't any smarter than I am! He isn't half so spry as I am, and I can jump three times as far as he can. I'll see for myself what this Great World is like, and then I'll go back to the Smiling Pool and stay there the rest of my life. Chugarum, how warm it is!"

It was warm. Jolly, round, bright Mr. Sun was smiling his broadest and pouring his warmest rays down on the Green Meadows. The Merry Little Breezes of Old Mother West Wind were taking a nap. You see, they had played so hard early in the morning that they were tired. So there was nobody and nothing to cool Grandfather Frog, and he just grew warmer and warmer with every jump. He began to grow thirsty, and how he did long for a plunge in the dear, cool Smiling Pool! But he was stubborn. He wouldn't turn back, no matter how uncomfortable he felt. He *would* see the Great World if it killed him. So he kept right on, jump, jump, jump, jump.

Grandfather Frog had been up the Laughing Brook and down the Laughing Brook, where he could swim when he grew tired of traveling on the bank, and where he could cool off whenever he became too warm, but never before had he been very far away from water, and he found this a very different matter. At first he had made great jumps, for that is what his long legs were given him for; but the long grass bothered him, and after a little the jumps grew shorter and shorter and shorter, and with every jump he puffed and puffed and presently began to grunt. You see he never before had made more than a few jumps at a time without resting, and his legs grew tired in a very little while.

Now if Grandfather Frog had known as much about the Green Meadows as the little people who live there all the time do, he would have taken the Lone Little Path, where the going was easy. But he didn't. He just started right out without knowing where he was going, and of course the way was hard, very hard indeed. The grass was so tall that he couldn't see over it, and the ground was so rough that it hurt his tender feet, which were used to the soft, mossy bank of the Smiling Pool. He had gone only a little way before he wished with all his might that he had never thought of seeing the Great World. But he had said that he was going to and he would, so he kept right on—jump, jump, rest, jump, jump, jump, rest, jump, and then a long rest.

It was during one of these rests that he heard footsteps, and then a dreadful sound that made cold chills run all over him. Sniff, sniff, sniff! It was coming nearer. Grandfather Frog flattened himself down as close to the ground as he could get. But it was of no use, no use at all. The sniffing came nearer and nearer, and then right over him stood Bowser the Hound! Bowser looked just as surprised as he felt. He put out one paw and turned Grandfather Frog over on his back. Grandfather Frog struggled to his feet and made two frightened jumps.

"Bow, wow!" cried Bowser and rolled him over again. Bowser thought it great fun, but Grandfather Frog thought that his last day had come.

XII. Grandfather Frog Keeps On

"Grandfather Frog is old and wise,
But even age is foolish.
I'm sure you'll all agree with me
His stubbornness was mulish."

That his very last day had come Grandfather Frog was sure. He didn't have the least doubt about it. Here he was at the mercy of Bowser the Hound out on the Green Meadows far from the dear, safe Smiling Pool. Every time he moved, Bowser flipped him over on his back and danced around him, barking with joy. Every minute Grandfather Frog expected to feel Bowser's terrible teeth, and he grew cold at the thought. When he found that he couldn't get away, he just lay still. He was too tired and frightened to do much of anything else, anyway.

Now when he lay still, he spoiled Bowser's fun, for it was seeing him jump and kick his long legs that tickled Bowser so. Bowser tossed him up in the air two or three times, but Grandfather Frog simply lay where he fell without moving.

"Bow, wow, wow!" cried Bowser, in his great deep voice. Grandfather Frog didn't so much as blink his great goggly eyes. Bowser sniffed him all over. "I guess I've frightened him to death," said Bowser, talking to himself. "I didn't mean to do that. I just wanted to have some fun with him." With that, Bowser took one more sniff and then trotted off to try to find something more exciting. You see, he hadn't had the least intention in the world of really hurting Grandfather Frog.

Grandfather Frog kept perfectly still until he was sure that Bowser was nowhere near. Then he gave a great sigh of relief and crawled under a big mullein leaf to rest, and think things over.

"Chugarum, that was a terrible experience; it was, indeed!" said he to himself, shivering at the very thought of what he had been through. "Nothing like that ever happened to me in the Smiling Pool. I've always said that the Smiling Pool is a better place in which to live than is the Great World, and now I know it. The question is, what had I best do now?"

Now right down in his heart Grandfather Frog knew the answer. Of course the best thing to do was to go straight back to the Smiling Pool as fast as he could. But Grandfather Frog is stubborn. Yes, Sir, he certainly is stubborn. And stubbornness is often just another name for foolishness. He had told Jerry Muskrat that he was going out to see the Great World. Now if he went back, Jerry would laugh at him.

"I won't!" said Grandfather Frog.

"What won't you do?" asked a voice so close to him that Grandfather Frog made a long jump before he thought. You see, at the Smiling Pool he always jumped at the least hint of danger, and because one jump always took him into the water, he was always safe. But there was no water here, and that jump took him right out where anybody passing could see him. Then he turned around to see who had startled him so. It was Danny Meadow Mouse.

"I won't go back to the Smiling Pool until I have seen the Great World," replied Grandfather Frog gruffly.

"You won't see much of the Great World if you jump like that every time you get a scare," said Danny, shaking his head. "No, Sir, you won't see much of the Great World, because one of these times you'll jump right into the claws of old Whitetail the Marsh Hawk, or his cousin Redtail, or Reddy Fox. You take my advice, Grandfather Frog, and go straight back to the Smiling Pool. You don't know enough about the Great World to take care of yourself."

But Grandfather Frog was set in his ways, and nothing that Danny Meadow Mouse could say changed his mind in the least. "I started out to see the Great World, and I'm going to keep right on," said he.

"All right," said Danny at last. "If you will, I suppose you will. I'll go a little way with you just to get you started right."

"Thank you," replied Grandfather Frog. "Let's start right away."

*"You won't see much of the Great World if you jump
like that every time you get a scare," said Danny.*
See page 169.

XIII. Danny Meadow Mouse Feels Responsible

Responsible is a great big word. But it is just as big in its meaning as it is in its looks, and that is the way words should be, I think, don't you? Anyway, re-spon-sible is the way Danny Meadow Mouse felt when he found Grandfather Frog out on the Green Meadows so far from the Smiling Pool and so stubborn that he would keep on to see the Great World instead of going back to his big green lily-pad in the Smiling Pool, where he could take care of himself. You remember Peter Rabbit felt re-spon-sible when he brought little Miss Fuzzytail down from the Old Pasture to the dear Old Briar-patch. He felt that it was his business to see to it that no harm came to her, and that is just the way Danny Meadow Mouse felt about Grandfather Frog.

You see, Danny knew that if Grandfather Frog was going to jump like that every time he was frightened, he wouldn't get very far in the Great World. It might be the right thing to do in the Smiling Pool, where the friendly water would hide him from his enemies, but it was just the wrong thing to do on the Green Meadows or in the Green Forest. Danny had learned, when a very tiny fellow, that there the only safe thing to do when danger was near was to sit perfectly still and hardly breathe.

Now Danny Meadow Mouse is fond of Grandfather Frog, and he couldn't bear to think that something dreadful might happen to him. So when he found that he couldn't get Grandfather Frog to go back to the Smiling Pool, he made up his mind that he just *had* to go along with Grandfather Frog to try to keep him out of danger. Yes, Sir, he just *had* to do it. He felt re-sponsible for Grandfather Frog's safety. So here they were, Danny Meadow Mouse running ahead, anxious and worried and watching sharply for signs of danger, and Grandfather Frog puffing along behind, bound to see the Great World which his cousin, old Mr. Toad, said was a better place to live in than the Smiling Pool.

Now Danny has a great many private little paths under the grass all over the Green Meadows, and along these he can scamper ever so fast without once showing himself to those who may be looking for him. Of course he started to take Grandfather Frog along one of these little paths. But Grandfather Frog doesn't walk or run; he jumps. There wasn't room in Danny's little paths for jumping, as they soon found out. Grandfather Frog simply couldn't follow Danny along those little paths. Danny sat down to think, and puckered his brows anxiously. He was more worried than ever. It was very clear that Grandfather Frog would have to travel out in the open, where there was room for him to jump, and where also he would be right out in plain sight of all who happened along. Once more Danny urged him to go back to the Smiling Pool, but he might just as well have talked to a stick or a stone. Grandfather Frog had started out to see the Great World, and he was going to see it.

Danny sighed. "If you will, you will, I suppose," said he, "and I guess the only place you can travel in any comfort is the Lone Little Path. It is dangerous, very dangerous, but I guess you will have to do it."

"Chugarum!" replied Grandfather Frog, "I'm not afraid. You show me the Lone Little Path and then go about your business, Danny Meadow Mouse."

So Danny led the way to the Lone Little Path, and Grandfather Frog sighed with relief, for here he could jump without getting all tangled up in long grass and without hurting his tender feet on sharp stubble where the grass had been cut. But Danny felt more worried than ever. He wouldn't leave Grandfather Frog because, you know, he felt re-spon-sible for him, and at the same time he was terribly afraid, for he felt sure that some of their enemies would see them. He wanted to go back, but he kept right on, and that shows just what a brave little fellow Danny Meadow Mouse was.

XIV. Grandfather Frog Has a Strange Ride

"A thousand things may happen to,
Ten thousand things befall,
The traveler who careless is,
Or thinks he knows it all."

Grandfather Frog, jumping along behind Danny Meadow Mouse up the Lone Little Path, was beginning to think that Danny was the most timid and easiest frightened of all the little meadow people of his acquaintance. Danny kept as much under the grass that overhung the Lone Little Path as he could. When there were perfectly bare places, Danny looked this way and looked that way anxiously and then scampered across as fast as he could make his little legs go. When he was safely across, he would wait for Grandfather Frog. If a shadow passed over the grass, Danny would duck under the nearest leaf and hold his breath.

"Foolish!" muttered Grandfather Frog. "Foolish, foolish to be so afraid! Now, I'm not afraid until I see something to be afraid of. Time enough then. What's the good of looking for trouble all the time? Now, here I am out in the Great World, and I'm not afraid. And here's Danny Meadow Mouse, who has lived here all his life, acting as if he expected something dreadful to happen any minute. Pooh! How very, very foolish!"

Now Grandfather Frog is old and in the Smiling Pool he is accounted very, very wise. But the wisest sometimes become foolish when they think that they know all there is to know. It was so with Grandfather Frog. It was he who was foolish and not Danny Meadow Mouse. You see Danny knew all the dangers on the Green Meadows, and how many sharp eyes were all the time watching for him. He had long ago learned that the only way to feel safe was to feel afraid. You see, then he was watching for danger every minute, and so he wasn't likely to be surprised by his hungry enemies.

So while Grandfather Frog was looking down on Danny for being so timid, Danny was really doing the wisest thing. More than that, he was really very, very brave. He was showing Grandfather Frog the way up the Lone Little Path to see the Great World, when he himself would never, never have thought of traveling anywhere but along his own secret little paths, just because Grandfather Frog couldn't jump anywhere excepting where the way was fairly clear, as in the Lone Little Path, and Danny was afraid that unless Grandfather Frog had some one with him to watch out for him, he would surely come to a sad end.

The farther they went with nothing happening, the more foolish Danny's timid way of running and hiding seemed to Grandfather Frog, and he was just about to tell Danny just what he thought, when Danny dived into the long grass and warned Grandfather Frog to do the same. But Grandfather Frog didn't.

"Chugarum!" said he, "I don't see anything to be afraid of, and I'm not going to hide until I do."

So he sat still right where he was, in the middle of the Lone Little Path, looking this way and that way, and seeing nothing to be afraid of. And just then around a turn in the Lone Little Path came—who do you think? Why Farmer Brown's boy! He saw Grandfather Frog and with a whoop of joy he sprang for him. Grandfather Frog gave a frightened croak and jumped, but he was too late. Before he could jump again Farmer Brown's boy had him by his long hind-legs.

"Ha, ha!" shouted Farmer Brown's boy, "I believe this is the very old chap I have tried so often to catch in the Smiling Pool. These legs of yours will be mighty fine eating, Mr. Frog. They will, indeed."

With that he tied Grandfather Frog's legs together and went on his way across the Green Meadows with poor old Grandfather Frog dangling from the end of a string. It was a strange ride and a most uncomfortable one, and with all his might Grandfather Frog wished he had never thought of going out into the Great World.

XV. Grandfather Frog Gives Up Hope

With his legs tied together, hanging head down from the end of a string, Grandfather Frog was being carried he knew not where by Farmer Brown's boy. It was dreadful. Half-way across the Green Meadows the Merry Little Breezes of Old Mother West Wind came dancing along. At first they didn't see Grandfather Frog, but presently one of them, rushing up to tease Farmer Brown's boy by blowing off his hat, caught sight of Grandfather Frog.

Now the Merry Little Breezes are great friends of Grandfather Frog. Many, many times they have blown foolish green flies over to him as he sat on his big green lily-pad, and they are very fond of him. So when this one caught sight of him in such a dreadful position, he forgot all about teasing Farmer Brown's boy. He raced away to tell the other Merry Little Breezes. For a minute they were perfectly still. They forgot all about being merry.

"It's awful, just perfectly awful!" cried one.

"We must do something to help Grandfather Frog!" cried another.

"Of course we must," said a third.

"But what can we do?" asked a fourth.

Nobody replied. They just thought and thought and thought. Finally the first one spoke. "We might try to comfort him a little," said he.

"Of course we will do that!" they shouted all together.

"And if we throw dust in the face of Farmer Brown's boy and steal his hat, perhaps he will put

Grandfather Frog down," continued the Merry Little Breeze.

"The very thing!" the others cried, dancing about with excitement.

"Then we can rush about and tell all Grandfather Frog's friends what has happened to him and where he is. Perhaps some of them can help us," the Little Breeze continued.

They wasted no more time talking, but raced after Farmer Brown's boy as fast as they could go. One of them, who was faster than the others, ran ahead and whispered in Grandfather Frog's ear that they were coming to help him. But poor old Grandfather Frog couldn't be comforted. He couldn't see what there was that the Merry Little Breezes could do. His legs smarted where the string cut into the skin, and his head ached, for you know he was hanging head down. No, Sir, Grandfather Frog couldn't be comforted. He was in a terrible fix, and he couldn't see any way out of it. He hadn't the least bit of hope left. And all the time Farmer Brown's boy was trudging along, whistling merrily. You see, it didn't occur to him to think how Grandfather Frog must be suffering and how terribly frightened he must be. He wasn't cruel. No, indeed, Farmer Brown's boy wasn't cruel. That is, he didn't mean to be cruel. He was just thoughtless, like a great many other boys, and girls too.

So he went whistling on his way until he reached the Long Lane leading from the Green Meadows up to Farmer Brown's dooryard. No sooner was he in the Long Lane than something happened. A great cloud of dust and leaves and tiny sticks was dashed in his face and nearly choked him. Dirt got in his eyes. His hat was snatched from his head and went sailing over into the garden. He dropped Grandfather Frog and felt for his handkerchief to wipe the dirt from his eyes.

"Phew!" exclaimed Farmer Brown's boy, as he started after his hat. "It's funny where that wind came from so suddenly!"

But you know and I know that it was the Merry Little Breezes working together who made up that sudden wind. And Grandfather Frog ought to have known it too, but he didn't. You see the dust had got in his nose and eyes just as it had in those of Farmer Brown's boy, and he was so frightened and confused that he couldn't think. So he lay just where Farmer Brown's boy dropped him, and he didn't have any more hope than before.

XVI. The Merry Little Breezes Work Hard

The Merry Little Breezes almost shouted aloud with delight when they saw Farmer Brown's boy drop Grandfather Frog to feel for his handkerchief and wipe out the dust which they had thrown in his eyes. Then he had to climb the fence and chase his hat through the garden. They would let him almost get his hands on it and then, just as he thought that he surely had it, they would snatch it away. It was great fun for the Merry Little Breezes. But they were not doing it for fun. No, indeed, they were not doing it for fun! They were doing it to lead Farmer Brown's boy away from Grandfather Frog.

Just as soon as they dared, they dropped the hat and then separated and rushed away in all directions across the Green Meadows, over to the Green Forest, and down to the Smiling Pool. What were they going for? Why, to hunt for some of Grandfather Frog's friends and ask their help. You see, the Merry Little Breezes could make Farmer Brown's boy drop Grandfather Frog, but they couldn't untie a knot or cut a string, and this is just what had got to be done to set Grandfather Frog free, for his hind-legs were tied together. So now they were looking for some one with sharp teeth, who thought enough of Grandfather Frog to come and help him.

One thought of Striped Chipmunk and started for the old stone wall to look for him. Another went in search of Danny Meadow Mouse. A third headed for the dear Old Briar-patch after Peter Rabbit. A fourth remembered Jimmy Skunk and how he had once set Blacky the Crow free from a snare. A fifth remembered what sharp teeth Happy Jack Squirrel has and hurried over to the Green Forest to look for him. A sixth started straight for the Smiling Pool to tell Jerry Muskrat. And every one of them raced as fast as he could.

All this time Grandfather Frog was without hope. Yes, Sir, poor old Grandfather Frog was wholly in despair. You see, he didn't know what the Merry Little Breezes were trying to do, and he was so frightened and confused that he couldn't think. When Farmer Brown's boy dropped him, he lay right where he fell for a few minutes. Then, right close at hand, he saw an old board. Without really thinking, he tried to get to it, for there looked as if there might be room for him to hide under it. It was hard work, for you know his long hind-legs, which he uses for jumping, were tied together. The best he could do was to crawl and wriggle and pull himself along. Just as Farmer Brown's boy started to climb the fence back into the Long Lane, his hat in his hand, Grandfather Frog reached the old board and crawled under it.

Now when the Merry Little Breezes had thrown the dust in Farmer Brown's boy's face and snatched his hat, he had dropped Grandfather Frog in such a hurry that he didn't notice just where he did drop him, so now he didn't know the exact place to look for him. But he knew pretty near, and he hadn't the least doubt but that he would find him. He had just started to look when the dinner horn sounded. Farmer Brown's boy hesitated. He was hungry. If he was late, he might lose his dinner. He could come back later to look for Grandfather Frog, for with his legs tied Grandfather Frog couldn't get far. So, with a last look to make sure of the place, Farmer Brown's boy started for the house.

If the Merry Little Breezes had known this, they would have felt ever so much better. But they didn't. So they hurried as fast as ever they could to find Grandfather Frog's friends and worked until they were almost too tired to move, for it seemed as if every single one of Grandfather Frog's friends had taken that particular day to go away from home. So while Farmer Brown's boy ate his dinner, and Grandfather Frog lay hiding under the old board in the Long Lane, the Merry Little Breezes did their best to find help for him.

XVII. Striped Chipmunk Cuts the String

"Hippy hop! Flippy flop! All on a summer day
    My mother turned me from the house and
        sent me out to play!"

Striped Chipmunk knew perfectly well that that
was just nonsense, but Striped Chipmunk learned
a long time ago that when you are just bubbling right
over with good feeling, there is fun in saying and
doing foolish things, and that is just how he was feeling. So he ran along the old rail fence on one side of
the Long Lane, saying foolish things and cutting up
foolish capers just because he felt so good, and all
the time seeing all that those bright little eyes of his
could take in.

Now Striped Chipmunk and the Merry Little
Breezes of Old Mother West Wind are great friends,
very great friends, indeed. Almost every morning
they have a grand frolic together. But this morning
the Merry Little Breezes hadn't come over to the old
stone wall where Striped Chipmunk makes his home.
Anyway, they hadn't come at the usual time. Striped
Chipmunk had waited a little while and then,
because he was feeling so good, he had decided to
take a run down the Long Lane to see if anything
new had happened there. That is how it happened
that when one of the Merry Little Breezes did go to
look for him, and was terribly anxious to ask him to
come to the help of Grandfather Frog, he was
nowhere to be found.

But Striped Chipmunk didn't know anything about
that. He scampered along the top rails of the old

fence, jumped up on top of a post, and sat up to wash his face and hands, for Striped Chipmunk is very neat and cannot bear to be the least bit dirty. He looked up and winked at Ol' Mistah Buzzard, sailing round and round way, way up in the blue, blue sky. He chased his own tail round and round until he nearly fell off of the post. He made a wry face in the direction of Redtail the Hawk, whom he could see sitting in the top of a tall tree way over on the Green Meadows. He scolded Bowser the Hound, who happened to come trotting up the Long Lane, and didn't stop scolding until Bowser was out of sight. Then he kicked up his heels and whisked along the old fence again.

Half-way across a shaky old rail, he suddenly stopped. His bright eyes had seen something that filled him with curiosity, quite as much curiosity as Peter Rabbit would have had. It was a piece of string. Yes, Sir, it was a piece of string. Now Striped Chipmunk often had found pieces of string, so there was nothing particularly interesting in the string itself. What did interest him and make him very curious was the fact that this piece of string kept moving. Every few seconds it gave a little jerk. Whoever heard of a piece of string moving all by itself? Certainly Striped Chipmunk never had. He couldn't understand it.

For a few minutes he watched it from the top rail of the old fence. Then he scurried down to the ground and, a few steps at a time, stopping to watch sharply between each little run, he drew nearer and nearer to that queer acting string. It gave him a funny feeling inside to see a string acting like that, so he was very careful not to get too near. He looked at it from one side, then ran around and looked at it from the other side. At last he got where he could see that one end of the string was under an old board, and then he began to understand. Of course there was somebody hiding under that old board and jerking the string.

Striped Chipmunk sat down and scratched his head thoughtfully. Whoever was pulling that string couldn't be very big, or they would never have been able to crawl under that old board, therefore he needn't be afraid. A gleam of mischief twinkled in Striped Chipmunk's eyes. He seized the other end of the string and began to pull. Such a jerking and yanking as began right away! But he held on and pulled harder. Then out from under the old board appeared the queer webbed feet of Grandfather Frog tied together. Striped Chipmunk was so surprised that he let go of the string and nearly fell over backward.

"Why, Grandfather Frog, what under the sun are you doing here?" he shouted.

When Striped Chipmunk let go of the string, Grandfather Frog promptly drew his feet back under the old board, but when he heard Striped Chipmunk's voice, he slowly and painfully crawled out. He told how he had been caught and tied by Farmer Brown's boy and finally dropped near the old board. He told how terribly frightened he was, and how sore his legs were. Striped Chipmunk didn't wait for him to finish. In a flash he was at work with his sharp teeth and had cut the cruel string before Grandfather Frog had finished his story.

He seized the other end of the string and began to pull.
See page 183.

XVIII. Grandfather Frog Hurries Away

When Striped Chipmunk cut the string that bound the long legs of Grandfather Frog together, Grandfather Frog was so relieved that he hardly knew what to do. Of course he thanked Striped Chipmunk over and over again. Striped Chipmunk said that it was nothing, just nothing at all, and that he was very glad indeed to help Grandfather Frog.

"We folks who live out in the Great World have to help one another," said Striped Chipmunk, "because we never know when we may need help ourselves. Now you take my advice, Grandfather Frog, and go back to the Smiling Pool as fast as you can. The Great World is no place for an old fellow like you, because you don't know how to take care of yourself."

Now when he said that, Striped Chipmunk made a great mistake. Old people never like to be told that they are old or that they do not know all there is to know. Grandfather Frog straightened up and tried to look very dignified.

"Chugarum!" said he, "I'd have you to know, Striped Chipmunk, that people were coming to me for advice before you were born. It was just an accident that Farmer Brown's boy caught me, and I'd like to see him do it again. Yes, Sir, I'd like to see him do it again!"

Dear me, dear me! Grandfather Frog was boasting. If he had been safe at home in the Smiling Pool, there might have been some excuse for boasting, but way over here in the Long Lane, not even knowing the way back to the Smiling Pool, it was foolish, very foolish indeed. No one knew that better than Striped Chipmunk, but he has a great deal of respect for Grandfather Frog, and he knew too that Grandfather Frog was feeling very much out of sorts and very much mortified to think that he had been caught in such a scrape, so he put a hand over his mouth to hide a smile as he said:

"Of course he isn't going to catch you again. I know how wise and smart you are, but you look to me very tired, and there are so many dangers out here in the Great World that it seems to me that the very best thing you can do is to go back to the Smiling Pool."

But Grandfather Frog is stubborn, you know. He had started out to see the Great World, and he didn't want the little people of the Green Meadows and the Green Forest to think that he was afraid. The truth is, Grandfather Frog was more afraid of being laughed at than he was of the dangers around him, which shows just how foolish wise people can be sometimes. So he shook his head.

"Chugarum!" said he, "I am going to see the Great World first, and then I am going back to the Smiling Pool. Do you happen to know where there is any water? I am very thirsty."

Now over on the other side of the Long Lane was a spring where Farmer Brown's boy filled his jug with clear cold water to take with him to the cornfield when he had to work there. Striped Chipmunk knew all about that spring, for he had been there for a drink many times. So he told Grandfather Frog just where the spring was and how to get to it. He even offered to show the way, but Grandfather Frog said that he would rather go alone.

"Watch out, Grandfather Frog, and don't fall in, because you might not be able to get out again," warned Striped Chipmunk.

Grandfather Frog looked up sharply to see if Striped Chipmunk was making fun of him. The very idea of any one thinking that he, who had lived in the water all his life, couldn't get out when he pleased! But Striped Chipmunk looked really in earnest, so Grandfather Frog swallowed the quick retort on the tip of his tongue, thanked Striped Chipmunk, and hurried away to look for the spring, for he was very, very thirsty. Besides, he was very, very hot, and he hurried still faster as he thought of the cool bath he would have when he found that spring.

XIX. Grandfather Frog Jumps into More Trouble

Some people are heedless and run into trouble. Some people are stupid and walk into trouble. Grandfather Frog was both heedless and stupid and jumped into trouble. When Striped Chipmunk told him where the spring was, it seemed to him that he couldn't wait to reach it. You see, Grandfather Frog had spent all his life in the Smiling Pool, where he could get a drink whenever he wanted it by just reaching over the edge of his big green lily-pad. Whenever he was too warm, all he had to do was to say "Chugarum!" and dive head first into the cool water. So he wasn't used to going a long time without water.

Jump, jump, jump! Grandfather Frog was going as fast as ever he could in the direction Striped Chipmunk had pointed out. Every three or four jumps he would stop for just a wee, wee bit of rest, then off he would go again, jump, jump, jump! And each jump was a long one. Peter Rabbit certainly would have been envious if he could have seen those long jumps of Grandfather Frog.

At last the ground began to grow damp. The farther he went, the damper it grew. Presently it became fairly wet, and there was a great deal of soft, cool, wet moss. How good it did feel to Grandfather Frog's poor tired feet!

"Must be I'm 'most there," said Grandfather Frog to himself, as he scrambled up on a big mossy hummock, so as to look around. Right away he saw a little path from the direction of the Long Lane. It led straight past the very hummock on which Grandfather Frog was sitting, and he noticed that where the ground was very soft and wet, old boards had been laid down. That puzzled Grandfather Frog a great deal.

"It's a sure enough path," said he. "But what under the blue, blue sky does any one want to spoil it for by putting those boards there?"

You see, Grandfather Frog likes the soft wet mud, and he couldn't understand how any one, even Farmer Brown's boy, could prefer a hard dry path. Of course he never had worn shoes himself, so he couldn't understand why any one should want dry feet when they could just as well have wet ones. He was still puzzling over it when he heard a sound that made him nearly lose his balance and tumble off the hummock. It was a whistle, the whistle of Farmer Brown's boy! Grandfather Frog knew it right away, because he often had heard it over by the Smiling Pool. The whistle came from over in the Long Lane. Farmer Brown's boy had had his dinner and was on his way back to look for Grandfather Frog where he had been dropped.

Grandfather Frog actually grinned as he thought how surprised Farmer Brown's boy was going to be when he could find no trace of him. Suddenly the smile seemed to freeze on Grandfather Frog's face. That whistle was coming nearer! Farmer Brown's boy had left the Long Lane and was coming along the little path. The truth is, he was coming for a drink at the spring, but Grandfather Frog didn't think of this. He was sure that in some way Farmer Brown's boy had found out which way he had gone and was coming after him. He crouched down as flat as he could on the big hummock and held his breath. Farmer Brown's boy went straight past. Just a few steps beyond, he stopped and knelt down. Peeping through the grass, Grandfather Frog saw him dip up beautiful clear water in an old cup and drink. Then Grandfather Frog knew just where the spring was.

A few minutes later, Farmer Brown's boy passed again, still whistling, on his way to the Long Lane. Grandfather Frog waited only long enough to be sure that he had really gone. Then, with bigger jumps than ever, he started for the spring. A dozen long jumps, and he could see the water. Two more jumps and then a long jump, and he had landed in the spring with a splash!

"Chugarum!" cried Grandfather Frog. "How good the water feels!"

And all the time, Grandfather Frog had jumped straight into more trouble.

XX. Grandfather Frog Loses Heart

"Look before you leap;
The water may be deep."

That is the very best kind of advice, but most people find that out when it is too late. Grandfather Frog did. Of course he had heard that little verse all his life. Indeed, he had been very fond of saying it to those who came to the Smiling Pool to ask his advice. But Grandfather Frog seemed to have left all his wisdom behind him when he left the Smiling Pool to go out into the Great World. You see, it is very hard work for any one whose advice has been sought to turn right around and take advice themselves. So Grandfather Frog had been getting into scrapes ever since he started out on his foolish journey, and now here he was in still another, and he had landed in it head first, with a great splash.

Of course, when he had seen the cool, sparkling water of the spring, it had seemed to him that he just couldn't wait another second to get into it. He was so hot and dry and dreadfully thirsty and uncomfortable! And so—oh, dear me!—Grandfather Frog didn't look at all before he leaped. No, Sir, he didn't! He just dived in with a great long jump. Oh, how good that

water felt! For a few minutes he couldn't think of anything else. It was cooler than the water of the Smiling
Pool, because, as you know, it was a spring. But it felt
all the better for that, and Grandfather Frog just
closed his eyes and floated there in pure happiness.

Presently he opened his eyes to look around. Then
he blinked them rapidly for a minute or so. He
rubbed them to make sure that he saw aright. His
heart seemed to sink way, way down towards his
toes. "Chugarum!" exclaimed Grandfather Frog,
"Chugarum!" And after that for a long time he didn't
say a word.

You see, it was this way. All around him rose perfectly straight smooth walls. He could look up and
see a little of the blue, blue sky right overhead and
whispering leaves of trees and bushes. Over the edge
of the smooth straight wall grasses were bending.
But they were so far above his head, so dreadfully
far! *There wasn't any place to climb out!* Grandfather
Frog was in a prison! He didn't understand it at all,
but it was so.

Of course, Farmer Brown's boy could have told
him all about it. A long time before Farmer Brown
himself had found that spring, and because the water
was so clear and cold and pure, he had cleared away
all the dirt and rubbish around it. Then he had
knocked the bottom out of a nice clean barrel and
had dug down where the water bubbled up out of the
sand and had set the barrel down in this hole and
had filled in the bottom with clean white sand for the
water to bubble up through. About half-way up the
barrel he had cut a little hole for the water to run out
as fast as it bubbled in at the bottom. Of course the

water never could fill the barrel, because when it reached that hole, it ran out. This left a straight, smooth wall up above, a wall altogether too high for Grandfather Frog to jump over from the inside.

Poor old Grandfather Frog! He wished more than ever that he never, never had thought of leaving the Smiling Pool to see the Great World. Round and round he swam, but he couldn't see any way out of it. The little hole where the water ran out was too small for him to squeeze through, as he found out by try-ing and trying. So far as he could see, he had just got to stay there all the rest of his life. Worse still, he knew that Farmer Brown's boy sometimes came to the spring for a drink, for he had seen him do it. That meant that the very next time he came, he would find Grandfather Frog, because there was no place to hide. When Grandfather Frog thought of that, he just lost heart. Yes, Sir, he just lost heart. He gave up all hope of ever seeing the Smiling Pool again, and two big tears ran out of his big goggly eyes.

XXI. The Merry Little Breezes Try to Comfort Grandfather Frog

When the Merry Little Breezes of Old Mother West Wind had left Grandfather Frog in the Long Lane where Farmer Brown's boy had dropped him, and had hurried as fast as ever they could to try to find some of his friends to help him, not one of them had been successful. No one was at home, and no one was in any of the places where they usually were to be found. The Merry Little Breezes looked and looked. Then, one by one, they sadly turned back to the Long Lane. They felt so badly that they just hated to go back where they had left Grandfather Frog.

When they got there, they found Striped Chipmunk, who now was scolding Farmer Brown's boy as fast as his tongue could go.

"Where is he?" cried the Merry Little Breezes excitedly.

Striped Chipmunk stopped scolding long enough to point to Farmer Brown's boy, who was hunting in the grass for some trace of Grandfather Frog.

"We don't mean him, you stupid! We can see him for ourselves. Where's Grandfather Frog?" cried the Merry Little Breezes, all speaking at once.

"I don't know," replied Striped Chipmunk, "and what's more, I don't care!"

Now this wasn't true, for Striped Chipmunk isn't that kind. It was mostly talk, and the Merry Little Breezes knew it. They knew that Striped Chipmunk really thinks a great deal of Grandfather Frog, just as they do. So they pretended not to notice what he said or how put out he seemed. After a while, he told them that he had set Grandfather Frog free and that then he had started for the spring on the other side of the Long Lane. The Merry Little Breezes were delighted to hear the good news, and they said such a lot of nice things to Striped Chipmunk that he quite forgot to scold Farmer Brown's boy. Then they started for the spring, dancing merrily, for they felt sure that there Grandfather Frog was all right, and they expected to find him quite at home.

"Hello, Grandfather Frog!" they shouted, as they

peeped into the spring. "How do you like your new home?"

Grandfather Frog made no reply. He just rolled his great goggly eyes up at them, and they were full of tears.

"Why—why—why, Grandfather Frog, what is the matter now?" they cried.

"Chugarum," said Grandfather Frog, and his voice sounded all choky, "I can't get out."

Then they noticed for the first time how straight and smooth the walls of the spring were and how far down Grandfather Frog was, and they knew that he spoke the truth. They tried bending down the grasses that grew around the edge of the spring, but none were long enough to reach the water. If they had stopped to think, they would have known that Grandfather Frog couldn't have climbed up by them, anyway. Then they tried to lift a big stick into the spring, but it was too heavy for them, and they couldn't move it. However, they did manage to blow an old shingle in, and this gave Grandfather Frog something to sit on, so that he began to feel a little better. Then they said all the comforting things they could think of. They told him that no harm could come to him there, unless Farmer Brown's boy should happen to see him.

"That's just what I am afraid of!" croaked Grandfather Frog. "He is sure to see me if he comes for a drink, for there is no place for me to hide."

"Perhaps he won't come," said one of the Little Breezes hopefully.

"If he does come, you can hide under the piece of shingle, and then he won't know you are here at all," said another.

"That's just what I am afraid of!"
croaked Grandfather Frog.
See page 194.

Grandfather Frog brightened up. "That's so!" said he. "That's a good idea, and I'll try it."

Then one of the Merry Little Breezes promised to keep watch for Farmer Brown's boy, and all the others started off on another hunt for some one to help Grandfather Frog out of this new trouble.

XXII. Grandfather Frog's Troubles Grow

> "Head first in; no way out;
> It's best to know what you're about!"

Grandfather Frog had had plenty of time to realize how very true this is. As he sat on the old shingle which the Merry Little Breezes had blown into the spring where he was a prisoner, he thought a great deal about that little word "if." *If* he hadn't left the Smiling Pool, *if* he hadn't been stubborn and set in his ways, *if* he hadn't been in such a hurry, *if* he had looked to see where he was leaping—well, any one of these *ifs* would have kept him out of his present trouble.

It really wasn't so bad in the spring. That is, it wouldn't have been so bad but for the fear that Farmer Brown's boy might come for a drink and find him there. That was Grandfather Frog's one great fear, and it gave him bad dreams whenever he tried to take a nap. He grew cold all over at the very thought of being caught again by Farmer Brown's boy, and when at last one of the Merry Little Breezes hurried up to tell him that Farmer Brown's boy actually was coming, pool old Grandfather Frog was so frightened that the Merry Little Breeze had to tell him twice to hide under the old shingle as it floated on the water.

At last he got it through his head, and drawing a very long breath, he dived into the water and swam under the old shingle. He was just in time. Yes, Sir, he was just in time. If Farmer Brown's boy hadn't been thinking of something else, he certainly would have noticed the little rings on the water made by Grandfather Frog when he dived in. But he was thinking of something else, and it wasn't until he dipped a cup in for the second time that he even saw the old shingle.

"Hello!" he exclaimed. "That must have blown in since I was here yesterday. We can't have anything like that in our nice spring."

With that he reached out for the old shingle, and Grandfather Frog, hiding under it, gave himself up for lost. But the anxious Little Breeze had been watching sharply and the instant he saw what Farmer Brown's boy was going to do, he played the old, old trick of snatching his hat from his head. The truth is, he couldn't think of anything else to do. Farmer Brown's boy grabbed at his hat, and then, because he was in a hurry and had other things to do, he started off without once thinking of the old shingle again.

"Chugarum!" cried Grandfather Frog, as he swam out from under the shingle and climbed up on it, "That certainly was a close call. If I have many more like it, I certainly shall die of fright."

Nothing more happened for a long time, and Grandfather Frog was wondering if it wouldn't be safe to take a nap when he saw peeping over the edge above him two eyes. They were greenish yellow eyes, and they stared and stared. Grandfather Frog stared

and stared back. He just couldn't help it. He didn't
know who they belonged to. He couldn't remember
ever having seen them before. He was afraid, and yet
somehow he couldn't make up his mind to jump. He
stared so hard at the eyes that he didn't notice a long
furry paw slowly, very slowly, reaching down
towards him. Nearer it crept and nearer. Then suddenly it moved like a flash. Grandfather Frog felt
sharp claws in his white and yellow waistcoat, and
before he could even open his mouth to cry
"Chugarum," he was sent flying through the air and
landed on his back in the grass. Pounce! Two paws
pinned him down, and the greenish yellow eyes were
not an inch from his own. They belonged to Black
Pussy, Farmer Brown's cat.

XXIII. The Dear Old Smiling Pool Once More

Black Pussy was having a good time. Grandfather
Frog wasn't. It was great fun for Black Pussy to
slip a paw under Grandfather Frog and toss him up
in the air. It was still more fun to pretend to go away,
but to hide instead, and the instant Grandfather Frog
started off, to pounce upon him and cuff him and roll
him about. But there wasn't any fun in it for Grandfather Frog. In the first place, he didn't know
whether or not Black Pussy liked Frogs to eat, and
he was terribly frightened. In the second place,
Black Pussy didn't always cover up her claws, and
they pricked right through Grandfather Frog's white
and yellow waistcoat and hurt, for he is very tender
there.

At last Black Pussy grew tired of playing, so catching up Grandfather Frog in her mouth, she started along the little path from the spring to the Long Lane. Grandfather Frog didn't even kick, which was just as well, because if he had, Black Pussy would have held him tighter, and that would have been very uncomfortable indeed.

"It's all over, and this is the end," moaned Grandfather Frog. "I'm going to be eaten now. Oh, why, why did I ever leave the Smiling Pool?"

Just as Black Pussy slipped into the Long Lane, Grandfather Frog heard a familiar sound. It was a whistle, a merry whistle. It was the whistle of Farmer Brown's boy. It was coming nearer and nearer. A little bit of hope began to stir in the heart of Grandfather Frog. He didn't know just why, but it did. Always he had been in the greatest fear of Farmer Brown's boy, but now—well, if Farmer Brown's boy should take him, he might get away from him as he did before, but he was very sure that he never, never could get away from Black Pussy.

The whistle drew nearer. Black Pussy stopped. Then she began to make a queer whirring sound deep down in her throat.

"Hello, Black Pussy! Have you been hunting? Come here and show me what you've got," cried a voice.

Black Pussy arched up her back and began to rub against the legs of Farmer Brown's boy, and all the time the whirring sound in her throat grew louder and louder. Farmer Brown's boy stooped down to see what she had in her mouth.

"Why," he exclaimed, "I do believe this is the very same old frog that got away from me! You don't want him, Puss. I'll just put him in my pocket and take him up to the house by and by."

With that he took Grandfather Frog from Black Pussy and dropped him in his pocket. He patted Black Pussy, called her a smart cat, and then started on his way, whistling merrily. It was dark and rather close in that pocket, but Grandfather Frog didn't mind this. It was a lot better than feeling sharp teeth and claws all the time. He wondered how soon they would reach the house and what would happen to him then. After what seemed a long, long time, he felt himself swung through the air, and then he landed on the ground with a thump that made him grunt. Farmer Brown's boy had taken off his coat and thrown it down.

The whistling stopped. Everything was quiet. Grandfather Frog waited and listened, but not a sound could he hear. Then he saw a little ray of light creeping into his prison. He squirmed and pushed, and all of a sudden he was out of the pocket. The bright light made him blink. As soon as he could see, he looked to see where he was. Then he rubbed his eyes with both hands and looked again. He wasn't at Farmer Brown's house at all. Where do you think he was? Why, right on the bank of the Smiling Pool, and a little way off was Farmer Brown's boy fishing!

"Chugarum!" cried Grandfather Frog, and it was the loudest, gladdest chugarum that the Smiling Pool ever had heard. "Chugarum!" he cried again, and with a great leap he dived with a splash into the dear old Smiling Pool, which smiled more than ever.

And never again has Grandfather Frog tried to see the Great World. He is quite content to leave it to those who like to dwell there. And since his own wonderful adventures, he has been ready to believe anything he is told about what happens there.

THE END

The Adventures of
Buster Bear

by
Thornton W. Burgess

Buster blinked his greedy little eyes rapidly
and looked again.
See page 252.

I. Buster Bear Goes Fishing

Buster Bear yawned as he lay on his comfortable bed of leaves and watched the first early morning sunbeams creeping through the Green Forest to chase out the Black Shadows. Once more he yawned, and slowly got to his feet and shook himself. Then he walked over to a big pine-tree, stood up on his hind-legs, reached as high up on the trunk of the tree as he could, and scratched the bark with his great claws. After that he yawned until it seemed as if his jaws would crack, and then sat down to think what he wanted for breakfast.

While he sat there, trying to make up his mind what would taste best, he was listening to the sounds that told of the waking of all the little people who live in the Green Forest. He heard Sammy Jay way off in the distance screaming, "Thief! Thief!" and grinned. "I wonder," thought Buster, "if some one has stolen Sammy's breakfast, or if he has stolen the breakfast of some one else. Probably he is the thief himself."

He heard Chatterer the Red Squirrel scolding as fast as he could make his tongue go and working himself into a terrible rage. "Must be that Chatterer got out of bed the wrong way this morning," thought he.

He heard Blacky the Crow cawing at the top of his lungs, and he knew by the sound that Blacky was getting into mischief of some kind. He heard the sweet voices of happy little singers, and they were good to hear. But most of all he listened to a merry, low, silvery laugh that never stopped but went on and on, until he just felt as if he must laugh too. It was the voice of the Laughing Brook. And as Buster listened it suddenly came to him just what he wanted for breakfast.

"I'm going fishing," said he in his deep grumbly-rumbly voice to no one in particular. "Yes, Sir, I'm going fishing. I want some fat trout for my breakfast."

He shuffled along over to the Laughing Brook, and straight to a little pool of which he knew, and as he drew near he took the greatest care not to make the teeniest, weeniest bit of noise. Now it just happened that early as he was, some one was before Buster Bear. When he came in sight of the little pool, who should he see but another fisherman there, who had already caught a fine fat trout. Who was it? Why, Little Joe Otter to be sure. He was just climbing up the bank with the fat trout in his mouth. Buster Bear's own mouth watered as he saw it. Little Joe sat down on the bank and prepared to enjoy his breakfast. He hadn't seen Buster Bear, and he didn't know that he or any one else was anywhere near.

Buster Bear tiptoed up very softly until he was right behind Little Joe Otter. "Woof, woof!" said he in his deepest, most grumbly-rumbly voice. "That's a very fine looking trout. I wouldn't mind if I had it myself."

Little Joe Otter gave a frightened squeal and without even turning to see who was speaking dropped his fish and dived headfirst into the Laughing Brook. Buster Bear sprang forward and with one of his big paws caught the fat trout just as it was slipping back into the water.

"Here's your trout, Mr. Otter," said he, as Little Joe

"Here's your trout, Mr. Otter," said he.
See page 206.

put his head out of water to see who had frightened him so. "Come and get it."

But Little Joe wouldn't. The fact is, he was afraid to. He snarled at Buster Bear and called him a thief and everything bad he could think of. Buster didn't seem to mind. He chuckled as if he thought it all a great joke and repeated his invitation to Little Joe to come and get his fish. But Little Joe just turned his back and went off down the Laughing Brook in a great rage.

"It's too bad to waste such a fine fish," said Buster thoughtfully. "I wonder what I'd better do with it." And while he was wondering, he ate it all up. Then he started down the Laughing Brook to try to catch some for himself.

II. Little Joe Otter Gets Even with Buster Bear

Little Joe Otter was in a terrible rage. It was a bad beginning for a beautiful day and Little Joe knew it. But who wouldn't be in a rage if his breakfast was taken from him just as he was about to eat it? Anyway, that is what Little Joe told Billy Mink. Perhaps he didn't tell it quite exactly as it was, but you know he was very badly frightened at the time.

"I was sitting on the bank of the Laughing Brook beside one of the little pools," he told Billy Mink, "and was just going to eat a fat trout I had caught, when who should come along but that great big bully, Buster Bear. He took that fat trout away from me and ate it just as if it belonged to him! I hate him! If I live long enough I'm going to get even with him!"

Of course that wasn't nice talk and anything but a nice spirit, but Little Joe Otter's temper is sometimes pretty short, especially when he is hungry, and this time he had had no breakfast, you know.

Buster Bear hadn't actually taken the fish away from Little Joe. But looking at the matter as Little Joe did, it amounted to the same thing. You see, Buster knew perfectly well when he invited Little Joe to come back and get it that Little Joe wouldn't dare do anything of the kind.

"Where is he now?" asked Billy Mink.

"He's somewhere up the Laughing Brook. I wish he'd fall in and get drowned!" snapped Little Joe.

Billy Mink just had to laugh. The idea of great big Buster Bear getting drowned in the Laughing Brook was too funny. There wasn't water enough in it anywhere except down in the Smiling Pool, and that was on the Green Meadows, where Buster had never been known to go. "Let's go see what he is doing," said Billy Mink.

At first Little Joe didn't want to, but at last his curiosity got the better of his fear, and he agreed. So the two little brown-coated scamps turned down the Laughing Brook, taking the greatest care to keep out of sight themselves. They had gone only a little way when Billy Mink whispered: "Sh-h! There he is."

Sure enough, there was Buster Bear sitting close beside a little pool and looking into it very intently.

"What's he doing?" asked Little Joe Otter, as Buster Bear sat for the longest time without moving.

Just then one of Buster's big paws went into the water as quick as a flash and scooped out a trout that had ventured too near.

"He's fishing!" exclaimed Billy Mink.

And that is just what Buster Bear was doing, and it was very plain to see that he was having great fun. When he had eaten the trout he had caught, he moved along to the next little pool.

"They are *our* fish!" said Little Joe fiercely. "He has no business catching *our* fish!"

"I don't see how we are going to stop him," said Billy Mink.

"I do!" cried Little Joe, into whose head an idea had just popped. "I'm going to drive all the fish out of the little pools and muddy the water all up. Then we'll see how many fish he will get! Just you watch me get even with Buster Bear."

Little Joe slipped swiftly into the water and swam straight to the little pool that Buster Bear would try next. He frightened the fish so that they fled in every direction. Then he stirred up the mud until the water was so dirty that Buster couldn't have seen a fish right under his nose. He did the same thing in the next pool and the next. Buster Bear's fishing was spoiled for that day.

III. Buster Bear Is Greatly Puzzled

Buster Bear hadn't enjoyed himself so much since he came to the Green Forest to live. His fun began when he surprised Little Joe Otter on the bank of a little pool in the Laughing Brook and Little Joe was so frightened that he dropped a fat trout he had just caught. It had seemed like a great joke to Buster Bear, and he had chuckled over it all the time he was eating the fat trout. When he had finished it, he started on to do some fishing himself.

Presently he came to another little pool. He stole up to it very, very softly, so as not to frighten the fish. Then he sat down close to the edge of it and didn't move. Buster learned a long time ago that a fisherman must be patient unless, like Little Joe Otter, he is just as much at home in the water as the fish themselves, and can swim fast enough to catch them by chasing them. So he didn't move so much as an eye lash. He was so still that he looked almost like the stump of an old tree. Perhaps that is what the fish thought he was, for pretty soon, two or three swam right in close to where he was sitting. Now Buster Bear may be big and clumsy looking, but there isn't anything that can move much quicker than one of those big paws of his when he wants it to. One of them moved now, and quicker than a wink had scooped one of those foolish fish out on to the bank.

Buster's little eyes twinkled, and he smacked his lips as he moved on to the next little pool, for he knew that it was of no use to stay longer at the first one. The fish were so frightened that they wouldn't come back for a long, long time. At the next little pool the same thing happened. By this time Buster Bear was in fine spirits. It was fun to catch the fish, and it was still more fun to eat them. What finer breakfast could any one have than fresh-caught trout? No wonder he felt good! But it takes more than three trout to fill Buster Bear's stomach, so he kept on to the next little pool.

But this little pool, instead of being beautiful and

clear so that Buster could see right to the bottom of it and so tell if there were any fish there, was so muddy that he couldn't see into it at all. It looked as if some one had just stirred up all the mud at the bottom.

"Huh!" said Buster Bear. "It's of no use to try to fish here. I would just waste my time. I'll try the next pool."

So he went on to the next little pool. He found this just as muddy as the other. Then he went on to another, and this was no better. Buster sat down and scratched his head. It was puzzling. Yes, Sir, it was puzzling. He looked this way and he looked that way suspiciously, but there was no one to be seen. Everything was still save for the laughter of the Laughing Brook. Somehow, it seemed to Buster as if the Brook were laughing at him.

"It's very curious," muttered Buster, "very curious indeed. It looks as if my fishing is spoiled for to-day. I don't understand it at all. It's lucky I caught what I did. It looks as if somebody is trying to—ha!" A sudden thought had popped into his head. Then he began to chuckle and finally to laugh. "I do believe that scamp Joe Otter is trying to get even with me for eating that fat trout!"

And then, because Buster Bear always enjoys a good joke even when it is on himself, he laughed until he had to hold his sides, which is a whole lot better than going off in a rage as Little Joe Otter had done. "You're pretty smart, Mr. Otter! You're pretty smart, but there are other people who are smart too," said Buster Bear, and still chuckling, he went off to think up a plan to get the best of Little Joe Otter.

IV. Little Joe Otter Supplies Buster Bear with a Breakfast

"Getting even just for spite
Doesn't always pay.
Fact is, it is very apt
To work the other way."

That is just how it came about that Little Joe Otter furnished Buster Bear with the best breakfast he had had for a long time. He didn't mean to do it. Oh, my, no! The truth is, he thought all the time that he was preventing Buster Bear from getting a breakfast. You see he wasn't well enough acquainted with Buster to know that Buster is quite as smart as he is, and perhaps a little bit smarter. Spite and selfishness were at the bottom of it. You see Little Joe and Billy Mink had had all the fishing in the Laughing Brook to themselves so long that they thought no one else had any right to fish there. To be sure Bobby Coon caught a few little fish there, but they didn't mind Bobby. Farmer Brown's boy fished there too, sometimes, and this always made Little Joe and Billy Mink very angry, but they were so afraid of him that they didn't dare do anything about it. But when they discovered that Buster Bear was a fisherman, they made up their minds that something had got to be done. At least, Little Joe did.

"He'll try it again to-morrow morning," said Little Joe. "I'll keep watch, and as soon as I see him coming, I'll drive out all the fish, just as I did to-day. I guess that'll teach him to let our fish alone."

So the next morning Little Joe hid before daylight

close by the little pool where Buster Bear had given him such a fright. Sure enough, just as the Jolly Sunbeams began to creep through the Green Forest, he saw Buster Bear coming straight over to the little pool. Little Joe slipped into the water and chased all the fish out of the little pool, and stirred up the mud on the bottom so that the water was so muddy that the bottom couldn't be seen at all. Then he hurried down to the next little pool and did the same thing.

Now Buster Bear is very smart. You know he had guessed the day before who had spoiled his fishing. So this morning he only went far enough to make sure that if Little Joe were watching for him, as he was sure he would be, he would see him coming. Then, instead of keeping on to the little pool, he hurried to a place way down the Laughing Brook, where the water was very shallow, hardly over his feet, and there he sat chuckling to himself. Things happened just as he had expected. The frightened fish Little Joe chased out of the little pools up above swam down the Laughing Brook, because, you know, Little Joe was behind them, and there was nowhere else for them to go. When they came to the place where Buster was waiting, all he had to do was to scoop them out on to the bank. It was great fun. It didn't take Buster long to catch all the fish he could eat. Then he saved a nice fat trout and waited.

By and by along came Little Joe Otter, chuckling to think how he had spoiled Buster Bear's fishing. He was so intent on looking behind him to see if Buster was coming that he didn't see Buster waiting there until he spoke.

"I'm much obliged for the fine breakfast you have

given me," said Buster in his deepest, most grumbly-rumbly voice. "I've saved a fat trout for you to make up for the one I ate yesterday. I hope we'll go fishing together often."

Then he went off laughing fit to kill himself. Little Joe couldn't find a word to say. He was so surprised and angry that he went off by himself and sulked. And Billy Mink, who had been watching, ate the fat trout.

V. Grandfather Frog's Common Sense

There is nothing quite like common sense to smooth out troubles. People who have plenty of just plain common sense are often thought to be very wise. Their neighbors look up to them and are forever running to them for advice, and they are very much respected. That is the way with Grandfather Frog. He is very old and very wise. Anyway, that is what his neighbors think. The truth is, he simply has a lot of common sense, which after all is the very best kind of wisdom.

Now when Little Joe Otter found that Buster Bear had been too smart for him and that instead of spoiling Buster's fishing in the Laughing Brook he had really made it easier for Buster to catch all the fish he wanted, Little Joe went off down to the Smiling Pool in a great rage.

Billy Mink stopped long enough to eat the fat fish Buster had left on the bank and then he too went down to the Smiling Pool.

When Little Joe Otter and Billy Mink reached the

Smiling Pool, they climbed up on the Big Rock, and there Little Joe sulked and sulked, until finally Grandfather Frog asked what the matter was. Little Joe wouldn't tell, but Billy Mink told the whole story. When he told how Buster had been too smart for Little Joe, it tickled him so that Billy had to laugh in spite of himself. So did Grandfather Frog. So did Jerry Muskrat, who had been listening. Of course this made Little Joe angrier than ever. He said a lot of unkind things about Buster Bear and about Billy Mink and Grandfather Frog and Jerry Muskrat, because they had laughed at the smartness of Buster.

"He's nothing but a great big bully and thief!" declared Little Joe.

"Chugarum! He may be a bully, because great big people are very apt to be bullies, and though I haven't seen him, I guess Buster Bear is big enough from all I have heard, but I don't see how he is a thief," said Grandfather Frog.

"Didn't he catch my fish and eat them?" snapped Little Joe. "Doesn't that make him a thief?"

"They were no more your fish than mine," protested Billy Mink.

"Well, *our* fish, then! He stole *our* fish, if you like that any better. That makes him just as much a thief, doesn't it?" growled Little Joe.

Grandfather Frog looked up at jolly, round, bright Mr. Sun and slowly winked one of his great, goggly eyes. "There comes a foolish green fly," said he. "Who does he belong to?"

"Nobody!" snapped Little Joe. "What have foolish green flies got to do with my—I mean *our* fish?"

"Nothing, nothing at all," replied Grandfather Frog mildly. "I was just hoping that he would come near enough for me to snap him up; then he would belong to me. As long as he doesn't, he doesn't belong to any one. I suppose that if Buster Bear should happen along and catch him, he would be stealing from me, according to Little Joe."

"Of course not! What a silly idea! You're getting foolish in your old age," retorted Little Joe.

"Can you tell me the difference between the fish that you haven't caught and the foolish green flies that I haven't caught?" asked Grandfather Frog.

Little Joe couldn't find a word to say.

"You take my advice, Little Joe Otter," continued Grandfather Frog, "and always make friends with those who are bigger and stronger and smarter than you are. You'll find it pays."

VI. Little Joe Otter Takes Grandfather Frog's Advice

"Who makes an enemy a friend,
    To fear and worry puts an end."

Little Joe Otter found that out when he took Grandfather Frog's advice. He wouldn't have admitted that he was afraid of Buster Bear. No one ever likes to admit being afraid, least of all Little Joe Otter. And really Little Joe has a great deal of courage. Very few of the little people of the Green Forest or the Green Meadows would willingly quarrel with him, for Little Joe is a great fighter when he has to fight. As for all those who live in or along the

"You take my advice, Little Joe Otter,"
continued Grandfather Frog.
See page 217.

Laughing Brook or in the Smiling Pool, they let Little Joe have his own way in everything.

Now having one's own way too much is a bad thing. It is apt to make one selfish and thoughtless of other people and very hard to get along with. Little Joe Otter had his way too much. Grandfather Frog knew it and shook his head very soberly when Little Joe had been disrespectful to him.

"Too bad. Too bad! Too bad! Chugarum! It is too bad that such a fine young fellow as Little Joe should spoil a good disposition by such selfish heedlessness. Too bad," said he.

So, though he didn't let on that it was so, Grandfather Frog really was delighted when he heard how Buster Bear had been too smart for Little Joe Otter. It tickled him so that he had hard work to keep a straight face. But he did and was as grave and solemn as you please as he advised Little Joe always to make friends with any one who was bigger and stronger and smarter than he. That was good common sense advice, but Little Joe just sniffed and went off declaring that he would get even with Buster Bear yet. Now Little Joe is good-natured and full of fun as a rule, and after he had reached home and his temper had cooled off a little, he began to see the joke on himself,—how when he had worked so hard to frighten the fish in the little pools of the Laughing Brook so that Buster Bear should not catch any, he had all the time been driving them right into Buster's paws. By and by he grinned. It was a little sheepish grin at first, but at last it grew into a laugh.

"I believe," said Little Joe as he wiped tears of laughter from his eyes, "that Grandfather Frog is right, and that the best thing I can do is to make friends with Buster Bear. I'll try it to-morrow morning."

So very early the next morning Little Joe Otter went to the best fishing pool he knew of in the Laughing Brook, and there he caught the biggest trout he could find. It was so big and fat that it made Little Joe's mouth water, for you know fat trout are his favorite food. But he didn't take so much as one bite. Instead he carefully laid it on an old log where Buster Bear would be sure to see it if he should come along that way. Then he hid near by, where he could watch. Buster was late that morning. It seemed to Little Joe that he never would come. Once he nearly lost the fish. He had turned his head for just a minute, and when he looked back again, the trout was nowhere to be seen. Buster couldn't have stolen up and taken it, because such a big fellow couldn't possibly have gotten out of sight again.

Little Joe darted over to the log and looked on the other side. There was the fat trout, and there also was Little Joe's smallest cousin, Shadow the Weasel, who is a great thief and altogether bad. Little Joe sprang at him angrily, but Shadow was too quick and darted away. Little Joe put the fish back on the log and waited. This time he didn't take his eyes off it. At last, when he was almost ready to give up, he saw Buster Bear shuffling along towards the Laughing Brook. Suddenly Buster stopped and sniffed. One of the Merry Little Breezes had carried the scent of that fat trout over to him. Then he came straight over to where the fish lay, his nose wrinkling, and his eyes twinkling with pleasure.

"Now I wonder who was so thoughtful as to leave this fine breakfast ready for me," said he out loud.

"Me," said Little Joe in a rather faint voice. "I caught it especially for you."

"Thank you," replied Buster, and his eyes twinkled more than ever. "I think we are going to be friends."

"I—I hope so," replied Little Joe.

VII. Farmer Brown's Boy Has No Luck at All

Farmer Brown's boy tramped through the Green Forest, whistling merrily. He always whistles when he feels light-hearted, and he always feels light-hearted when he goes fishing. You see, he is just as fond of fishing as is Little Joe Otter or Billy Mink or Buster Bear. And now he was making his way through the Green Forest to the Laughing Brook, sure that by the time he had followed it down to the Smiling Pool he would have a fine lot of trout to take home. He knew every pool in the Laughing Brook where the trout love to hide, did Farmer Brown's boy, and it was just the kind of a morning when the trout should be hungry. So he whistled as he tramped along, and his whistle was good to hear.

When he reached the first little pool he baited his hook very carefully and then, taking the greatest care to keep out of sight of any trout that might be in the little pool, he began to fish. Now Farmer Brown's boy learned a long time ago that to be a successful fisherman one must have a great deal of patience, so though he didn't get a bite right away as he had expected to, he wasn't the least bit discouraged. He kept very quiet and fished and fished, patiently waiting for a foolish trout to take his hook. But he didn't get so much as a nibble. "Either the trout have lost their appetite or they have grown very wise," muttered Farmer Brown's boy, as after a long time he moved on to the next little pool.

There the same thing happened. He was very patient, very, very patient, but his patience brought no reward, not so much as the faintest kind of a nibble. Farmer Brown's boy trudged on to the next pool, and there was a puzzled frown on his freckled face. Such a thing never had happened before. He didn't know what to make of it. All the night before he had dreamed about the delicious dinner of fried trout he would have the next day, and now—well, if he didn't catch some trout pretty soon, that splendid dinner would never be anything but a dream.

"If I didn't know that nobody else comes fishing here, I should think that somebody had been here this very morning and caught all the fish or else frightened them so that they are all in hiding," said he, as he trudged on to the next little pool. "I never had such bad luck in all my life before. Hello! What's this?"

There, on the bank beside the little pool, were the heads of three trout. Farmer Brown's boy scowled down at them more puzzled than ever. "Somebody *has* been fishing here, and they have had better luck than I have," thought he. He looked up at the Laughing Brook and down the Laughing Brook and this way and that way, but no one was to be seen. Then he picked up one of the little heads and looked at it sharply. "It wasn't cut off with a knife; it was bitten off!" he exclaimed. "I wonder now if Billy Mink is the scamp who has spoiled my fun."

Thereafter he kept a sharp lookout for signs of Billy Mink, but though he found two or three more trout heads, he saw no other signs and he caught no fish. This puzzled him more than ever. It didn't seem possible that such a little fellow as Billy Mink could have caught or frightened all the fish or have eaten so many. Besides, he didn't remember ever having known Billy to leave heads around that way. Billy sometimes catches more fish than he can eat, but then he usually hides them. The farther he went down the Laughing Brook, the more puzzled Farmer Brown's boy grew. It made him feel very queer. He would have felt still more queer if he had known that all the time two other fishermen who had been before him were watching him and chuckling to themselves. They were Little Joe Otter and Buster Bear.

VIII. Farmer Brown's Boy Feels His Hair Rise

"'Twas just a sudden odd surprise
Made Farmer Brown's boy's hair to rise."

That's a funny thing for hair to do—rise up all of a sudden—isn't it? But that is just what the hair on Farmer Brown's boy's head did the day he went fishing in the Laughing Brook and had no luck at all. There are just two things that make hair rise—anger and fear. Anger sometimes makes the hair on the back and neck of Bowser the Hound and of some other little people bristle and stand up, and you know the hair on the tail of Black Pussy stands on end until her tail looks twice as big as it really is. Both anger and fear make it do that. But there is only one thing that can make the hair on the head of Farmer Brown's boy rise, and as it isn't anger, of course it must be fear.

It never had happened before. You see, there isn't much of anything that Farmer Brown's boy is really afraid of. Perhaps he wouldn't have been afraid this time if it hadn't been for the surprise of what he found. You see when he had found the heads of those trout on the bank he knew right away that some one else had been fishing, and that was why he couldn't catch any; but it didn't seem possible that little Billy Mink could have eaten all those trout, and Farmer Brown's boy didn't once think of Little Joe Otter, and so he was very, very much puzzled.

He was turning it all over in his mind and studying what it could mean, when he came to a little muddy place on the bank of the Laughing Brook, and there he saw something that made his eyes look as if they would pop right out of his head, and it was right then that he felt his hair rise. Anyway, that is what he said when he told about it afterward. What was it he saw? What do you think? Why, it was a footprint in the soft mud. Yes, Sir, that's what it was, and all it was. But it was the biggest footprint Farmer Brown's boy ever had seen, and it looked as if it had been made only a few minutes before. It was the footprint of Buster Bear.

Now Farmer Brown's boy didn't know that Buster Bear had come down to the Green Forest to live. He never had heard of a Bear being in the Green Forest.

And so he was so surprised that he had hard work to believe his own eyes, and he had a queer feeling all over,—a little chilly feeling, although it was a warm day. Somehow, he didn't feel like meeting Buster Bear. If he had had his terrible gun with him, it might have been different. But he didn't, and so he suddenly made up his mind that he didn't want to fish any more that day. He had a funny feeling, too, that he was being watched, although he couldn't see any one. He *was* being watched. Little Joe Otter and Buster Bear were watching him and taking the greatest care to keep out of his sight.

All the way home through the Green Forest, Farmer Brown's boy kept looking behind him, and he didn't draw a long breath until he reached the edge of the Green Forest. He hadn't run, but he had wanted to.

"Huh!" said Buster Bear to Little Joe Otter, "I believe he was afraid!"

And Buster Bear was just exactly right.

IX. Little Joe Otter Has Great News to Tell

Little Joe Otter was fairly bursting with excitement. He could hardly contain himself. He felt that he had the greatest news to tell since Peter Rabbit had first found the tracks of Buster Bear in the Green Forest. He couldn't keep it to himself a minute longer than he had to. So he hurried to the Smiling Pool, where he was sure he would find Billy Mink and Jerry Muskrat and Grandfather Frog and Spotty the Turtle, and he hoped that perhaps some of the little people who live in the Green Forest might be there too. Sure enough, Peter Rabbit was there on one side of the Smiling Pool, making faces at Reddy Fox, who was on the other side, which, of course, was not at all nice of Peter. Mr. and Mrs. Redwing were there, and Blacky the Crow was sitting in the big hickory-tree.

Little Joe Otter swam straight to the Big Rock and climbed up to the very highest part. He looked so excited, and his eyes sparkled so, that every one knew right away that something had happened.

"Hi!" cried Billy Mink. "Look at Little Joe Otter! It must be that for once he has been smarter than Buster Bear."

Little Joe made a good-natured face at Billy Mink and shook his head. "No, Billy," said he, "you are wrong, altogether wrong. I don't believe anybody can be smarter than Buster Bear."

Reddy Fox rolled his lips back in an unpleasant grin. "Don't be too sure of that!" he snapped. "I'm not through with him yet."

"Boaster! Boaster!" cried Peter Rabbit.

Reddy glared across the Smiling Pool at Peter. "I'm not through with you either, Peter Rabbit!" he snarled. "You'll find it out one of these fine days!"

> "Reddy, Reddy, smart and sly,
> Couldn't catch a buzzing fly!"

taunted Peter.

"Chugarum!" said Grandfather Frog in his deepest, gruffest voice. "We know all about that. What we want to know is what Little Joe Otter has got on his mind."

"It's news—great news!" cried Little Joe.

Reddy glared across the Smiling Pool at Peter.
See page 226.

"We can tell better how great it is when we hear what it is," replied Grandfather Frog testily. "What is it?"

Little Joe Otter looked around at all the eager faces watching him, and then in the slowest, most provoking way, he drawled: "Farmer Brown's boy is afraid of Buster Bear."

For a minute no one said a word. Then Blacky the Crow leaned down from his perch in the big hickory-tree and looked very hard at Little Joe as he said:

"I don't believe it. I don't believe a word of it. Farmer Brown's boy isn't afraid of any one who lives in the Green Forest or on the Green Meadows or in the Smiling Pool, and you know it. We are all afraid of him."

Little Joe glared back at Blacky. "I don't care whether you believe it or not; it's true," he retorted. Then he told how early that very morning he and Buster Bear had been fishing together in the Laughing Brook, and how Farmer Brown's boy had been fishing there too, and hadn't caught a single trout because they had all been caught or frightened before he got there. Then he told how Farmer Brown's boy had found a footprint of Buster Bear in the soft mud, and how he had stopped fishing right away and started for home, looking behind him with fear in his eyes all the way.

"Now tell me that he isn't afraid!" concluded Little Joe. "For once he knows just how we feel when he comes prowling around where we are. Isn't that great news? Now we'll get even with *him!*"

"I'll believe it when I see it for myself!" snapped Blacky the Crow.

X. Buster Bear Becomes a Hero

The news that Little Joe Otter told at the Smiling Pool,—how Farmer Brown's boy had run away from Buster Bear without even seeing him,—soon spread all over the Green Meadows and through the Green Forest, until every one who lives there knew about it. Of course, Peter Rabbit helped spread it. Trust Peter for that! But everybody else helped too. You see, they had all been afraid of Farmer Brown's boy for so long that they were tickled almost to pieces at the very thought of having some one in the Green Forest who could make Farmer Brown's boy feel fear as they had felt it. And so it was that Buster Bear became a hero right away to most of them.

A few doubted Little Joe's story. One of them was Blacky the Crow. Another was Reddy Fox. Blacky doubted because he knew Farmer Brown's boy so well that he couldn't imagine him afraid. Reddy doubted because he didn't want to believe. You see, he was jealous of Buster Bear, and at the same time he was afraid of him. So Reddy pretended not to believe a word of what Little Joe Otter had said, and he agreed with Blacky that only by seeing Farmer Brown's boy afraid could he ever be made to believe it. But nearly everybody else believed it, and there was great rejoicing. Most of them were afraid of Buster, very much afraid of him, because he was so big and strong. But they were still more afraid of Farmer Brown's boy, because they didn't know him or understand him, and because in the past he had tried to catch some of them in traps and had hunted some of them with his terrible gun.

So now they were very proud to think that one of their own number actually had frightened him, and they began to look on Buster Bear as a real hero. They tried in ever so many ways to show him how friendly they felt and went quite out of their way to do him favors. Whenever they met one another, all they could talk about was the smartness and the greatness of Buster Bear.

"Now I guess Farmer Brown's boy will keep away from the Green Forest, and we won't have to be all the time watching out for him," said Bobby Coon, as he washed his dinner in the Laughing Brook, for you know he is very neat and particular.

"And he won't dare set any more traps for me," gloated Billy Mink.

"Ah wish Brer Bear would go up to Farmer Brown's henhouse and scare Farmer Brown's boy so that he would keep away from there. It would be a favor to me which Ah cert'nly would appreciate," said Unc' Billy Possum when he heard the news.

"Let's all go together and tell Buster Bear how much obliged we are for what he has done," proposed Jerry Muskrat.

"That's a splendid idea!" cried Little Joe Otter. "We'll do it right away."

"Caw, caw, caw!" broke in Blacky the Crow. "I say, let's wait and see for ourselves if it is all true."

"Of course it's true!" snapped Little Joe Otter. "Don't you believe I'm telling the truth?"

"Certainly, certainly. Of course no one doubts your word," replied Blacky, with the utmost politeness.

"But you say yourself that Farmer Brown's boy didn't see Buster Bear, but only his footprint. Perhaps he didn't know whose it was, and if he had he wouldn't have been afraid. Now I've got a plan by which we can see for ourselves if he really is afraid of Buster Bear."

"What is it?" asked Sammy Jay eagerly.

Blacky the Crow shook his head and winked. "That's telling," said he. "I want to think it over. If you meet me at the big hickory-tree at sun-up to-morrow morning, and get everybody else to come that you can, perhaps I will tell you."

XI. Blacky the Crow Tells His Plan

"Blacky is a dreamer!
Blacky is a schemer!
His voice is strong;
When things go wrong
Blacky is a screamer!"

It's a fact. Blacky the Crow is forever dreaming and scheming and almost always it is of mischief. He is one of the smartest and cleverest of all the little people of the Green Meadows and the Green Forest, and all the others know it. Blacky likes excitement. He wants something going on. The more exciting it is, the better he likes it. Then he has a chance to use that harsh voice of his, and how he does use it!

So now, as he sat in the top of the big hickory-tree beside the Smiling Pool and looked down on all the little people gathered there, he was very happy. In the first place he felt very important, and you know

Blacky dearly loves to feel important. They had all come at his invitation to listen to a plan for seeing for themselves if it were really true that Farmer Brown's boy was afraid of Buster Bear.

On the Big Rock in the Smiling Pool sat Little Joe Otter, Billy Mink, and Jerry Muskrat. On his big, green lily-pad sat Grandfather Frog. On another lily-pad sat Spotty the Turtle. On the bank on one side of the Smiling Pool were Peter Rabbit, Jumper the Hare, Danny Meadow Mouse, Johnny Chuck, Jimmy Skunk, Unc' Billy Possum, Striped Chipmunk, and old Mr. Toad. On the other side of the Smiling Pool were Reddy Fox, Digger the Badger, and Bobby Coon. In the big hickory-tree were Chatterer the Red Squirrel, Happy Jack the Gray Squirrel, and Sammy Jay.

Blacky waited until he was sure that no one else was coming. Then he cleared his throat very loudly and began to speak. "Friends," said he.

Everybody grinned, for Blacky has played so many sharp tricks that no one is really his friend unless it is that other mischief-maker, Sammy Jay, who, you know, is Blacky's cousin. But no one said anything, and Blacky went on.

"Little Joe Otter has told us how he saw Farmer Brown's boy hurry home when he found the footprint of Buster Bear on the edge of the Laughing Brook, and how all the way he kept looking behind him, as if he were afraid. Perhaps he was, and then again perhaps he wasn't. Perhaps he had something else on his mind. You have made a hero of Buster Bear, because you believe Little Joe's story. Now I don't say that I don't believe it, but I do say that I will be a lot more sure that Farmer Brown's boy is afraid of Buster when I see him run away myself. Now here is my plan:

"To-morrow morning, very early, Sammy Jay and I will make a great fuss near the edge of the Green Forest. Farmer Brown's boy has a lot of curiosity, and he will be sure to come over to see what it is all about. Then we will lead him to where Buster Bear is. If he runs away, I will be the first to admit that Buster Bear is as great a hero as some of you seem to think he is. It is a very simple plan, and if you will all hide where you can watch, you will be able to see for yourselves if Little Joe Otter is right. Now what do you say?"

Right away everybody began to talk at the same time. It was such a simple plan that everybody agreed to it. And it promised to be so exciting that everybody promised to be there, that is, everybody but Grandfather Frog and Spotty the Turtle, who didn't care to go so far away from the Smiling Pool. So it was agreed that Blacky should try his plan the very next morning.

XII. Farmer Brown's Boy and Buster Bear Grow Curious

Ever since it was light enough to see at all, Blacky the Crow had been sitting in the top of the tallest tree on the edge of the Green Forest nearest to Farmer Brown's house, and never for an instant had he taken his eyes from Farmer Brown's back door. What was he watching for? Why, for Farmer Brown's boy to come out on his way to milk the cows. Meanwhile, Sammy Jay was slipping silently through the Green Forest, looking for Buster Bear, so that when the time came he could let his cousin, Blacky the Crow, know just where Buster was.

By and by the back door of Farmer Brown's house opened, and out stepped Farmer Brown's boy. In each hand he carried a milk pail. Right away Blacky began to scream at the top of his lungs. "Caw, caw, caw!" shouted Blacky. "Caw, caw, caw!" And all the time he flew about among the trees near the edge of the Green Forest as if so excited that he couldn't keep still. Farmer Brown's boy looked over there as if he wondered what all that fuss was about, as indeed he did, but he didn't start to go over and see. No, Sir, he started straight for the barn.

Blacky didn't know what to make of it. You see, smart as he is and shrewd as he is, Blacky doesn't know anything about the meaning of duty, for he never has to work excepting to get enough to eat. So, when Farmer Brown's boy started for the barn instead of for the Green Forest, Blacky didn't know what to make of it. He screamed harder and louder than ever, until his voice grew so hoarse he couldn't scream any more, but Farmer Brown's boy kept right on to the barn.

"I'd like to know what you're making such a fuss about, Mr. Crow, but I've got to feed the cows and milk them first," said he.

Now all this time the other little people of the Green Forest and the Green Meadows had been hiding where they could see all that went on. When Farmer Brown's boy disappeared in the barn, Chatterer the Red Squirrel snickered right out loud. "Ha, ha, ha! This is a great plan of yours, Blacky!

Ha, ha, ha!" he shouted. Blacky couldn't find a word to say. He just hung his head, which is something Blacky seldom does.

"Perhaps if we wait until he comes out again, he will come over here," said Sammy Jay, who had joined Blacky. So it was decided to wait. It seemed as if Farmer Brown's boy never would come out, but at last he did. Blacky and Sammy Jay at once began to scream and make all the fuss they could. Farmer Brown's boy took the two pails of milk into the house, then out he came and started straight for the Green Forest. He was so curious to know what it all meant that he couldn't wait another minute.

Now there was some one else with a great deal of curiosity also. He had heard the screaming of Blacky the Crow and Sammy Jay, and he had listened until he couldn't stand it another minute. He just *had* to know what it was all about. So at the same time Farmer Brown's boy started for the Green Forest, this other listener started towards the place where Blacky and Sammy were making such a racket. He walked very softly so as not to make a sound. It was Buster Bear.

XIII. Farmer Brown's Boy and Buster Bear Meet

"If you should meet with Buster Bear
While walking through the wood,
What would you do? Now tell me true.
I'd run the best I could."

That is what Farmer Brown's boy did when he met Buster Bear, and a lot of the little people of the

Green Forest and some from the Green Meadows saw him. When Farmer Brown's boy came hurrying home from the Laughing Brook without any fish one day and told about the great footprint he had seen in a muddy place on the bank deep in the Green Forest, and had said he was sure that it was the footprint of a Bear, he had been laughed at. Farmer Brown had laughed and laughed.

"Why," said he, "there hasn't been a Bear in the Green Forest for years and years and years, not since my own grandfather was a little boy, and that, you know, was a long, long, long time ago. If you want to find Mr. Bear, you will have to go to the Great Woods. I don't know who made that footprint, but it certainly couldn't have been a Bear. I think you must have imagined it."

Then he had laughed some more, all of which goes to show how easy it is to be mistaken, and how foolish it is to laugh at things you really don't know about. Buster Bear *had* come to live in the Green Forest, and Farmer Brown's boy *had* seen his footprint. But Farmer Brown laughed so much and made fun of him so much, that at last his boy began to think that he must have been mistaken after all. So when he heard Blacky the Crow and Sammy Jay making a great fuss near the edge of the Green Forest, he never once thought of Buster Bear, as he started over to see what was going on.

When Blacky and Sammy saw him coming, they moved a little farther in to the Green Forest, still screaming in the most excited way. They felt sure that Farmer Brown's boy would follow them, and they meant to lead him to where Sammy had seen Buster Bear that morning. Then they would find out for sure if what Little Joe Otter had said was true,—that Farmer Brown's boy really was afraid of Buster Bear.

Now all around, behind trees and stumps, and under thick branches, and even in tree tops, were other little people watching with round, wide-open eyes to see what would happen. It was very exciting, the most exciting thing they could remember. You see, they had come to believe that Farmer Brown's boy wasn't afraid of anybody or anything, and as most of them were very much afraid of him, they had hard work to believe that he would really be afraid of even such a great, big, strong fellow as Buster Bear. Every one was so busy watching Farmer Brown's boy that no one saw Buster coming from the other direction.

You see, Buster walked very softly. Big as he is, he can walk without making the teeniest, weeniest sound. And that is how it happened that no one saw him or heard him until just as Farmer Brown's boy stepped out from behind one side of a thick little hemlock-tree, Buster Bear stepped out from behind the other side of that same little tree, and there they were face to face! Then everybody held their breath, even Blacky the Crow and Sammy Jay. For just a little minute it was so still there in the Green Forest that not the least little sound could be heard. What was going to happen?

XIV. A Surprising Thing Happens

Blacky the Crow and Sammy Jay, looking down from the top of a tall tree, held their breath. Happy Jack the Gray Squirrel and his cousin,

Chatterer the Red Squirrel, looking down from another tree, held *their* breath. Unc' Billy Possum, sticking his head out from a hollow tree, held *his* breath. Bobby Coon, looking through a hole in a hollow stump in which he was hiding, held *his* breath. Reddy Fox, lying flat down behind a heap of brush, held *his* breath. Peter Rabbit, sitting bolt upright under a thick hemlock branch, with eyes and ears wide open, held *his* breath. And all the other little people who happened to be where they could see did the same thing.

You see, it was the most exciting moment ever was in the Green Forest. Farmer Brown's boy had just stepped out from behind one side of a little hemlock-tree and Buster Bear had just stepped out from behind the opposite side of the little hemlock-tree and neither had known that the other was anywhere near. For a whole minute they stood there face to face, gazing into each other's eyes, while everybody watched and waited, and it seemed as if the whole Green Forest was holding its breath.

Then something happened. Yes, Sir, something happened. Farmer Brown's boy opened his mouth and yelled! It was such a sudden yell and such a loud yell that it startled Chatterer so that he nearly fell from his place in the tree, and it made Reddy Fox jump to his feet ready to run. And that yell was a yell of fright. There was no doubt about it, for with the yell Farmer Brown's boy turned and ran for home, as no one ever had seen him run before. He ran just as Peter Rabbit runs when he has got to reach the dear Old Briar-patch before Reddy Fox can catch him, which, you know, is as fast as he can run. Once he stumbled and fell, but he scrambled to his feet in a twinkling, and away he went without once turning his head to see if Buster Bear was after him. There wasn't any doubt that he was afraid, very much afraid.

Everybody leaned forward to watch him. "What did I tell you? Didn't I say that he was afraid of Buster Bear?" cried Little Joe Otter, dancing about with excitement.

"You were right, Little Joe! I'm sorry that I doubted it. See him go! Caw, caw, caw!" shrieked Blacky the Crow.

For a minute or two everybody forgot about Buster Bear. Then there was a great crash which made everybody turn to look the other way. What do you think they saw? Why, Buster Bear was running away too, and he was running twice as fast as Farmer Brown's boy! He bumped into trees and crashed through bushes and jumped over logs, and in almost no time at all he was out of sight. Altogether it was the most surprising thing that the little people of the Green Forest ever had seen.

Sammy Jay looked at Blacky the Crow, and Blacky looked at Chatterer, and Chatterer looked at Happy Jack, and Happy Jack looked at Peter Rabbit, and Peter looked at Unc' Billy Possum, and Unc' Billy looked at Bobby Coon, and Bobby looked at Johnny Chuck, and Johnny looked at Reddy Fox, and Reddy looked at Jimmy Skunk, and Jimmy looked at Billy Mink, and Billy looked at Little Joe Otter, and for a minute nobody could say a word. Then Little Joe gave a funny little gasp.

"Why, why-e-e!" said he, "I believe Buster Bear is

Buster Bear was running away too.
See page 239.

afraid too!" Unc' Billy Possum chuckled. "Ah believe yo' are right again. Brer Otter," said he. "It cert'nly does look so. If Brer Bear isn't scared, he must have remembered something impo'tant and has gone to attend to it in a powerful hurry."

Then everybody began to laugh.

XV. Buster Bear Is a Fallen Hero

A fallen hero is some one to whom every one has looked up as very brave and then proves to be less brave than he was supposed to be. That was the way with Buster Bear. When Little Joe Otter had told how Farmer Brown's boy had been afraid at the mere sight of one of Buster Bear's big footprints, they had at once made a hero of Buster. At least some of them had. As this was the first time, the very first time, that they had ever known any one who lives in the Green Forest to make Farmer Brown's boy run away, they looked on Buster Bear with a great deal of respect and were very proud of him.

But now they had seen Buster Bear and Farmer Brown's boy meet face to face; and while it was true that Farmer Brown's boy had run away as fast as ever he could, it was also true that Buster Bear had done the same thing. He had run even faster than Farmer Brown's boy, and had hidden in the most lonely place he could find in the very deepest part of the Green Forest. It was hard to believe, but it was true. And right away everybody lost a great deal of the respect for Buster which they had felt. It is always that way. They began to say unkind things about him. They said them among themselves, and some of them even said them to Buster when they met him, or said them so that he would hear them.

Of course Blacky the Crow and Sammy Jay, who, because they can fly, have nothing to fear from Buster, and who always delight in making other people uncomfortable, never let a chance go by to tell Buster and everybody else within hearing what they thought of him. They delighted in flying about through the Green Forest until they had found Buster Bear and then from the safety of the tree tops screaming at him.

> "Buster Bear is big and strong;
> His teeth are big; his claws are long;
> In spite of these he runs away
> And hides himself the livelong day!"

A dozen times a day Buster would hear them screaming this. He would grind his teeth and glare up at them, but that was all he could do. He couldn't get at them. He just had to stand it and do nothing. But when impudent little Chatterer the Red Squirrel shouted the same thing from a place just out of reach in a big pine-tree, Buster could stand it no longer. He gave a deep, angry growl that made little shivers run over Chatterer, and then suddenly he started up that tree after Chatterer. With a frightened little shriek Chatterer scampered to the top of the tree. He hadn't known that Buster could climb. But Buster is a splendid climber, especially when the tree is big and stout as this one was, and now he went up after Chatterer, growling angrily.

How Chatterer did wish that he had kept his tongue still! He ran to the very top of the tree, so frightened that his teeth chattered, and when he looked down and saw Buster's great mouth coming nearer and nearer, he nearly tumbled down with terror. The worst of it was there wasn't another tree near enough for him to jump to. He was in trouble this time, was Chatterer, sure enough! And there was no one to help him.

XVI. Chatterer the Red Squirrel Jumps for His Life

It isn't very often that Chatterer the Red Squirrel knows fear. That is one reason that he is so often impudent and saucy. But once in a while a great fear takes possession of him, as when he knows that Shadow the Weasel is looking for him. You see, he knows that Shadow can go wherever he can go. There are very few of the little people of the Green Forest and the Green Meadows who do not know fear at some time or other, but it comes to Chatterer as seldom as to any one, because he is very sure of himself and his ability to hide or run away from danger.

But now as he clung to a little branch near the top of a tall pine-tree in the Green Forest and looked down at the big sharp teeth of Buster Bear drawing nearer and nearer, and listened to the deep, angry growls that made his hair stand on end, Chatterer was too frightened to think. If only he had kept his tongue still instead of saying hateful things to Buster Bear! If only he had known that Buster could climb a tree! If only he had chosen a tree near enough to other trees for him to jump across! But he *had* said hateful things, he *had* chosen to sit in a tree which stood quite by itself, and Buster Bear *could* climb! Chatterer was in the worst kind of trouble, and there was no one to blame but himself. That is usually the case with those who get into trouble.

Nearer and nearer came Buster Bear, and deeper and angrier sounded his voice. Chatterer gave a little frightened gasp and looked this way and looked that way. What should he do? What *could* he do! The ground seemed a terrible distance below. If only he had wings like Sammy Jay! But he hadn't.

"Gr-r-r-r!" growled Buster Bear. "I'll teach you manners! I'll teach you to treat your betters with respect! I'll swallow you whole, that's what I'll do. Gr-r-r-r!"

"Oh!" cried Chatterer.

"Gr-r-r-r! I'll eat you all up to the last hair on your tail!" growled Buster, scrambling a little nearer.

"Oh! Oh!" cried Chatterer, and ran out to the very tip of the little branch to which he had been clinging. Now if Chatterer had only known it, Buster Bear couldn't reach him way up there, because the tree was too small at the top for such a big fellow as Buster. But Chatterer didn't think of that. He gave one more frightened look down at those big teeth, then he shut his eyes and jumped—jumped straight out for the far-away ground.

It was a long, long, long way down to the ground, and it certainly looked as if such a little fellow as Chatterer must be killed. But Chatterer had learned from Old Mother Nature that she had given him certain things to help him at just such times, and one of them is the power to spread himself very flat. He did it now. He spread his arms and legs out just as far as he could, and that kept him from falling as fast and as hard as he otherwise would have done, because being spread out so flat that way, the air held him up a little. And then there was his tail, that funny little tail he is so fond of jerking when he scolds. This helped him too. It helped him keep his balance and keep from turning over and over.

Down, down, down he sailed and landed on his feet. Of course, he hit the ground pretty hard, and for just a second he quite lost his breath. But it was only for a second, and then he was scurrying off as fast as a frightened Squirrel could. Buster Bear watched him and grinned.

"I didn't catch him that time," he growled, "but I guess I gave him a good fright and taught him a lesson."

XVII. Buster Bear Goes Berrying

Buster Bear is a great hand to talk to himself when he thinks no one is around to overhear. It's a habit. However, it isn't a bad habit unless it is carried too far. Any habit becomes bad if it is carried too far. Suppose you had a secret, a real secret, something that nobody else knew and that you didn't want anybody else to know. And suppose you had the habit of talking to yourself. You might, without thinking, you know, tell that secret out loud to yourself, and some one might, just might happen to overhear! Then there wouldn't be any secret. That is the way that a habit which isn't bad in itself can become bad when it is carried too far.

Now Buster Bear had lived by himself in the Great Woods so long that this habit of talking to himself had grown and grown. He did it just to keep from being lonesome. Of course, when he came down to the Green Forest to live, he brought all his habits with him. That is one thing about habits,—you always take them with you wherever you go. So Buster brought this habit of talking to himself down to the Green Forest, where he had many more neighbors than he had in the Great Woods.

"Let me see, let me see, what is there to tempt my appetite?" said Buster in his deep, grumbly-rumbly voice. "I find my appetite isn't what it ought to be. I need a change. Yes, Sir, I need a change. There is something I ought to have at this time of year, and I haven't got it. There is something that I used to have and don't have now. Ha! I know! I need some fresh fruit. That's it—fresh fruit! It must be about berry time now, and I'd forgotten all about it. My, my, my, how good some berries would taste! Now if I were back up there in the Great Woods I could have all I could eat. Um-m-m-m! Makes my mouth water just to think of it. There ought to be some up in the Old Pasture. There ought to be a lot of 'em up there. If I wasn't afraid that some one would see me, I'd go up there."

Buster sighed. Then he sighed again. The more he thought about those berries he felt sure were growing in the Old Pasture, the more he wanted some. It seemed to him that never in all his life had he wanted berries as he did now. He wandered about uneasily. He was hungry—hungry for berries and nothing else. By and by he began talking to himself again.

"If I wasn't afraid of being seen, I'd go up to the Old

Pasture this very minute. Seems as if I could taste those berries." He licked his lips hungrily as he spoke. Then his face brightened. "I know what I'll do! I'll go up there at the very first peep of day to-morrow. I can eat all I want and get back to the Green Forest before there is any danger that Farmer Brown's boy or any one else I'm afraid of will see me. That's just what I'll do. My, I wish to-morrow morning would hurry up and come."

Now though Buster didn't know it, some one had been listening, and that some one was none other than Sammy Jay. When at last Buster lay down for a nap, Sammy flew away, chuckling to himself. "I believe I'll visit the Old Pasture to-morrow morning myself," thought he. "I have an idea that something interesting may happen if Buster doesn't change his mind."

Sammy was on the lookout very early the next morning. The first Jolly Little Sunbeams had only reached the Green Meadows and had not started to creep into the Green Forest, when he saw a big, dark form steal out of the Green Forest where it joins the Old Pasture. It moved very swiftly and silently, as if in a great hurry. Sammy knew who it was: it was Buster Bear, and he was going berrying. Sammy waited a little until he could see better. Then he too started for the Old Pasture.

XVIII. Somebody Else Goes Berrying

Isn't it funny how two people will often think of the same thing at the same time, and neither one know that the other is thinking of it? That is just what happened the day that Buster Bear first thought of going berrying. While he was walking around in the Green Forest, talking to himself about how hungry he was for some berries and how sure he was that there must be some up in the Old Pasture, some one else was thinking about berries and about the Old Pasture too.

"Will you make me a berry pie if I will get the berries to-morrow?" asked Farmer Brown's boy of his mother.

Of course Mrs. Brown promised that she would, and so that night Farmer Brown's boy went to bed very early that he might get up early in the morning, and all night long he dreamed of berries and berry pies. He was awake even before jolly, round, red Mr. Sun thought it was time to get up, and he was all ready to start for the Old Pasture when the first Jolly Little Sunbeams came dancing across the Green Meadows. He carried a big tin pail, and in the bottom of it, wrapped up in a piece of paper, was a lunch, for he meant to stay until he filled that pail, if it took all day.

Now the Old Pasture is very large. It lies at the foot of the Big Mountain, and even extends a little way up on the Big Mountain. There is room in it for many people to pick berries all day without even seeing each other, unless they roam about a great deal. You see, the bushes grow very thick there, and you cannot see very far in any direction. Jolly, round, red Mr. Sun had climbed a little way up in the sky by the time Farmer Brown's boy reached the Old Pasture, and was smiling down on all the Great World, and all the Great World seemed to be smiling back. Farmer Brown's boy started to whistle, and then he stopped.

"If I whistle," thought he, "everybody will know just where I am, and will keep out of sight, and I never can get acquainted with folks if they keep out of sight."

You see, Farmer Brown's boy was just beginning to understand something that Peter Rabbit and the other little people of the Green Meadows and the Green Forest learned almost as soon as they learned to walk,—that if you don't want to be seen, you mustn't be heard. So he didn't whistle as he felt like doing, and he tried not to make a bit of noise as he followed an old cow-path towards a place where he knew the berries grew thick and oh, so big, and all the time he kept his eyes wide open, and he kept his ears open too.

That is how he happened to hear a little cry, a very faint little cry. If he had been whistling, he wouldn't have heard it at all. He stopped to listen. He never had heard a cry just like it before. At first he couldn't make out just what it was or where it came from. But one thing he was sure of, and that was that it was a cry of fright. He stood perfectly still and listened with all his might. There it was again—"Help! Help! Help!"—and it was very faint and sounded terribly frightened. He waited a minute or two, but heard nothing more. Then he put down his pail and began a hurried look here, there, and everywhere. He was sure that it had come from somewhere on the ground, so he peered behind bushes and peeped behind logs and stones, and then just as he had about given up hope of finding where it came from, he went around a little turn in the old cow-path, and there right in front of him was little Mr. Gartersnake, and what do you think he was doing? Well, I don't like to tell you, but he was trying to swallow one of the children of Stickytoes the Tree Toad. Of course Farmer Brown's boy didn't let him. He made little Mr. Gartersnake set Master Stickytoes free and held Mr. Gartersnake until Master Stickytoes was safely out of reach.

XIX. Buster Bear Has a Fine Time

Buster Bear was having the finest time he had had since he came down from the Great Woods to live in the Green Forest. To be sure, he wasn't in the Green Forest now, but he wasn't far from it. He was in the Old Pasture, one edge of which touches one edge of the Green Forest. And where do you think he was, in the Old Pasture? Why, right in the middle of the biggest patch of the biggest blueberries he ever had seen in all his life! Now if there is any one thing that Buster Bear had rather have above another, it is all the berries he can eat, unless it be honey. Nothing can quite equal honey in Buster's mind. But next to honey give him berries. He isn't particular what kind of berries. Raspberries, blackberries, or blueberries, either kind, will make him perfectly happy.

"Um-m-m, my, my, but these are good!" he mumbled in his deep grumbly-rumbly voice, as he sat on his haunches stripping off the berries greedily. His little eyes twinkled with enjoyment, and he didn't mind at all if now and then he got leaves and some green berries in his mouth with the big ripe berries. He didn't try to get them out. Oh, my, no! He just chomped them all up together and patted his stomach from sheer delight. Now Buster had reached the Old Pasture just as jolly, round, red Mr. Sun had crept out of bed, and he had fully made up his mind that he would be back in the Green Forest before Mr. Sun had climbed very far up in the blue, blue sky. You see, big as he is and strong as he is, Buster Bear is very shy and bashful, and he has no desire to meet Farmer Brown, or Farmer Brown's boy, or any other of those two-legged creatures called men. It seems funny, but he actually is afraid of them. And he had a feeling that he was a great deal more likely to meet one of them in the Old Pasture than deep in the Green Forest.

So when he started to look for berries, he made up his mind that he would eat what he could in a great hurry and get back to the Green Forest before Farmer Brown's boy was more than out of bed. But when he found those berries he was so hungry that he forgot his fears and everything else. They tasted so good that he just had to eat and eat and eat. Now you know that Buster is a very big fellow, and it takes a lot to fill him up. He kept eating and eating and eating, and the more he ate the more he wanted. You know how it is. So he wandered from one patch of berries to another in the Old Pasture, and never once thought of the time. Somehow, time is the hardest thing in the world to remember, when you are having a good time.

Jolly, round, red Mr. Sun climbed higher and higher in the blue, blue sky. He looked down on all the Great World and saw all that was going on. He saw Buster Bear in the Old Pasture, and smiled as he saw what a perfectly glorious time Buster was having.

And he saw something else in the Old Pasture that made his smile still broader. He saw Farmer Brown's boy filling a great tin pail with blueberries, and he knew that Farmer Brown's boy didn't know that Buster Bear was anywhere about, and he knew that Buster Bear didn't know that Farmer Brown's boy was anywhere about, and somehow he felt very sure that he would see something funny happen if they should chance to meet.

"Um-m-m, um-m-m," mumbled Buster Bear with his mouth full, as he moved along to another patch of berries. And then he gave a little gasp of surprise and delight. Right in front of him was a shiny thing just full of the finest, biggest, bluest berries! There were no leaves or green ones there. Buster blinked his greedy little eyes rapidly and looked again. No, he wasn't dreaming. They were real berries, and all he had got to do was to help himself. Buster looked sharply at the shiny thing that held the berries. It seemed perfectly harmless. He reached out a big paw and pushed it gently. It tipped over and spilled out a lot of the berries. Yes, it was perfectly harmless. Buster gave a little sigh of pure happiness. He would eat those berries to the last one, and then he would go home to the Green Forest.

XX. Buster Bear Carries Off the Pail
of Farmer Brown's Boy

The question is, did Buster Bear steal Farmer Brown's boy's pail? To steal is to take something which belongs to some one else. There is no doubt that he stole the berries that were in the pail when he found it, for he deliberately ate them. He knew well enough that some one must have picked them—for whoever heard of blueberries growing in tin pails? So there is no doubt that when Buster took them, he stole them. But with the pail it was different. He took the pail, but he didn't mean to take it. In fact, he didn't want that pail at all.

You see it was this way: When Buster found that big tin pail brimming full of delicious berries in the shade of that big bush in the Old Pasture, he didn't stop to think whether or not he had a right to them. Buster is so fond of berries that from the very second that his greedy little eyes saw that pailful, he forgot everything but the feast that was waiting for him right under his very nose. He didn't think anything about the right or wrong of helping himself. There before him were more berries than he had ever seen together at one time in all his life, and all he had to do was to eat and eat and eat. And that is just what he did do. Of course he upset the pail, but he didn't mind a little thing like that. When he had gobbled up all the berries that rolled out, he thrust his nose into the pail to get all that were left in it. Just then he heard a little noise, as if some one were coming. He threw up his head to listen, and somehow, he never did know just how, the handle of the pail slipped back over his ears and caught there.

This was bad enough, but to make matters worse, just at that very minute he heard a shrill, angry voice shout, "Hi, there! Get out of there!" He didn't need to be told whose voice that was. It was the voice of Farmer Brown's boy. Right then and there Buster Bear nearly had a fit. There was that awful pail fast over his head so that he couldn't see a thing. Of course, that meant that he couldn't run away, which was the thing of all things he most wanted to do, for big as he is and strong as he is, Buster is very shy and bashful when human beings are around. He growled and whined and squealed. He tried to back out of the pail and couldn't. He tried to shake it off and couldn't. He tried to pull it off, but somehow he couldn't get hold of it. Then there was another yell. If Buster hadn't been so frightened himself, he might have recognized that second yell as one of fright, for that is what it was. You see Farmer Brown's boy had just discovered Buster Bear. When he had yelled the first time, he had supposed that it was one of the young cattle who live in the Old Pasture all summer, but when he saw Buster, he was just as badly frightened as Buster himself. In fact, he was too surprised and frightened even to run. After that second yell he just stood still and stared.

Buster clawed at that awful thing on his head more frantically than ever. Suddenly it slipped off, so that he could see. He gave one frightened look at Farmer Brown's boy, and then with a mighty "Woof!" he started for the Green Forest as fast as his legs could take him, and this was very fast indeed, let me tell you. He didn't stop to pick out a path, but just crashed through the bushes as if they were nothing at all, just nothing at all. But the funniest thing of all is this—he took that pail with him! Yes, Sir, Buster Bear ran away with the big tin pail of Farmer's Brown's boy! You see when it slipped off his head, the handle was still around his neck, and there he was running away with a pail hanging from his neck! He didn't want it. He would have given anything to get rid of it. But he took it because he couldn't help it. And that brings us back to the question, did Buster steal Farmer Brown's boy's pail? What do you think?

XXI. Sammy Jay Makes Things Worse for Buster Bear

"Thief, thief, thief! Thief, thief, thief!" Sammy Jay was screaming at the top of his lungs, as he followed Buster Bear across the Old Pasture towards the Green Forest. Never had he screamed so loud, and never had his voice sounded so excited. The little people of the Green Forest, the Green Meadows, and the Smiling Pool are so used to hearing Sammy cry thief that usually they think very little about it. But every blessed one who heard Sammy this morning stopped whatever he was doing and pricked up his ears to listen.

Sammy's cousin, Blacky the Crow, just happened to be flying along the edge of the Old Pasture, and the minute he heard Sammy's voice, he turned and flew over to see what it was all about. Just as soon as he caught sight of Buster Bear running for the Green Forest as hard as ever he could, he understood what had excited Sammy so. He was so surprised that he almost forgot to keep his wings moving. Buster Bear had what looked to Blacky very much like a tin pail hanging from his neck! No wonder Sammy was excited. Blacky beat his wings fiercely and started after Sammy.

And so they reached the edge of the Green Forest, Buster Bear running as hard as ever he could, Sammy Jay flying just behind him and screaming, "Thief, thief, thief!" at the top of his lungs, and behind him Blacky the Crow, trying to catch up and yelling as loud as he could, "Caw, caw, caw! Come on, everybody! Come on! Come on!"

Poor Buster! It was bad enough to be frightened almost to death as he had been up in the Old Pasture when the pail had caught over his head just as Farmer Brown's boy had yelled at him. Then to have the handle of the pail slip down around his neck so that he couldn't get rid of the pail but had to take it with him as he ran, was making a bad matter worse. Now to have all his neighbors of the Green Forest see him in such a fix and make fun of him, was more than he could stand. He felt humiliated. That is just another way of saying shamed. Yes, Sir, Buster felt that he was shamed in the eyes of his neighbors, and he wanted nothing so much as to get away by himself, where no one could see him, and try to get rid of that dreadful pail. But Buster is so big that it is not easy for him to find a hiding-place. So when he reached the Green Forest, he kept right on to the deepest, darkest, most lonesome part and crept under the thickest hemlock-tree he could find.

But it was of no use. The sharp eyes of Sammy Jay and Blacky the Crow saw him. They actually flew into the very tree under which he was hiding, and how they did scream! Pretty soon Ol' Mistah Buzzard came dropping down out of the blue, blue sky and took a seat on a convenient dead tree, where he could see all that went on. Ol' Mistah Buzzard began to grin as soon as he saw that tin pail on Buster's neck. Then came others,—Redtail the Hawk, Scrapper the Kingbird, Redwing the Blackbird, Drummer the Woodpecker, Welcome Robin, Tommy Tit the Chickadee, Jenny Wren, Redeye the Vireo, and ever so many more. They came from the Old Orchard, the Green Meadows, and even down by the Smiling Pool, for the voices of Sammy Jay and Blacky the Crow carried far, and at the sound of them everybody hurried over, sure that something exciting was going on.

Presently Buster heard light footsteps, and peeping out, he saw Billy Mink and Peter Rabbit and Jumper the Hare and Prickly Porky and Reddy Fox and Jimmy Skunk. Even timid little Whitefoot the Wood Mouse was where he could peer out and see without being seen. Of course, Chatterer the Red Squirrel and Happy Jack the Gray Squirrel were there. There they all sat in a great circle around him, each where he felt safe, but where he could see, and every one of them laughing and making fun of Buster.

"Thief, thief, thief!" screamed Sammy until his throat was sore. The worst of it was Buster knew that everybody knew that it was true. That awful pail was proof of it.

"I wish I never had thought of berries," growled Buster to himself.

XXII. Buster Bear Has a Fit of Temper

"A temper is a bad, bad thing
When once it gets away.
There's nothing quite at all like it
To spoil a pleasant day."

Buster Bear was in a terrible temper. Yes, Sir, Buster Bear was having the worst fit of temper ever seen in the Green Forest. And the worst part of it all was that all his neighbors of the Green Forest and a whole lot from the Green Meadows and the Smiling Pool were also there to see it. It is bad enough to give way to temper when you are all alone, and there is no one to watch you, but when you let temper get the best of you right where others see you, oh, dear, dear, it certainly is a sorry sight.

Now ordinarily Buster is one of the most good-natured persons in the world. It takes a great deal to rouse his temper. He isn't one tenth so quick-tempered as Chatterer the Red Squirrel, or Sammy Jay, or Reddy Fox. But when his temper is aroused and gets away from him, then watch out! It seemed to Buster that he had had all that he could stand that day and a little more. First had come the fright back there in the Old Pasture. Then the pail had slipped down behind his ears and held fast, so he had run all the way to the Green Forest with it hanging about his neck. This was bad enough, for he knew just how funny he must look, and besides, it was very uncomfortable. But to have Sammy Jay call everybody within hearing to come and see him was more than he could stand. It seemed to Buster as if everybody who lives in the Green Forest, on the Green Meadows, or around the Smiling Pool, was sitting around his hiding-place, laughing and making fun of him. It was more than any self-respecting Bear could stand.

With a roar of anger Buster Bear charged out of his hiding-place. He rushed this way and that way! He roared with all his might! He was very terrible to see. Those who could fly, flew. Those who could climb, climbed. And those who were swift of foot, ran. A few who could neither fly nor climb nor run fast, hid and lay shaking and trembling for fear that Buster would find them. In less time than it takes to tell about it, Buster was alone. At least, he couldn't see any one.

Then he vented his temper on the tin pail. He cuffed at it and pulled at it, all the time growling angrily. He lay down and clawed at it with his hind feet. At last the handle broke, and he was free! He shook himself. Then he jumped on the helpless pail. With a blow of a big paw he sent it clattering against a tree. He tried to bite it. Then he once more fell to knocking it this way and that way, until it was pounded flat, and no one would ever have guessed that it had once been a pail.

Then, and not till then, did Buster recover his usual good nature. Little by little, as he thought it all over, a look of shame crept into his face. "I—I guess it wasn't the fault of that thing. I ought to have known enough to keep my head out of it," he said slowly and thoughtfully.

"You got no more than you deserve for stealing Farmer Brown's boy's berries," said Sammy Jay, who had come back and was looking on from the top of a

Those who could fly, flew.
Those who could climb, climbed.
See page 259.

tree. "You ought to know by this time that no good comes of stealing."

Buster Bear looked up and grinned, and there was a twinkle in his eyes. "You ought to know, Sammy Jay," said he. "I hope you'll always remember it."

"Thief, thief, thief!" screamed Sammy, and flew away.

XXIII. Farmer Brown's Boy Lunches on Berries

> "When things go wrong in spite of you
> To smile's the best thing you can do—
> To smile and say, 'I'm mighty glad
> They are no worse; they're not so bad!'"

That is what Farmer Brown's boy said when he found that Buster Bear had stolen the berries he had worked so hard to pick and then had run off with the pail. You see, Farmer Brown's boy is learning to be something of a philosopher, one of those people who accept bad things cheerfully and right away see how they are better than they might have been. When he had first heard some one in the bushes where he had hidden his pail of berries, he had been very sure that it was one of the cows or young cattle who live in the Old Pasture during the summer. He had been afraid that they might stupidly kick over the pail and spill the berries, and he had hurried to drive whoever it was away. It hadn't entered his head that it could be anybody who would eat those berries.

When he had yelled and Buster Bear had suddenly appeared, struggling to get off the pail which had caught over his head, Farmer Brown's boy had been too frightened to even move. Then he had seen Buster tear away through the brush even more frightened than he was, and right away his courage had begun to come back.

"If he is so afraid of me, I guess I needn't be afraid of him," said he. "I've lost my berries, but it is worth it to find out that he is afraid of me. There are plenty more on the bushes, and all I've got to do is to pick them. It might be worse."

He walked over to the place where the pail had been, and then he remembered that when Buster ran away he had carried the pail with him, hanging about his neck. He whistled. It was a comical little whistle of chagrin as he realized that he had nothing in which to put more berries, even if he picked them. "It's worse than I thought," cried he. "That bear has cheated me out of that berry pie my mother promised me." Then he began to laugh, as he thought of how funny Buster Bear had looked with the pail about his neck, and then because, you know, he is learning to be a philosopher, he once more repeated, "It might have been worse. Yes, indeed, it might have been worse. That bear might have tried to eat me instead of the berries. I guess I'll go eat that lunch I left back by the spring, and then I'll go home. I can pick berries some other day."

Chuckling happily over Buster Bear's great fright, Farmer Brown's boy tramped back to the spring where he had left two thick sandwiches on a flat stone when he started to save his pail of berries. "My, but those sandwiches will taste good," thought he. "I'm glad they are big and thick. I never was hungrier in my life. Hello!" This he exclaimed right out loud, for he had just come in sight of the flat stone where the sandwiches should have been, and they were not there. No, Sir, there wasn't so much as a crumb left of those two thick sandwiches. You see, Old Man Coyote had found them and gobbled them up while Farmer Brown's boy was away.

But Farmer Brown's boy didn't know anything about Old Man Coyote. He rubbed his eyes and stared everywhere, even up in the trees, as if he thought those sandwiches might be hanging up there. They had disappeared as completely as if they never had been, and Old Man Coyote had taken care to leave no trace of his visit. Farmer Brown's boy gaped foolishly this way and that way. Then, instead of growing angry, a slow smile stole over his freckled face. "I guess some one else was hungry too," he muttered. "Wonder who it was? Guess this Old Pasture is no place for me to-day. I'll fill up on berries and then I'll go home."

So Farmer Brown's boy made his lunch on blueberries and then rather sheepishly he started for home to tell of all the strange things that had happened to him in the Old Pasture. Two or three times, as he trudged along, he stopped to scratch his head thoughtfully. "I guess," said he at last, "that I'm not so smart as I thought I was, and I've got a lot to learn yet."

THE END